THE KINGDOM'S SANDCASTLE

THE KINGDOM'S SANDCASTLE

a novel based on true events

Luai Qubain

Rare Bird Books
Los Angeles, Calif.

THIS IS A GENUINE RARE BIRD BOOK

Rare Bird Books
453 South Spring Street, Suite 302
Los Angeles, CA 90013
rarebirdlit.com

FIRST HARDCOVER EDITION

Set in Minion
Printed in the United States

10 9 8 7 6 5 4 3 2 1

Library of Congress Cataloging-in-Publication Data available upon request.

For my mom

&

All LGBT+ people who are in danger for being themselves.
You are not alone.

Chapter One

WHEN I LEFT THE KINGDOM, I hadn't planned on going back, at least not for a long time. California was everything my homeland in the Middle East was not, and I was looking forward to four blissful years on the beaches of Santa Barbara. However, just two months later, I was stepping out of the capital's airport in the Kingdom. The polished roadways were cast in a hazy, orange light and the dry heat I had grown up in.

It was both a return and a regression. Here in the Kingdom, I had to hide, to blend in, to pretend to be someone that I wasn't. I hated it. The dread of seeing my cousins and father was an afterthought in comparison. Yet here I was, walking toward my waiting parents.

"Louie!" My mother's voice was the only thing that kept me moving. There she was, smiling and waving. Her electric hazel eyes beneath her iconic hair, colored dark blonde, were a beacon of hope in that soul-crushing march to the car. "Over here!" I didn't have to pretend to be someone I was not when I was with her. Her love for me was unconditional.

My father stood just behind her, an ever-present shadow, his manicured mustache resting motionless above his smoldering cigarette. He believed the rumor. I could see it in his flat expression, the tight lips, rigid gaze, and perfect posture. Why wouldn't he? He never knew the truth, my truth, but my mother did. In that moment, she was all I had.

My suitcase clattered on the sidewalk as my limbs shook, and I threw my arms around her. Burying my face in the crook of her shoulder as I had when I was a child, I began to sob. All of my frustration, fear, and rage went into those tears, and the only comfort I could find was my mother's sweet and familiar perfume.

"It's not true, Mom," I said softly between sobs. "It's all a lie."

"I know," she whispered, and she gave my back a comforting pat. "It's all going to be all right. You'll go back."

I pulled myself away after a time, not knowing how long I cried, only that I had exhausted all the tears there were to offer.

"Hello, Father," I said, wiping my eyes with my sleeve. The material was coarse and caught on my unshaven stubble.

"Son," he answered with his typical nod, adjusting his sunglasses like some sort of tip of the hat. Then he turned to the chauffeur waiting beside the Mercedes-Benz and beckoned him to take my luggage. "Let's go home."

Home was a whitewashed compound at the end of an elegant street that snaked up a hill overlooking the Kingdom's capital. It was a megalopolis, home to some four million people at that time, and the majority of its inhabitants lived in extremely close proximity to each other in the eastern part of the city. Houses and apartments were crammed throughout the valleys and hills they sprawled over. The neighbors called out to one another, smiling over clotheslines and the rumble of a million motorized scooters that never ceased to buzz about the ancient streets.

By contrast, the western part of the city boasted chic residential neighborhoods where many of the upper-middle-class, and some of the upper-class lived. Corporate and bank headquarters sat alongside gleaming avenues and boulevards with their tall and lush palm trees. Many of the city's five-star hotels, restaurants, and luxurious shopping malls also called that part of the city home. It was a vibrant, massive city full of life, secrets, and regrets.

But that was not the case where we lived. Our affluent area was secluded. Each compound distinctly cut off from their neighbors by beautifully designed tall stone walls that protected the secrets of those inside. There was no community, only family, and that had been made clear to me from an early age.

Our property included three villas, with a grand swimming pool that sat in the center of the arrangement. The first housed my brother, our parents, and me. Next door lived my uncle, his wife, and my three derelict cousins. The younger two were a year apart from me, one older and one younger. The oldest, Nathan, was much older and already done with university, still living at home like a good boy was supposed to. The last villa was my aunt's house. Five housekeepers worked on the compound—they were from Sri Lanka—and a groundskeeper from Egypt. He was more of a guard than a gardener, and he gave us a friendly smile every time we passed through the front gate.

Our villa was always immaculate. My mother saw to that. She went to enormous lengths to keep everything spotless and arranged just the way she wanted. Intricate and beautiful flower arrangements were delivered weekly, and she would walk around the house humming as she adjusted each vase just so. Our furniture was modern, sleek, and clean. My mother kept things so neatly arranged and polished that sometimes it felt awkward to sit on a couch for fear of upsetting the room's perfect posing.

Growing up, dinner parties were frequent, and every Thursday was poker night. The whole family would come over for a lavish dinner, then set to cards and laughter. The cigarette smoke would cloud thick, the drinks would clink relentlessly, and the chips would clatter on and on between the three tables late into the evening hours. The men of the family sat at one, the women at another, and all us kids had our own. I still love playing poker, and I like to think I'm pretty good.

On the weekends, we would pile into father's black Mercedes-Benz and take a forty-minute drive out to the country home. It looked out of place there in the Kingdom, more like something one might find in some mountain resort in Colorado, or some actor's house in the Hollywood Hills of California. It was a bright white, huge, modern concrete building, outfitted with all the accessories. The enormous floor-to-ceiling windows flooded the interior with warm sunlight and painted a perfect picture of what felt like everlasting scenery. It perched on a rocky hill with breathtaking views of tree-covered mountains and far-flung villages in the valleys beneath. The rest of the family would meet us there, and I would play on the massive immaculate lawn with my cousins and brother while the adults sat and talked over more cigarette smoke and scotch.

Sometimes my best friend would tag along. We would take the ATV out on the dirt trails, winding up at the same spot overlooking a huge man-made lake. We would sit up there and talk about our future, throwing sticks and stones absently like the kids we were. It was a beautiful spot. We always said that we would build our homes next to one another and have a bridge or a tunnel connecting them. We were more than just best friends. We were almost brothers.

I think of those times fondly. Life was simple, and I enjoyed it. I felt loved and blessed.

Things were uncomplicated before school started, before I realized who I was, and before I had to pretend to be someone I was not. School changed everything. It was one of those exclusive private schools, with navy-blue uniforms, and teachers strict with rules and homework. It felt like a prison.

Back then, I started to realize I was different from everyone else in the classroom, and different from my brother and my cousins. I was in touch with my feminine side and I didn't understand why. To make things even more interesting, I had a squeaky voice that physically set me apart.

Growing up, before cell phones were common, my brother and his friends had me call their girlfriends at their houses and pretend to be their classmate.

"Hello?"

"Hello, is Sarah available?" I calmly asked with my girl voice.

"Who is calling?"

"This is Dina, her schoolmate. I have some questions about the homework. Can she talk for a bit?"

"Of course, wait just a moment. Good for you for reaching out. I am glad she has such studious friends," her mom pleasantly responded.

My brother›s friends were all quietly laughing and giving me the thumbs-up as I handed the phone over. It always worked and I walked away smiling, feeling victorious.

I love my brother, I always have, but growing up we were never that close. He spent his time hunched over his top-end gaming PC, scorning video game consoles, while he looked through pictures of hot rods on the internet and snuck around back to smoke cigarettes. Sure, we had fun on Thursday nights and on our weekend getaways, but the older we got, the more apparent our dissimilar interests became. Eventually, I realized it was just one of those things.

My father was always distant. Our conversations were short, shallow, and infrequent. He was practically never home, frequently away on some business trip to Europe or somewhere. The days he was at home, he spent his time in his office behind his prized grand wooden desk, nursing a glass of scotch while a thin wisp of cigarette smoke drifted up from his ever-active ashtray. His windows overlooked the expansive, manicured garden. The light from outside reflected off the marble floor with a brutal persistence that would burn your eyes if you looked at it the wrong way. The couch and chairs in the room were brown, like the desk, and the whole place reflected his permanent, pessimistic frown. He left the door open, and whenever I walked by, I could feel him staring at me, as if he were trying to sort out where he had gone wrong, inflicting this pervasive feeling of inadequacy.

In that house, my refuge was my mother. She was the only one who understood me, who supported me, and was proud of my accomplishments. I spent a ton of time with her as a child because she recognized who I truly was and didn't try to change me.

I spent hours playing in her big walk-in closet, looking at her massive collection of exquisite shoes and designer dresses, all organized by color and style. Everything inside smelled like her, that specific perfume she wore, and I loved being surrounded by it.

Everyone admired and respected her. She had a passion for charity work. She helped many people all over the Kingdom with tuition fees and medical bills for their kids and even helped others with housing. She was elegantly soft spoken—but not in a weak way, it was more of a tactful grace—and she was beautiful. She had gorgeous olive skin that complemented her warm and kind eyes. She had an appointment with the hair stylist every Monday, Wednesday, and Friday, and I always went with her. Her hair always looked stunning! I would come into my parents' room and sleep next to her, all the way up to sixth grade. No doubt that had something to do with my father's permanent look of disappointment.

When I was seven, I wandered over to my aunt's house on the compound. She had a wig from Paris with long, silky black hair. It was expensive as hell. I saw it there on its stand, and I was mesmerized. There was a welling gravity to it, pulling me in faster than I could process. I put it on and looked in the mirror. It was perfect and I felt so happy, as if I had seen a true reflection of myself in that mirror for the very first time.

I ended up wearing it back over to our house, and my mother saw me. She got this huge smile on her face and spent the rest of the day dressing me up in her clothes. We were laughing and joking as we went through dress after dress, and that moment was the most fun I had ever had. I'm sure that's the time she knew I was gay. Or maybe she had always known. Either way, she was there for me.

However, she also knew where we lived. Luckily, you couldn't be thrown in jail for being gay anymore, but you could still suffer for it. You could be shunned and assaulted. Shit, you could even get killed. The Kingdom was religiously conservative, and although we had westernized shopping malls and billboards, holding a man's hand was still unaccepted and something a cop could ticket you for.

"Don't tell your father," she said, snapping another Polaroid as I posed in my boa, and I understood.

Growing up gay in the Kingdom means living a double life, but you can't do it alone. Doing it alone will eventually eat you alive, mentally and emotionally, until there's nothing left but crushing and crippling depression, sometimes the kind you can't climb out of.

My first huge crush was my seventh grade physics teacher. That guy was something else. The first time I saw him walking down the hall I nearly fell over. He was handsome, almost impossibly so, and his face had kind, thoughtful features. He had deep-set, light green eyes, and a slender build with strong-looking arms that filled out his short-sleeved, button-down blue shirt. I was excited when I found out I was in his class. I dreamt about him during the day, and stayed up late thinking about him. In class, I was perfectly behaved, watching him walk through the room, drinking it in. I worked harder in that class than I ever did in any other, all to impress him. The funny thing was I actually got pretty good at physics because of him.

My best friend was Robert. We had been tight since we were four and went to school together our whole lives. We tried really hard to be the cool kids, and in all honesty, we were. People were always trying to hang out with us, trying to get into our little two-man group, but we never let it happen. That space we shared was our only sanctuary back then, and letting anybody else in would corrupt and destroy it. In public, we joked about girls and talked about cars and sports, but in private, we would give each other makeovers and blast Britney Spears.

We lived for Britney. To us, she was a goddess. Robert would come over for sleepovers, and we would stay up all night choreographing our own dances while we watched the DVD of her landmark 2000 Hawaii concert on repeat. We also fell in love with Shania Twain. Our favorite song was "Up!" We would sing along as loud as we could, jumping on the bed and pretending to be on stage performing for thousands of people. Fortunately for us, homes in the Middle East are built using heavy and insulated concrete blocks that helped in dampening the noise of our imaginary but legendary concerts.

It was Robert whom I came out to first. We were in seventh grade, and he was over for one of our customary sleepovers. I was lying on my stomach, with my elbows propped up on a pillow in front of him. He was sitting cross-legged with his back against a big leather armchair. I don't know why I chose that moment, and I'm not sure I even knew what I was saying, but I knew that I had to say something. And if I could say it to anyone, it was Robert.

"You know our physics teacher," I said, my feet bouncing together behind me nervously.

"Yeah," Robert said, glancing up from the DVDs he was shuffling through.

"I think he's really cute."

"You do?" he said, putting the movies down. He looked at me for a long time, and I was so nervous. I thought I may have ruined everything, but then he said, "Yeah, me too."

"I think a lot of guys are cute," I went on, emboldened by this confirmation of our sanctuary. "I don't really like girls, I don't think. Just guys."

"I don't know," he replied, "I think girls and guys are both cute. I think I like them both."

"That's cool," I said.

"Yeah," he said, his face working into a grin. "But just liking guys, you know, that's cool too."

"Yeah," I said back, matching his smile. We held eye contact for a long time in silence, only understanding the gravity of our words after we had said them and grinning wildly at each other as we came to realize just how special our friendship was.

It wasn't long after that we cut our thumbs open with an X-ACTO knife from my dad's office and sealed our bond as blood brothers. We were inseparable. Nobody else understood our lives, and honestly, neither did we. We leaned on each other for support as we discovered how different we were from the rest. We would stay up late talking about which guys we thought were cute in our classes, and we wrote secret love poems to our physics teacher that we never did anything with. Together, we slowly grew into understanding who we truly were.

Life got a lot more interesting when I was fourteen. My family took a long vacation to California. It was the first time I had been to the United States as a self-aware person, able to realize the extreme differences between California and the Kingdom. I felt so free there, so happy and full of warmth. Gone was the constant social oppression of the Kingdom, the rigid classrooms, and school uniforms. In their place was a carefree feeling of joy. I knew I wanted to live there, and I worked hard to make that a reality.

The trip changed my mother as well. She had been in banking all my life, and always arranged her light brown hair in a professional way. But when we got back to the Kingdom, she colored it dark blonde, wore it looser, and quit her job at the bank to go back to school. She got into running, training for full marathons. I was proud of her for doing that. She had the courage to pursue what she wanted, and I try to carry that courage with me today. It took a long time for me to find it, but now it's there, and I know that's because of her.

That same year, 2000, Robert and I started getting into internet chat rooms. They were new back then, and all the rage. To us, they were a playground of self-expression, and a time we cherished. I got my first cell phone that year too. It was a loaded combination!

Robert and I would hang around these chat rooms, pretending we were girls, talking to guys all over the region. I had been blessed with that girly voice, so why not use it to our advantage? If we liked someone, we would exchange phone numbers. I pretended to be a girl named Alicia to get a guy's number. It was just for fun, and to flirt. At least for him. To me, it was different. Although I was pretending to be a girl, it felt good talking to guys who, at least over the phone, seemed to be genuinely into me.

One time I accidentally rerouted my cell phone calls to the house phone, and some dude called asking for Alicia. My mother asked him what number he had dialed, and when he read mine back to her, she gave me a friendly, scorning look before taking my phone away for a month. I remember being crushed without it. Without that phone, I was isolated once again, unable to express myself.

When I got a little older, around sixteen, Robert and I started finding the gay chat rooms that other people in hiding used. It was a major breakthrough. I never knew how many people like me were in the Kingdom, and it gave me hope.

The first time I tried sleeping with a guy was because of the chat rooms, a man named Pablo. He was Italian, in the Kingdom on some business trip. We were talking, and he invited me to his hotel room.

He was staying at the Sheraton. Robert went with me. We walked into the lobby and Robert gave me this look, and said, "You really going to do this?"

I thought about it for maybe half of a second and then answered, "Yeah, I am."

Robert waited for me in the lobby. I got up to the room and was nervous as hell when I knocked on the door. Pablo opened it, and the second I walked in I froze, unable to move and unsure of what to do. I had gotten in over my head, and it was obvious. Pablo was nice about it though, and we ended up just sitting and talking for a while. Then Robert and I went home.

It became pretty normal for us to meet people for coffee. The gay chat rooms were our link to that hidden world, and we wanted to explore it as much as possible. One time I was talking to this Palestinian guy with the richest, most handsome voice I had ever heard. His voice was so enchanting it gave me chills! I used to daydream about what he looked like. Was he tall? Was he handsome? Was he muscular? Those unanswered questions kept bouncing around in my head. He kept asking about meeting in person, so eventually Robert and I set it up. He flew to the Kingdom from Israel just to meet us for coffee.

It was the worst! I had never seen anyone so ugly! I sat across from him in that coffee shop silently, perplexed and horrified by what I had gotten myself into. Robert was trying to carry on the conversation, just to be polite, and kept nudging me under the table. I couldn't say shit. I was so embarrassed. At the time, I didn't realize how blissful my life was. My biggest disappointment in the world was that this man with the sexiest voice I had ever heard was horribly ugly. If I had known then how cruelly my life would turn, I would have cherished that man and those happy times. I would have found something nice to say.

Robert's brother had this friend named Joseph, and we hung out with him once in a while. He was sort of what you could call a "goth" kid, but I don't think he thought of himself that way. I started talking to him a lot, and we built up this mutual attraction. It was different from the physics teacher because I could tell Joseph liked me too. He would slip me little notes and walk by the classes I was in, just to check in on me. I remember making eye contact with him as he passed the open doors, and I would melt in my seat as he gave me a little wink or a smile.

Then I was seventeen. It was the last year of school, and my family transferred me to a new, private British school a little bit outside of the capital because they had had a disagreement with my previous school's administration. I was terrified! I didn't know anybody there and Robert was still at our old school. I had to figure out a way to fit in and I couldn't afford to reveal the real me to my new classmates. Maybe it was because I was so wrapped up in my cover story, and worried about my hidden life becoming public, I felt like I had to date the hottest girl in school, so that's what I did. It worked out great, at least for a while. We would talk on the phone a lot, and hang out after school in big groups of friends. Nobody thought I was gay.

Looking back, I feel bad for using her the way I did. I was just trying to eliminate suspicion. I only kissed her once, and I felt like I would throw up! I shouldn't have gone out with her for seven months, but that's what I had to do to protect myself.

Whenever I was talking to guys, I could close my door and say, "I'm talking to Lina, leave me alone please," and my father bought it. My mother didn't. While I was "dating" Lina I started seeing this guy from the city. He was in a metal band, really handsome, and he had a car. In other words, he was the complete teenage dreamboat package. The only thing was he was twenty-nine, but I thought that was cool at the time. What's an eleven-year age difference anyways?

He had this spot he would take me to. It was an isolated hilltop that looked out over a huge valley covered in thousands of twinkling lights. The views were tremendous from up there. You could see into the next governorate. Little did you know that those spectacular views and twinkling lights were actually from an established refugee camp where most people had no running water and used generators to power their homes. It looked so peaceful from afar.

We would sit on the hood of his car, his arm around my shoulders, and do a lot of talking and kissing. It wasn't really what I thought of as a real relationship, but I guess he did because he lost it when I broke things off.

He threatened to out me to my family. It would have been a disaster. Sure, my mother knew the truth, but my father, my brother, my cousins, and uncles would have exiled me. It would have been the end of everything.

I ended up calling Joseph. I told him what was going on, and he said, "Don't worry, I'll take care of it. What's his phone number?" Joseph called him, pretending to be a police officer. I'm not sure what he told him, but he scared the crap out of that guy. I never heard from him again. I owe Joseph everything for being there for me and protecting me. He told me not to worry about it. "Like it never happened," he said, calmly deleting the number from my phone. If Robert was my sanctuary, Joseph was my protector.

I graduated high school in 2004. I was thrilled because I was accepted into the University of California at Santa Barbara. Everything seemed to be lining up. I was getting out of the Kingdom! I was going to be free! I couldn't stand the wait. I was finally going to be me and date whoever I wanted, and in public!

I told my mom that I wanted to become a plastic surgeon.

"So, you'll give me a new face for free?" she asked, smiling with that glitter in her eyes.

"When you're sixty," I answered, grinning back. "Sure, I will."

"Sixty?" she scoffed. "I'll need one sooner than that. Do you see these wrinkles? You had best get to work!"

I was in California for less than two months.

My uncle hated me, and so did his wife. I remember when I was just a kid, walking out of the restaurant on Easter Sunday—I must have been ten or eleven—hearing them talk about me.

My mother was always proud of how I did in school, just like any mother would be. I got the top marks in my classes every year. It wasn't hard. School was easy, it's just that the people I was with in school were lazy. They didn't care how much their parents spent on their education, they knew their families had money, and lots of it.

"Louie is the top student again this year," my mother had said as we walked out of the door toward the waiting cars. "I am so proud of him."

"We'll see how long that lasts," my uncle's wife shot back.

She was jealous. They were all jealous. My cousins were, in kinder terms, a couple of knuckleheads, at least the younger two. They couldn't do anything right, and I never understood why they acted so stupid and irresponsible. They were content to goof-off constantly and slowly await their inheritance. Their older brother Nathan was different, he was kind of a creep, but he was smart and seemed motivated. He had gone to school in the UK and walked around the compound like he was the coolest guy in the Heights.

He worked with my uncle, in their pharmaceutical empire, and always played a game of tag or hide-and-seek with the groundskeepers' children when they brought them to work. When I was still in elementary school he took me aside and offered to tutor me. I didn't know what tutoring was, but my mom told me I was smart and didn't need him in my life, and that when I was older I would understand why. Eventually, he stopped being nice to me and fell in line with his parents, treating me like some phony golden boy undeserving of my own accomplishments.

The older I got, the resentment of my uncle and his wife grew. For some reason, my success was the problem, and not the failings of their own kids. I guess they just couldn't blame themselves for raising a bunch of screwups. Then I went to the States for college, enrolling in the premed program, and that was the last straw.

My uncle started spreading the rumor that I was hooked on drugs. It wasn't a run-of-the-mill drug problem either, it was full-blown, heavy-duty addiction, the kind where I prostituted myself for more cocaine. I didn't even know anything about cocaine. The same couldn't be said for my cousins though. Maybe that's why my uncle started it, anything to make him feel better about his train-wreck children. The rumor ran through my family like wildfire. Less than two months after my arrival in the States, I was on a plane back to the Kingdom.

There was nothing I could do. My father called the school and canceled my tuition, then calmly informed me of my departure date. I was in utter shock and disbelief! I had not even begun my classes. I was still going through orientation. Everything I had been working toward suddenly seemed meaningless as I boarded that plane and sunk into the cramped, economy seat with my eyes bawling. I couldn't bear the thought of losing my freedom and myself.

Then I was at the airport crying into my mother's arms, and my father sternly said, "Let's go home."

I was home for a couple of months before the unthinkable happened. The whitewashed compound, which once seemed so bright, was suddenly void of cheer and color. Every shadow was longer. My room looked the same as it always had. It was as if I had gone nowhere. My dad didn't even give me the chance to explain what had happened and why. My mom couldn't do anything either. She knew everything but wasn't able to change the situation. The Kingdom had me in her steely clutches in that closeted purgatory.

I went about my days absently. Friends wanted to see me, but I couldn't bear the thought. I had no ambition after that defeat. They did not know why I had returned, but all my family members cast me horrified, cruel glances. Even if the supposed drug binge had been real, they did nothing to comfort me. They offered no support or love. They only looked at me like I was a grotesque mistake, a mar on their good name. Especially my cokehead cousins.

My mother and brother were the only ones who believed me. If there was one single thing that I was happy about that month, it was seeing my mother finish a marathon she had been training for. I clapped, hollered, and hooted until my voice gave way as she crossed the finish line.

I spent more time with my brother than I had growing up, trying to learn more about his passions. If I was going to live in the Kingdom longer, I had to become a more typical Middle Eastern young man. It was all sports cars, cigarettes, and in my brother's case, gaming PCs.

"Fuck Xbox," he would say. "Why would I buy a computer that can only do one thing? That's what it is, you know, it's just a computer, but they put limits on it! Why would I buy that?"

I started attending a university in the Kingdom. It was a fine enough school, but it didn't have the freedom that California had offered me. It put a real gray tint on the whole experience, but I still put my best foot forward with my studies. I always had. Anything to keep showing up my uncle and his kids.

It was Sunday, November 21, 2004—a day I will never forget. School weeks in the Kingdom started on Sunday and ran through Thursday, and I had an exam that morning. I started the day really early and had some time before I left for the campus.

I was in the media room watching MTV when my mom came down the stairs with a gym bag over her shoulder. Her hair looked amazing even in the early mornings. She didn't say anything, just lied down on the couch beside me and watched the screen for a little bit. Eventually I got up and told her I had to get to school early for some last-minute studying.

She stood up, gave me a kiss on my forehead, hugged me and said, "Good Luck. I'll see you when you're back," then she straightened out her shirt and patted her hands against the sides of her legs. "I'm off to the gym myself," she said.

"You're going to the Four Seasons?" I asked, shouldering my backpack.

"Oh no," she said. "Just next door." Our compound had a big gym complex that took up half of the basement of my aunt's villa and looked out over the city.

"All right," I said, walking out the door. "See you. I love you!"

"Good luck! I love you more," she called again after me.

My family's chauffeur was waiting in the courtyard. He was still driving me everywhere because I didn't have a driver's license.

"Another day in hell for me, Ron." I said as I sat right next to him in the front passenger seat.

"Why is that?" He asked.

"You know very well why. I'm stuck here, and I can't undo what happened to me," I complained.

"Your dad was just trying to protect you. He loves you. He's a very good man," he said to me as I thought to myself what a bunch of crap that was. If he loved me, he would've supported me and believed me.

Later that day, in my Arabic 101 lecture, a campus security officer came to get me out of class. "What's going on?" I asked.

"Bring your bag," he answered.

Ron was waiting out front with a police officer. He looked broken, his eyes red and glazed. I had known him all my life, and it hurt me to see him so distraught.

"What's happening?" I asked him, looking nervously between the police officer and Ron.

"We have to go home," he said, and then took me into a firm hug as he began crying. My fear got more intense. Had something happened to my father? Something with his plane? He was supposed to get back from London that day.

I knew something was very wrong as we got into the car. The police officer drove us back to the compound, and Ron was crying the whole way, gripping my hand and saying, "It's going to be all right, Louie. Whatever happens, it will be all right."

I stopped asking what was going on. I knew it was something bad, and I knew I was about to find out what. There was nothing to do but sit in that leather seat and wait while the anxiety built up in my chest like a cold iron ball.

The gate was open. That was the first thing I saw. Then I saw the cars, so many cars. They were parked all around the swimming pool like some ridiculous Mercedes commercial. So many cars that they went out through the gate and down the side of the road.

We pulled up into the courtyard and Ron got out to open my door. I was stuck. I could not face whatever travesty was waiting for me, not with so many people. I recognized most of the vehicles. It was the entire family, both sides, and it could only mean something devastating had happened.

I was freaking out now, sweating and bouncing my leg rapidly, staring out the open car door at the ominously waiting villa. I had to get out of the car. I had to find out what was happening. I had to move my legs.

Finally, I swung them around and stood up. As the sunlight in the courtyard struck me, I passed out.

I woke up in the house with a cold sweat at the nape of my neck. The room was full of people. Everyone was there, sitting around the living room, watching me. The house was deathly still, and the only sound I could hear was the distant ticking of the clock in my father's office.

Cigarette smoke drifted carelessly up from the tobacco in everyone's hands. My father was clutching his glass of scotch. Once people seemed to notice that I was fine, their heads all swung back down to the floor. Everyone was there. Everyone except my mother.

"What's going on?" I asked, my voice cracking through the stillness. My fingers clenched into sweaty fists as I sat upright. I blinked my eyes twice, just to make sure it was all real. It seemed like a dream, some staged painting of an extended Middle Eastern family. But it was real, it was horribly real.

"Louie," my father said, looking up from his untouched scotch. His eyes were blank, as if there was nothing inside to fill them. "Your mother is dead."

Chapter Two

MY MOM HAD BEEN my sole sanctuary in that house. She had been the light and joy of my life. The shield that protected my sandcastle. Now she was gone. It was the realization of my worst fear, and I was powerless to change it. It was like a twisted nightmare, only real.

They told me that she had suffered from a heart attack, then fell down the stairs. I received the news blankly. Everything was gone. I felt like a shell of a person, like there was nothing left inside, and all I could do was stand there with a dumb, vacant face, blinking over and over. I could see people's mouths moving, I knew they were talking to me, but I couldn't hear any of it. It was all a soft hum ringing through my ears, delivered through the haze of fifty stifling cigarettes.

There were two clear groups. My father's side of the family sat in the grand living room with their silent scotch and smoke, while my mother's side of the family was in the kitchen, crying. Those sobs and wails rose above the murmuring and pulled me forward. That was where I belonged.

Each step was heavy, and the thud of my heels on the marble floor were the loudest thing I could hear through a strange buzzing. Nothing made sense. There was no thinking. Automatically my slow steps moved me toward the kitchen, and my mom sister's cries of despair.

I don't know how long I was in the kitchen. I only remember sharing a few hugs with my aunt and grandma. They clutched at me and cried, but tears didn't run down my face. I had no tears, just as I had no heart, just as I had no brain or stomach. I was empty, drifting through the mourning villa.

I had never felt loss like that. I didn't know what to do. I felt as though I should do something, but there was nothing to be done. I dragged my legs up the stairs, running my hand along the banister, then froze halfway up the flight. Was this where she fell? Where was her body? What had really happened? Was it after the gym? I stood like that for twenty minutes or so, trying to get to the top of the stairs, but unable to move. A heart attack? She was fit. She had just run a marathon. If she could run a marathon, then I could get to the top of the stairs.

I sat in my room for a long time, looking at the ceiling. It wasn't real yet. The whole thing was still in that strange limbo, where it had complete control of me, but it felt like a bad dream. Half of me expected to see her the next time I went downstairs, positioning one of her beautiful flower arrangements, and the other half of me just wanted to stare at the ceiling.

What kind of sick joke was this? She couldn't be dead. They were pulling one over on me, punishing me for my supposed drug abuse. That had to be it. They were shunning me. If I went downstairs, she would be there, watching TV on the couch, right where I had left her.

There was a little tap at my door and Nathan shuffled in, his face long and somber. "How are you holding up?" he asked softly, moving to where I sat on the bed. I couldn't muster any words, so I just shook my head a little bit. "Yeah," he said. "I get it," and he sat down on the edge of the bed beside me. "I didn't think you should be all alone up here."

He slid over a little bit until he was right next to me and put his arm around my shoulders. All I could smell were his thick layers of cologne. He really heaped it on. Then he leaned into my ear as he rubbed my shoulders and whispered, "Are you one, Louie?"

I was completely confused by the question. It didn't make any sense, and my brain was still trying to figure out that my mom was never coming home. I existed in a blank, dark space, but suddenly I jumped in surprise as his lips started kissing my neck, and his hand reached down to my groin.

"What the fuck!" I yelled, standing abruptly.

"Louie—" he started saying, but I left my bedroom before he could finish saying anything. I felt sticky and disgusting on top of all the pain and sorrow. I didn't want to think about it, I just wanted everything to go away.

Nathan followed me out of the room and down the hall to the top of the stairs. He looked concerned, no doubt worried that I would tell someone what he was trying to pull, but I couldn't even think that far. As I started down the stairs I turned to him and said, "Just leave me alone, for fuck's sake! Use the other stairs and don't come near me!" My voice came out shaky and weak, and he backed up a few paces, his face twisted in thought like he was trying to figure out something to say. Then he disappeared, and I heard the backdoor slam. I went down the stairs into the mournful mingling that occupied our house.

That was the moment it all became real, and Nathan suddenly didn't matter. A sudden tidal wave of stress and grief filled my emptiness as I stepped down the stairs. Most of the lights were off, but I could still see the empty glasses and brimming ashtrays scattered around the living room. My mother wasn't there, and she wouldn't ever be there again, and I began to cry.

The clutter my family had left began to nag at me while I cried. My mother had always kept the house spotless. It really wasn't dirty, but in the dim light the empty scotch glasses cast enormous shadows. They were taunting me, those tyrannical stout towers of fired sand, sneering with their finger smudges and discarded coasters.

I was still crying as I began to clean. I don't think I stopped crying until I fell asleep, hours later. I cleaned the villa from top to bottom, neatly arranging everything the way she would have liked it. I clutched my knees to my chest on the kitchen floor, rocking against the cabinets, just waiting for the dishwasher to finish so I could put everything away. It was the only thing that made sense.

The funeral was two days later. The time between when I found out she was dead and the funeral was a strange haze of tears and solitude. My grandmother was at the house, and my mom's sister, but I couldn't speak with anyone. All I could do was lie down on the floor of my mom's walk-in closet, where I had spent so much time growing up, and cry as I clutched a pillow from the bed. It was the last thing that still smelled like her, and I couldn't stop holding it.

She had been the anchor in my chaotic, uncertain life. With her, I had been sure of myself, confident and excited, and now I felt intimidated and weak. It didn't help that I wasn't eating. I didn't remember the last time I had something to eat. She had been the only person in my family who truly understood me, who supported me, who was proud of me. Now she was a memory, and I was alone.

My brother carried it like he was expected to. He threw back his shoulders, cast his eyes downward, and went about his days in silence. The morning of the funeral he found me on the floor of her closet, clutching the pillow. The smell wasn't as strong as before, but it was still there, and I didn't want to let it go.

"Come on," he said softly. "You have to get dressed for the funeral."

I was really weak then—I hadn't eaten for three days, and I was emotionally vacant—but I was determined to stand strong for her. I had no idea how hard that was going to be.

It was a traditional Catholic funeral, which meant they laid her open casket out in our living room for the viewing. It was horrible. There were people everywhere, one at a time walking up and whispering a few words to her blank face and folded hands. When I looked down at her there, all prepped for burial, I broke down completely and almost fell over, but my brother caught me, gently steering me toward the couch. She looked beautiful in her funeral dress—the same gorgeous white designer dress she wore for my high school graduation—but it was a false sense of beauty. It was a mask, and it was too much to bear.

I took a small pair of scissors from the kitchen and cut a piece of her hair. I'm not sure why I did it, but it felt right. I tucked the hair into my shirt pocket, and then I started crying. I cried all the way to the church. We had a police escort because the caravan from our house to the church was so massive.

"What's all this?" my uncle muttered, peering curiously out the window as we pulled up to the church.

There were hundreds and hundreds of people waiting in the courtyard. Our family was large, but not that large. It was an entirely different group of mourners, and there were far more of them than we had family members and friends. At first, I couldn't make sense of it, but then I began recognizing a few scattered faces.

"So many unfortunates," my uncle's wife said with her typical arrogance. "I hope they know they won't all fit in the church."

"Well, we can't tell them to leave," my uncle said, sighing.

I had seen them in photos that my mother had shown me from her charity work. Whenever she helped people, she got a picture with them, looking all happy. Sometimes we would sit by the pool and she would go through a set of them with me, talking about the different ways she had helped them. For some it was medical bills, for others it was tuition fees, and even others had been given help with housing. They had all come, over five hundred of them, and seeing them there brought me such pride.

It was the only glimmer of something besides sorrow that day, but I held onto it. All those faces in my memory still bring me joy. She had truly been a good person. I knew it, and all those people knew it. I felt like they were on my side.

The car stopped in the courtyard and all the people shuffled to the side, clearing a path to the church steps. A lot of them were smoking and talking in soft voices as the doors on the hearse opened. The casket made its way into the church with my family proceeding in a ceremonial manner, but I hung back. Something about the finality of the grand church doors stopped me. They stood over the courtyard, ornate and intricate, the portal to the next chapter in my life, and I couldn't go through.

As I drifted through the churchyard, the people there kept coming up to me. I guess my mom had shown them pictures of me, because they all knew who I was. They were crying too, unlike my family, and they shared my overwhelming pain. They kept touching my hand softly and saying short things like, "She was our guardian angel," or "Your mother is the reason my child is alive." I felt so proud of her and such admiration for all these grateful people. It was that strength that got me through the doors and into my seat.

The church was packed to the brim. It was so full that many of the mourners had to wait in the courtyard while the service got underway. I was still crying in the pews when the priest started talking, and I cried the whole time. My dad kept giving me these looks, like, "Pull yourself together," but I kept on crying. There was nothing else to do.

I don't remember what was said at the funeral service. I cried and kept my eyes locked on the casket. Then the service was ending, and they clicked the lid shut on that heavy wooden case. The sound of the latches had a terrible finality, and it broke me completely.

I sprung from my seat and ran to the casket, crying and screaming as I threw my arms around it. All I wanted was to hug her, to hold her, for her to tell me everything was all right. But it wasn't, and she couldn't. This was the end of all that.

"I want my mama!" I shouted, clawing at the polished oak lid. "Give her back! Don't keep me away from her! Mama!"

My brother and uncle grabbed my arms and pulled me backward. I tried to fight against them, I didn't want to leave her in that glorified box, but I was too weak from my lack of food and days of crying and heartache. They pulled me out of the church, through those huge doors and down the steps, through the crowds of mourners outside, and sat me in the car.

"Wait here," my uncle said gruffly.

"It will be all right," my brother offered, touching my shoulder. Then they shut the door and left me in the back seat as they went back into the church.

My hands shook like crazy as I cried and pressed my forehead against the glass. Everyone in the courtyard could see me, but they did not shun me. They understood. I loved them for that.

The chauffeur was crying as he got in the car, but my uncle and father weren't. They were playing the role of a typical Middle Eastern man, not showing any emotions as we pulled away from the church and took off toward the cemetery.

"Such a splendid funeral," my uncle remarked as we turned out of the church courtyard. "So many people came."

"Yes, more than I expected," my father agreed, cleaning his sunglasses with a small patch of cloth.

"Are we going to open our homes to all those unfortunates?" my uncle asked, glancing toward my father for an answer. In the Kingdom, it's customary after a funeral to leave your house open for three days, so that mourners can come and pay their respects to the family. Clearly, my uncle was worried they didn't have enough food, and he didn't seem interested in buying more.

I snapped before my dad could answer. I turned to my uncle with a snarl and shouted back, "Of course! She loved them! All of them! She would have wanted them there! Christ! What is wrong with you?" The rest of that twenty-minute drive was completely silent as I felt my sorrow turn slowly to rage.

When we got to the cemetery I sat in the car, watching everybody trickle out of their black vehicles one at a time. I saw Joseph coming up to our car, and he gently opened the door. I was in the middle seat.

"Hey, Louie," he said, leaning his head into the car. "You need a hand?" Then I started crying again, really crying, like I had at the church. "Come on," he nudged, reaching out for my hand. "Let's get you out of this car."

Joseph pulled me out of the car, and put his arm around my shoulder, slowly walking me toward the burial plot. People were already clustered beside the casket and the grave. Joseph placed me in between Robert's mom and my brother and kept his arm around me. If he hadn't been there, I'm not sure what I would have done.

I had been crying for what felt like the whole day, and I showed no signs of stopping as they lowered the casket into the grave. I wanted to tell them to stop, to open it up once more so I could say goodbye one last time, but I was stuck. I couldn't move or speak, I could only cry.

Then they started shoveling the dirt over, and I lost it again. She hated being dirty, she always kept everything clean. The casket was so clean compared to the dirt they were throwing on top of it, and I couldn't cope with that. I could hear the dishwasher as they threw each lump over the casket, and I screamed out, "She doesn't want this! She hates dirt! Stop it! Stop!"

Joseph led me away. He parked me underneath a tree this time. "If you want to cry," he said, "then cry. Fuck them, this is bullshit. If anything is worth crying over, it's this." So I cried.

In the Kingdom, the family is supposed to line up at the funeral so that everyone can come by, shake their hand, pay their respects, and say sorry for their loss. I guess that's what my family was doing while I cried under the tree with Joseph before Nathan's younger brothers came to find me. They were fucking high, I could see it. Fucking cokeheads. Nathan was standing a ways off, watching his brothers harass me with a cold stare.

"Come on, Louie," they said, marching over with their rolled-up sleeves. "You have to stand in line with us. Dry those eyes, man, be a man!"

"Fuck you!" I screamed back, standing up so fast I got a head rush and almost fell back down, but Joseph caught me. "Fuck you!"

"Louie—" one of them reached out to grab my shoulder, but I swatted his hand away.

"Don't fucking touch me!" I shouted, seething, practically foaming at the mouth. "Leave me the fuck alone! I'll fucking kill you!"

"Jesus," they shrugged it off, "Fucking fine, freak, whatever you want," and then they left me alone.

"You're all right," Joseph said, rubbing my back. "You're all right now."

After the burial we had a huge lunch at our compound for everyone who showed up. In the Kingdom, these events are always segregated by gender, just like our poker tables. The men were all supposed to be at my father's villa, and all the women were supposed to be at my uncle's.

Joseph dropped me off at the compound gates, and asked, "You want me to come in?"

"It's all right," I said back, trying to get my eyes dry for the first time that day, "I'm just going to go to sleep."

"All right, man," he said, clapping me on the shoulder once more. "Call me."

"I will."

The pool in the middle of the compound reflected the midday sun in a brilliant way, and I could barely see as I walked across the courtyard, my dress shoes clicking on the limestone. When I opened the door to my house I was stunned. Instead of all the men, I was staring at a hundred or more women in black mourning gowns.

"Oh, Louie," my uncle's wife said, blinking at me strangely. "You didn't hear? Your uncle is hosting the men."

Of course he was, I thought, this was his chance to become the compound patriarch. What a bullshit power play. I slammed the door behind me, making it clear that I wasn't leaving, and some of the older ladies jumped in fright. I marched toward the stairs, and the little old ladies hurried out of my way, tossing me scared looks as I stomped my way to my bedroom. But first, I grabbed my mom's pillow from the walk-in closet.

As I lay down and gripped the pillow, I realized it had lost her smell and I started crying again. I knew it wouldn't last forever, but it still broke me down further. She was truly gone. All that was left was a messy patch of dirt nestled in that expanse of dry yellow grass.

I stayed up there for a long time, just clutching the pillow, and eventually I saw the sun set through my window. Then there was a knock at the door, and before I could answer, my uncle's wife opened it. She was standing with that slightly drunk tilt, a glass of wine in her hand, and her chin turned slightly downward.

"Louie," she said, "you know it's inappropriate for a man to be in this house tonight."

"Give us the room, dear," Robert's mom was suddenly behind her. My saving grace. "I'll talk to him."

"Oh," my uncle's wife looked surprised, "Well—"

"Thank you," Robert's mom shot back, stepping past her and shutting the door in her face. "How are you sweetie?" she asked, walking over and sitting down on the bed with me. I could tell she had been crying. She had a glass of wine in one hand, a cigarette in the other, and deep red bags beneath her eyes.

Robert's mom and my mom had always been close friends. I had known her since I was a small child, ever since Robert and I started hanging out. Sometimes I wondered if she was in the loop, if she understood that I was gay and Robert was bi. Looking back, she had to have known. Robert was a worse liar than I was.

"Can I have one of those?" I asked, nodding to her hand.

"A glass of wine?" she gestured with it. "Sure."

"No, a cigarette."

"Sure, sweetie," she pulled out one of those soft cigarette cases like you saw in old movies, lit up a Marlboro Light, and handed it to me. We stepped out onto my bedroom's balcony that looked over the capital under the murky dark skies and smoked. I coughed. She smiled and held my hand.

"Have you talked to Robert? He said he was trying to call you," she said finally, glancing my way.

"I lost my phone, I don't know when," I answered, staring ahead at the night sky. "But it's gone."

"Let's give him a call together," she said, pulling out her cell. "It's earlier in Texas."

"What's the time difference?"

"Eight hours."

We called Robert, and all three of us cried together. I asked him how school was going, and he told me some stories that I instantly forgot. Eventually he had to go, and the distraction was over.

"How did she die?" I whispered, staring ahead into the night sky. "I can't get my head around it."

"Sweetie," she said, stubbing her cigarette out on the balcony baluster. "I think you need to ask your dad about that. I still don't really know."

Her eyes were lying. I had to know. What kind of freak accident could take my mom away? Was she killed? What is everyone hiding from me? None of it made any sense. A heart attack? She had just run a marathon.

The next morning, my brother, Joseph, and Luke—one of my childhood friends—came into my room. My friends came around a lot those days, checking up on me. At the time I didn't realize how much that helped me. That day I was just lying in bed, staring at the ceiling.

"What?" I asked, glancing their way.

"You have to eat something," my brother said. "You haven't eaten anything for four days."

"I'm not hungry," I said, even though I felt horrible and had a terrible headache. I did need food, but I was too stubborn to admit it.

"Well, that's too bad," my brother shot back, "because you're going to eat something."

"You can't make me."

"Oh yeah?" Joseph challenged, crossing his arms. "Watch us."

"Fuck off, guys!" I yelled back. "Leave me alone."

"Okay then," my brother said, and gave Joseph and my friend a nod. My brother was way stronger than me on a normal day, and being malnourished, I really didn't have a chance. He pinned me down to the bed while Joseph and Luke stuffed small pieces of bread into my mouth.

"You can't get up until you eat it!" my brother said, easily keeping me down as they fed me like a baby bird. I resisted at first, then pretended to chew, and even made a fake swallowing sound. As soon as my brother let go, I shot up and spat all the food out onto Joseph's face.

The room fell silent as Joseph wiped the mushy bread from his eyebrow and looked at me really intensely. Then he started laughing, and my brother and Luke joined in. I found myself laughing along with them. It was the first time I had smiled or laughed since my mom had died, and it felt good.

The three of them finally got me out of my room. With Robert away for school in the States, my brother and Joseph were all I really had for emotional support. My dad might as well have been a cardboard cutout. Nathan seemed to always be on the edge of my view, keeping his distance, but always around. It really creeped me out.

I found out after I emerged from seclusion that my father had fired the maids, and that they had gone back to Sri Lanka. That broke my heart, because not only had I known them my entire life, but they had stolen a bunch of my mom's jewelry when they left, out of spite. Shit, if I were them, I might have done the same thing. So much for twenty-two years of service.

With the maids gone, I did most of the cleaning. Ever since that first night, staring at the dishwasher, I became obsessed with keeping the house clean. Everything had to be perfect, just the way my mother would've liked it. In the month that followed, I became intensely OCD. I'm still a clean freak, but it's better than it was. That month, I kept the villa perfect.

Joseph invited me out a few times, but I couldn't leave. I was stuck in the compound, just keeping the villa clean. It was the only thing that made sense. I was miserable, but it made sense. Just keep the house clean. Keep it very clean and she'll notice and appreciate it, wherever she was.

Christmas was right around the corner. The holiday was always a big deal around our compound. My mom had always gone all out on the decorations. One year we were even featured in a magazine. People were always stopping their cars to take pictures of all the lights. That year, Christmas felt hollow. We still had a big tree and a bunch of decorations, but for me it all felt fake. It was like some gross imitation of her absent Christmas spirit, and it made me sick.

After Christmas, I took all the decorations down. I was cleaning my dad's office one day—he was away in London on one of his frequent trips—when I found it. It was a big Manila envelope, already opened, just sitting in the middle of the desk. Inside was a single document.

It was my mother's death certificate. Under cause of death it read: asphyxia by strangulation—suicide by hanging.

I went into this crazy blur, not sure what to do, but knowing I needed to do something. I realized I was probably the only one kept in the dark on this, and that fucked me up even more. I knew at that moment, that in this family I was truly alone. My mom was the only one that had had my back, and now she was gone. It was as simple as that.

Grabbing a shitload of Valium from my dad's medicine cabinet, I washed them down with some vodka, and got in my mom's silver Mercedes. It had sat in the same spot since the funeral, and it was time to move it. At least I think that's what I was thinking.

I ended up speeding down the highway, going as fast as I could, screaming my lungs out over the top of the steering wheel. The radio was blaring some typical Middle Eastern shit, and I was jamming my thumb against the tuner trying to find something modern to blast. Then I clipped a bus, spun out, and smashed into the median.

The car was a mangled wreck. I could hear the sirens and see the flashing lights of emergency vehicles as I lay there with my head pressed against the twisted door. Shattered glass was everywhere, and I saw blood on the steering wheel, but I couldn't feel anything. It was some strange mix of the drugs and shock, and I felt like I could have sat there forever, nodding in and out of consciousness.

For a time I thought I was dead, but before long I was on the couch in my villa. My uncle was screaming at me about tarnishing the family name. His sons were doing that all on their own, but I didn't have the faculties to retort. I was beat to shit. I didn't have a driver's license. I should have been in jail, but my dad had pull with the prime minister.

Nathan sent a text out of the blue right after his dad left, reading, *I'm sorry about the other day, Louie, you know I love you. I hope you're okay.* In a furious panic I typed back, *Leave me the fuck alone, creep.* That seemed to settle it because he never replied.

I cried myself to sleep that night. I was outraged with myself for destroying her car. I knew I wouldn't see it in her usual parking spot anymore, and that broke my heart. Just like her pillow, the small things that reminded me of her were disappearing, and I didn't know how to cope.

Shortly after that, I got expelled from college. I had stopped attending my classes. I didn't care. All I did was keep the huge house in order. Rumors started flying around the Kingdom about our family. People in the upper classes love to talk all that shit.

They blamed me for it. My mom's family, my dad's family, and the condescending public. They said that my mom killed herself because she couldn't bear how disappointing I was, how I had failed school in California, how I had a drug problem, how I "just wasn't right." I knew it was bull, but it still tore into me like nothing else.

In February of 2005, my dad bought me this brand new S80 Volvo. I don't know why he bought me a car, maybe he was trying to get closer to me, or maybe he just didn't want me getting driven around by our chauffeur anymore. I know that he got me the Volvo specifically because it was the safest car you could buy, and he thought I was a bad driver. In all honesty, he was right about that.

I loved that car. People would snicker and call me a spoiled little brat. I'm not spoiled, I thought, I'm just secretly gay, depressed, and living in a cultural and physical prison. The compound stopped feeling like home. It was just a place that I went at night, and that place I had to keep clean.

I started going online a lot again. Those gay chat rooms were all I had left. I didn't even erase my browser history anymore. Nobody was looking. When I hit the letter "G" the first thing that popped up was Gaydar.co.uk. I would chat up a guy, set a meet, and whip off in my silver Volvo. We'd meet at a bar usually, and after a few drinks we'd spend a lot of time making out in cars or hotel rooms. It was mostly a distraction for me, so I didn't have to think about my mom being gone, but the distraction never lasted. Eventually I would end up crying, and the guy

I was with would leave. They would avoid me after, probably because I was such an emotional mess. I went through a lot of guys like that.

March 21, 2005 is Mother's Day in the Kingdom. My uncle and his wife had this big fucking inconsiderate party next door. I didn't want to go. Besides the holiday and my mom being dead, Nathan was over there, and I didn't want to be near him. But I had to go. Everyone had to go to everything when you lived on the compound. Everyone lived next door to each other, so there was no excuse.

I walked in the door, and Nathan's younger brothers looked up from the table, shouting in unison, "Louie's here!" They were obviously high. My uncle, his wife, my dad, his sister, my cousins, and my brother were all sitting around the big table. There was a huge cake in the middle of everything that said "Happy Mother's Day" in really big fancy lettering. There was a pile of presents piled next to it. I saw Nathan hurrying down the stairs, his eyes darting around the room as I settled in.

"Louie, we were beginning to wonder," my uncle said, turning halfway around to watch me enter the room. "We thought you weren't going to make it."

I stopped. It was all wrong. My mom literally died four months ago, and these people didn't love me, except for my brother, but he wasn't going to stand up to them. He had too much to lose.

I said, "Fuck this," and left.

Running back home, I threw a little bag of clothes together, grabbed a stack of cash from my dad's office, and hopped online to arrange a meet with this guy I had been talking to. His name was John, and he was in his late twenties, back from school in the UK. At least, that's what he had told me online. He agreed, gave me the spot and the make of his car, and logged off.

I got in my Volvo and took off through the gates. I wasn't going back. That wasn't my world anymore. It never had been.

It was night by the time I made it to the parking lot. There was a strong breeze whipping over the asphalt that tossed my hair around as

I got out of my car. The black Audi A6 had its lights on still, looking like some sort of car commercial in the windswept lot.

When I got close to it, the driver's door swung open. He was handsome, there was no denying that, but his eyes had this dangerous gleam I couldn't put my finger on. He made me nervous, but that only made everything more thrilling.

"I'm Louie," I said, stopping a few feet away from him.

"Hey, Louie," he said, tossing his hair back with a flick of his head. "I'm John."

Chapter Three

HE WAS SO COOL. In a lot of ways, he was pretty typical. The slick clothes, the flashy car, the cigarette he drew from effortlessly and relentlessly. All were hallmarks of an average and wealthy Middle Eastern man. I had met hundreds of people like him before, and I would meet hundreds more just like him in the future.

But there was something else about him, something magnetizing. He had an aura of waves crashing onto the beach. I was immediately into him, and each step I took closer to his car the more rapidly my heartbeat. It had been a hell of a day, emotionally, but the night showed no signs of slowing down.

"Hey John," I said, within a few feet of him. "I'm Louie."

"I'm John," he said with a coy smile. "And I know who you are, you told me online."

"Yeah," I said, stumbling with my words and feeling embarrassed. "I guess you're right."

"You're really a cute one, aren't you?" he asked, flashing a smile in between drags of his cigarette. I didn't know what to say back, so I didn't say anything.

We stood there in silence for a minute, looking each other up and down. He was taller than me, and I could feel his pressured gaze as his eyes flicked devilishly down the length of my body. I was so nervous. I don't know why, but I wanted him to like me so badly. It was as if all the validation I needed in the whole world could come from this guy right here, and I would be damned if I wasn't going to get it.

He flicked his cigarette onto the asphalt. "So you want to get in?"

"Yeah," I said, walking around the front of his car. "I do."

He popped the door open from the inside, and I slid down into his car. The seats were all leather, like some sort of moving high-class couch, and I instantly felt more relaxed as I leaned back. He leaned back too, and propped his arm up on my headrest, turning his head to look at me.

We locked eyes for a minute. I knew he wanted to kiss me. Shit, I wanted to kiss him and he knew it, too. His eyes were hypnotic reflecting pools, pulling me in deeper and deeper, yet showing nothing underneath. His facade was ironclad, but he was so cool I was becoming putty in his hand, just from looking into those wild, dangerous eyes.

"You like music?" he said, breaking our eye contact. I felt my heart flutter as he directed his attention to the sound system, pushing a few glowing buttons on the dash.

"Sure," I said, trying to calm down. I didn't want to be the guy that gets all sweaty and nervous, but I was having a hard time keeping it together.

"Yeah? What kind?" he asked, shooting me a sideways look, his finger poised just above the volume dial, waiting to strike.

"Umm, all kinds I guess," I said, trying to play it cool.

He reached into his jacket as he started clicking through the radio and pulled out his cigarettes, pulling two from the pack with his teeth like some character on TV. He lit them both at once, and slid one over to me. I didn't really smoke, but I took it anyway. I wanted to be like him.

Backlit buttons and digital displays lit up the console, and the car sat low to the ground. I felt like I was in some kind of submarine, as if the rest of the world didn't matter in that space. I ran my finger along the red stitching of the black leather seat as I awkwardly held the cigarette with my other hand. I took a drag and did everything in my power not to start hacking and coughing. I didn't know the guy, but I didn't want to fuck this up.

My ears perked as the radio landed on an Ace of Base song, and he said, "Aw shit, I love this track," as he turned up the glowing volume dial. Then I lost it. I couldn't get away from the sorrow and rage I was carrying, even with these distractions. I started sobbing.

"Whoa, whoa, what's wrong?" he asked, putting his arm back on my headrest and turning the music down. "You don't have to cry. What's going on?" His entire persona changed. The hard-bodied rouge had been replaced by some kind and caring sweetheart with the flip of a switch. It wasn't just his voice, it was his whole being, and I instantly felt like I could trust him with everything. So I did.

"I can't fucking do it!" I groaned out, trying to wipe away this sudden torrent of unwanted tears. "I just can't take it anymore."

"Take what?"

I bit my lip. How did I always manage to fuck these things up? Every time I got in a guy's car, I ended up crying. And we hadn't even gotten to making out yet. I was a wreck.

"Hey, hey," he said softly, brushing one of his fingers down the back of my ear. It sent a crazy shiver through me, and the tears sort of slowed down a bit, giving me a chance to catch my breath. "You can talk to me, if you need to," and I believed him.

"My fucking family," I said, shaking my head. I wiped my eyes on my sleeve and continued, "I can't deal with them anymore. I'm leaving."

"Leaving?" he asked, raising one eyebrow. "Do they know—"

"No," I said, "It's not like that."

"Well, what's it like?" he crooned.

"My mom took her own life," I blurted out, looking over to him. I met his eyes and

felt myself melting again in those dark pools. It felt so good to be vulnerable.

"Fuck," he said, moving his hand from my ear to the back of my head. He started gently rubbing the base of my neck with his thumb, and I began loosening up. I had known him for ten minutes, but I trusted him completely. "I'm so sorry."

"And my family, they don't seem to fucking notice," I said, raising my voice, and then I poured everything out. "My fucking uncle and my cousins, they don't care at all. They're happy, I think. My dad is a fucking statue that spends half his time at the British museum, and my brother, I love my brother, but it's not enough. I don't know. She was, like, all I had, and she's gone, and I crashed the shit out of her car, and now that's gone, and I just, I feel like there's nothing left."

He looked at me intensely. This was usually the part where the guy got out of the car and never talked to me again. But instead he gave me a sympathetic smile and said, "That sounds really hard."

"It is!" I cried out, feeling tears spring up again. "I can't fucking take it anymore!"

"Look," he said, stubbing out his cigarette in his littered ashtray. "I know who you are. I wasn't sure before, but now I know. I heard about you; I heard about your family."

"Who the fuck hasn't?" I groaned, leaning into his hand a bit more. It felt so good, so comforting.

"And I know enough," he went on, taking the unsmoked cigarette from my hand and relighting it. "To know that you can't leave."

"Can't leave?" I balked.

"Come on, Louie," he said, casting me a serious look. "You can't run away from a family like that. They won't let you."

"It's not running away if I'm not a child," I shot back. "I'm an adult. I can do whatever I want."

"They'll cut you off, you know."

"Fuck, I don't want their money."

"I know," he said, bobbing his head a bit. Then he reached out and touched his finger to the bottom of my chin, lifting it up to lock eyes once more. "But you do need it."

"I can get a job."

"Yeah, you can. But you don't have one. So don't leave just yet. Plus, do you really want to give them the satisfaction of pushing you out?"

"What?" I blinked. I hadn't thought like that before.

"Do they want you gone?"

"My uncle and his stupid wife do. I don't think my dad really cares."

"So fuck them!" he said, stomping his foot on the floor of the car. "Don't give it to them. Stick it in their faces that you are there. Be happy. Show them they aren't shit and can't keep you down. Go past them. But don't leave. They'll smear you forever if you do, and then what will you have?"

"Not everything is here in the Kingdom," I said, considering his words. He was so charismatic, so charming. I had never thought about what he had said, and now it was racketing around my brain.

"No, not everything," he said, "but I am." That shock of tenderness swept over me. I never had a guy listen to me like this before, especially such a hot one, and he had me eating out of the palm of his hand.

"You really think I should stay?" I asked, drinking from those pools.

"Yeah, I do," he said, brushing the back of my ear once more as he moved his hands back to the steering wheel. "Come on, let's go get a beer."

"All right," I said, breaking into an awkward, toothy smile. I felt warm inside, appreciated, and seen. "What about my car?" I asked as he turned his on.

"It's not going anywhere, not without you," he joked back. And we were off.

We sped down the highway in his sporty car like a couple of jackasses. I threw my head back laughing as he switched lanes over and over, weaving in and out of traffic for the hell of it with the windows down.

I stuck my hand out pointing and shouted over the noise, "That's where I crashed the car!"

"How'd you do that?" he asked, glancing over to the spot. There were still a few blemishes on the median from the wreck.

"I was high; I fucked up," I said back, feeling embarrassed, unsure of how he would take that, but I didn't want to lie. I trusted him.

"What were you high on?" he asked.

"Valium, a bunch of it."

"Badass, man," he said, grinning. Then I started feeling cool. I wanted to impress him so badly, and he thought I was a badass. It was the happiest moment I had had in a long time.

We drove around all night, popping in at different spots for a bite to eat or a quick beer. The whole time I kept wondering how we were still hanging out. Guys usually ran away long before this, but here we were, having a great time.

He kept listening to me, and I kept talking. I couldn't believe I was being heard, and I took full advantage. At the end of the night, I felt high off this emotional roller coaster, and I didn't want to go back home. I wanted to stay in his car forever.

I hadn't checked my phone the whole time we were together, and when I pulled it out of my pocket, I saw a list of texts and calls from my brother. I knew John was right. I couldn't just run away. Where would that get me?

"Shit," I said, looking over my texts. "I should get home."

"Yeah?" he asked, looking over his steering arm. "You're not going to run away on me?"

"No," I said, giving him a short smile. "I'm not."

"Good," he said, grinning back. "Because I like you."

"I like you too," I said, feeling my heart fluttering. Backstreet Boys' "More Than That" played in the background and he reached out and grabbed me, kissing me hard on the lips, and my heart exploded in a wave of comfort and excitement I had only dreamed of before that moment. I kissed him back with everything I had.

He took me back to my car. I didn't want to get out of those black leather seats, but I knew it was time. We exchanged phone numbers before I got out, and the second I saved his contact he texted me: *you're one sexy boy*. I looked up from my phone and smiled at him, sitting there next to me.

He smiled back and said, "What can I say? It's true."

It was almost midnight. I got back into my car and started driving home, and realized he was following me. My heart skipped another beat as his car stayed right behind mine every inch of the way. I felt protected, and I loved it.

I pulled up to the gate. The guard box was empty, so I hopped out of the driver's seat. His car pulled up behind mine, and he rolled down the window. I leaned down and he kissed me again, probably for a good thirty seconds, and then he abruptly pulled away.

"I'll text you when I'm home," he said, winking. Then he ripped out of the driveway and sped off like some outlaw on the run. It made me laugh.

I drove into our courtyard and parked in my spot. I was buzzing with excitement. I had found a guy that was actually into me. It seemed like an impossible dream suddenly realized. I didn't want to get out of the car, because if I did then I would be home and the day would be over. I was clinging to the whole thing as much as I could.

Sitting in my car smiling, I jammed out to Celine Dion's "Right in Front of You" for a while. I was so happy. I didn't think about my mom at all while I sat there, only about John. Replacing sorrow with romantic excitement had completely overhauled my entire being. I was alive and electric, and I loved it.

I finally shut off the car. I knew I couldn't sit there all night. When I stepped into the night air, though, a dark stillness came over me. The compound was silent. Almost all the villas had their lights turned off, but I could see a few from my uncle's second story. My cousins were probably watching TV or God knows what. The air was still, and the softly lit up pool reflected the moon in an eerie way that gave me chills. The whole place felt cursed, and I wanted to be back in John's car.

I started walking to the house, across the courtyard, and with each step, the reality of my world returned. My sorrow and rage built the closer I got to the front door as I thought about my mom and my family.

By the time I made it to my room, I was sobbing once more, and I collapsed onto my bed. I screamed into my pillow, drenching the pillowcases with my tears, and pounded my fists into the mattress.

Then my phone buzzed. I sat up on my bed, still crying, and fumbled to see what the disturbance was. I saw John's name on the screen, and my face lit up beneath the tears. I wiped my face on my blanket as best I could, trying to get a clear view of the screen. The text read:

I wish you were here in my arms.

Me too. I sent back.

I just want to hold you and take care of you. He replied.

That's all I want right now.

Maybe I should drive back over there.

Then that spark of happiness came roaring back, banishing my hateful and depressing thoughts. I started texting back, and every time I did he responded instantly.

I couldn't believe what was happening. He was my type and he was into me. We texted for hours, long after midnight. Eventually I fell asleep with my phone clutched in my hand like some toddler with a stuffed animal.

When I woke up, I thought for half a second it might have been a dream, but then I looked down at my phone. I had never responded to his last text because I had fallen asleep, and I felt horrified that he would be angry. I felt like everything I did for him had to be perfect because he was so perfect.

I sent an apology text: *I fell asleep! So sorry! Hope you have a good morning*, and for good measure I tacked on a smiley face. Then I sat there, staring at the screen waiting for his reply. I didn't have to wait long.

No worries! he texted. *But to make it up to me, we have to go out tonight.*

I sucked in my breath. Going out? Like a date? Where would we even go? What would we do? My experience of dates was making out in a parked car under a bridge or in an empty parking lot. I didn't know what to expect, but I knew I wanted to go out with him.

I'd love that. I replied.

I'll pick you up at 8.

After reading that, I jumped out of my bed like a bee stung me on the ass. I was so excited! How was I going to wait all day? I wanted to see him right then, to hold him and kiss him again, not wait until the evening.

I started blasting Britney Spears as loud as my speakers could handle, jumping around my room. I couldn't even get dressed. I was so excited. I went through my closet, throwing stuff onto my bed that I might end up wearing. It took me a good three hours to get out of my room that day. Everyone was already gone by the time I got downstairs, which was no surprise. I spent a lot of days alone on the compound avoiding everyone, including my friends. It was the way I liked it.

The day went by slower than any other. I paced the house, tapped my feet, made food I didn't eat, and surfed the web. When I thought a few hours had gone by, I checked the clock only to see that a measly thirty minutes had elapsed. It was driving me mad.

I ended up watching TV for most of the day. But then seven o'clock rolled around, and I was perched on the front step, waiting to see his headlights come into view.

I sat there for an hour, bouncing my leg, so excited and nervous that I kept running inside every twenty minutes to apply a new layer of deodorant, fix my hair, and check myself in the mirror. Finally, I saw the bright beams of his spaceship roll into view, and my heart started racing as I skipped out of the gate.

I slid into that comfortable leather seat, and he already had his hand up on the headrest. We kissed good and long, and then he pulled back and said, "You look fucking great."

"Thanks," I said, feeling myself blush, thankful for the darkness outside and the blue glow from the dashboard. "You look great, too." He was breathtaking.

"Not as cute as you, kiddo," he said, sparking up a cigarette with this big flashy Zippo.

"Where are we going?" I asked, settling into the seat.

"Come on," he said, backing out of the driveway. "I want you to meet some of my friends." And we sped off into the night.

Chapter Four

THE SUN WAS DOWN, but it wasn't fully dark yet as we zoomed down the highway. John drove fast, really fast, and for a while it freaked me out. I had never been a great driver, and the last time I had gone this fast I crashed. But John was cool and collected as he manipulated the stick shift, often leaving only two or three fingers on the wheel, or using his knees.

He wore that same leather jacket, and the whole time a cigarette hung lazily from his mouth, trailing a thin line of smoke past his face like some villain out of a comic book. I couldn't get enough of it. I didn't want to be weird by staring at him, so I kept darting my eyes between the driver's seat and the window. I think he could tell.

We started curving toward the exit ramp, and as he reached for another cigarette, he looked over at me and said, "Shift for me, give me fourth."

It was a simple request, but it had caught me completely by surprise. I didn't want to do anything wrong, to embarrass myself, but sitting there and not doing anything was worse. I reached out and grabbed hold of the stitched leather handle and popped it down into fourth gear as he toggled the clutched with his foot.

Before I took my hand off the stick, he laid his palm down over my knuckles and let it rest there. That simple accepting touch thrilled me, and I sat back in the seat with a big, goofy smile on my face.

Everything he did seemed flawless. When we got to our destination, he parallel parked with a single motion. When he flicked his cigarette, his foot came down on it the second it hit the ground. It was all of those little things that made him irresistible.

"Where are we?" I asked, climbing out of the car. Glancing around, I didn't recognize the area. There were a lot of shop fronts and small restaurants tucked around, and the street was narrow, indicating it was one of the older roads left in the city. I didn't really come around those parts of town, and I felt out of place.

"You've never been here?" he asked, raising his eyebrows like I was crazy.

"I don't know where here is," I said, feeling awkward. I wanted to impress him, and so far I wasn't off to a great start.

He grinned at me as he walked around the front of his car. As we stepped onto the sidewalk he put his arm around my shoulder. "Come on," he said, "I'll show you."

We walked to the corner toward a building with large double doors, and big windows. Concert posters covered the outside, many of them peeling away from the concrete, leaving that pale paper residue on the wall.

"What is this?" I asked, starting to feel a little weirded out.

"You're in for a treat," he replied. He slid his arm off my shoulder and pinched my cheek as his hand went by, then he swung the door open with a splash of bravado.

The interior took me by surprise. The high windows let in some of that bright moonlight, and the tall ceiling made the room feel bigger than it was. There were tables and chairs set up around the room, and a big oval bar in the back with stacks of ceramic coffee cups offsetting the liquor bottles.

Some off-brand nineties pop music played in the background. I didn't recognize the song, but it was catchy, and I instinctively bounced my heels as we walked in. Something about that place felt right.

There were a few people at the tables, talking to each other and laughing. Everyone seemed happy, like the little cafe was a space where stress could not persist, and I felt lighter because of it.

We found a small table in the corner, and as I sat down I looked around a little more. There was something different about the room, something I had never experienced before. It was so foreign to me that I could hardly believe it.

I looked at John, cocking my head to the side, and asked, "Is everyone, you know—"

"Gay?" He immediately responded, his mouth curling into a smile. He pulled another cigarette from his pack and sat the box down on the table with a purposeful slap. "That's why we're here, baby. I can't believe you've never been here."

I could hardly believe it. It was as if, after waiting and slogging through some purgatory, I had finally arrived. This was my new life, and I loved it.

"Hey John," the server said, walking up with a bottle of water for the table. "Got a new friend?"

"This is Louie," John answered, nodding my way. "How are you, Harold?"

"My feet are killing me, man," he said, setting two glasses down beside the water. "How are you doing, Louie?"

"Good," I replied, a little flustered.

"You want an upper or a downer?" he asked, giving me a playful look as he stood up straight.

"What?" I blinked. The newness of everything overwhelmed me, and I was terribly nervous about saying and doing the right thing. I was terrified of embarrassing myself in front of John, but that ship was actively pulling away from port.

"Coffee or alcohol," John said, giving me a smile. His leg drifted over to mine under the table, and I could feel his foot gently touch my calf. The embarrassment started fading, and a strange, warm confidence poured into its place.

"What are you having?" I asked, leaning back a little in my chair.

"Two beers, Harold," John said, tapping a long stick of ash into the tray.

"Sure thing, John," Harold said. He turned to go back to the bar, but right before he did, he gave me a wink and said, "Welcome."

That was the confirmation I needed. I knew I was in the right place. On the surface the place was nothing special—four walls, a few bookshelves, a small bar, and a cluster of tables. To the average passerby, it was a typical cafe, filled with the pleasant bubbling of casual chatter, the smell of roasting coffee, and the soft clinking of ceramic dishes and drinking glasses being rearranged behind the bar. But in the Kingdom, we were not the average pedestrians. We were a secret underclass, hunted and defamed, and to us that small space with its warm light was not a cafe. It was a sanctuary.

"There he is!" A loud voice came from the door, and I turned to see three guys walking in, one with his hand up, waving to John. I could tell that they were like him—good hair, nice clothes, late twenties, and an overall cool demeanor. I felt my nerves creeping back. What if I wasn't cool enough for his friends? It was hard enough to make him think I was cool, but now there were three more just like him to impress.

"Hey guys, grab chairs," John said, letting a long strand of smoke leak up from his lips. "Meet Louie."

"Louie, huh?" the loud one asked, pulling up a seat from a nearby empty table. "You look young, how old are you? I'm Omar. You gonna drink that?" and he pointed at my untouched beer.

"I—" I fumbled with my words, totally disarmed by the blatant extrovert suddenly in my face.

"Hush up, Omar," another one said, pulling two more chairs to the table. Shooting me a smile, he added, "He's only teasing."

"I am not," Omar said, putting on a dramatic pouting face. Then he glanced over his shoulder at the bartender. "Harold takes years to do anything."

"Depends who you are, I think," John said, smiling. "Guys, this is Louie. Louie, this is George, David, and Omar."

"I'm eighteen," I said, trying to keep up with the conversation.

"Wow, what a catch, John," Omar said, leaning back in his chair as he snagged a cigarette from John's pack on the table. "I had a boy like that once."

"Yeah, how'd you scare him off?" David interjected, folding his leg over the other.

"Fuck off, David," Omar said, rolling his eyes.

"I remember that one," George said, a devilish look in his eyes. "You scared him off good."

"Scared him off?" I asked, nervously holding my beer with both hands like an idiot. I knew I was blowing this. I wasn't cool, but something about these guys gave me weird vibes, and I didn't know how to carry myself around them.

"Ignore these idiots," John said, rubbing my leg a little more with his foot. "They're jealous, is all."

"Jealous of your beer," Omar grunted, scooting his chair forward a bit. "Seriously, can I have it?"

"Let the kid drink his beer, Omar," Harold's voice entered the conversation as he walked up, casting an irritated look toward Omar. "You all want the same?"

"Coffee for me," George said, glancing up from his cell phone. "I have a late one tonight."

"Sure thing," Harold nodded. He came back with the drinks, setting Omar's beer down last.

"So where are you from, Louie?" David asked, taking a sip of his beer.

"The Heights," I said, trying to move one of my hands back to my lap as casually as possible.

"Rich boy too," Omar said, casting a sideways look John's way. "How do you do it?"

"Seriously," John said, looking at Omar with that dark, dangerous veneer he adopted in a split second, "That's enough." The look gave me chills.

"All right, all right, big man," Omar said, holding up his hands in a mocking gesture. "You made your point."

We sat there and drank a few beers together, talking about random stuff, almost none of which I could relate to. As they talked and bitched about the troubles in their lives, I got the impression that none of them had jobs or any real responsibilities. Who were these strange people? What did they do? How did they know John? All questions I wanted to ask, but felt too intimidated to do so.

I knew they weren't trying to intimidate me, but I couldn't help feeling small between them. It didn't help that they were all about ten years older than me and did everything with total confidence. That was something I had never been able to do.

At the end of the night John settled the tab, which couldn't have been small given the way his friends had been going at those beers. Before John and I walked back to his car, all four got up and went to the restroom together and came out wiping their noses. Was that part of our gay culture too? Was I supposed to join them? I felt so lost.

"What did you think?" he asked, sliding his arm back over my shoulder.

"About what?" I asked, glad to have him so close.

"Oh, come on," he said with a laugh. "What did you think of my friends?"

"They're—" I trailed off. What did I think? Honestly, they had creeped me out, but I didn't want to tell him that.

"It's all right," he said, laughing a bit more. "I know, they're all assholes."

I smiled as we got back into his car. As soon as I shut the door, he leaned over, grabbed me by the collar, and pressed me up against the tinted window. I was startled, but I didn't have time to say anything before he kissed me. My heart raced with excitement, and his deep, piercing eyes usurped my body. He eventually pulled away and lit up a cigarette without saying anything.

He drove me back to my house, and the whole time I was buzzing inside. I still didn't understand why he was into me, but I wasn't going to question it. He was everything I had ever wanted, and for some strange reason he was mine.

We got to my gate, and he left the car running while he gave me another kiss. Then as I went to open the door, he said, "Wait a minute."

"What's up?" I asked, turning back around.

"Yesterday you said you liked Valium, right?" he asked, kicking back in the driver's seat to fish something out of his pocket.

"I mean—" I started to refute him, but he pulled out an orange prescription pill bottle.

"I got these for you," he said, gesturing toward me. "Go on, take one."

"I don't really—"

"Aw come on," he said, cutting off my protest. "You don't have to be ashamed of it. I love them too. Here, we'll take one together," and he popped off the lid. He poured two into my hand, and two into his. "Well, two are more fun," he said, giving off a little laugh. Then he downed the pills with a little bit of water from the bottle in his cup holder and offered it to me.

I didn't love Valium. I had only taken a bunch of them the night of the crash because I was losing it and they were there. I didn't really want to take the pills in my hand, but then he swallowed his down, and I knew I had to if I wanted him to think I was cool. So I took them.

"Wait," I said, "you still have to drive home."

"I'll drive really fast," he said, giving me a wicked grin. "I'll text you when I get home. We'll see who can stay up the latest."

"Okay," I said, smiling sheepishly. "That sounds good."

"Goodnight," he said, leaning back against the driver's side door. I thought he was going to lean over and kiss me again. I wanted him to. But he didn't. He just sort of looked at me, like he was waiting for me to get out of his car.

"Goodnight," I said back, finally opening the door.

That night I lay in bed stoned, smiling from ear to ear each time my phone buzzed, and by the time I fell asleep I was even more enchanted than I had been the previous day. After that night, we started hanging out a lot.

We would go to the cafe frequently. It was a place we could laugh, have a few beers, and make out in the corner. It was unlike any place I had known before, and it became like a second home.

Every night he would drop me off, we would take some Valium together, and I would text him as long as I could while the drugs lulled me to sleep. Before I knew what was happening, I was drinking a couple of glasses of white wine and taking some Valium every day, but I didn't mind that at all. It provided me with the escape I needed while I was away from John. Those magical discs numbed my pain and blurred the compound's sad and ugly reality.

I would look at the pills in the palm of my hand before I swallowed them. What would I do without them? I didn't think I had it in me to live another day if it weren't for those pills and John. He always had another bottle of Valium for me, one way or another. I still don't know how he got them so easily.

One night we were making out in his car down the block from the cafe. We had been hanging out for a few weeks by then, and I was about as in love with John as I could be. Every moment I was awake, my thoughts swirled around him, and half the time I was asleep I dreamed of him.

I hardly ever saw any of my friends anymore. I had been drifting away from them since my mom died, but now with such a magnetic distraction added to the mix, I had all but forgotten them. They would text, and I would forget to text back. Eventually, they stopped texting, and I didn't really care. I only cared about John. Looking back, I'm sure the drugs had something to do with that. Robert and I still talked occasionally. He was in the States for school, and we would text each other sometimes, but I felt the oceans between us growing larger and larger.

I had stopped going to mom's resting place, too. For the first forty days after she died, I had gone to the cemetery every day. I would stand there and cry, tell her I missed her, and ask for strength. Now, I hadn't been there in a few weeks. I was busy. I was with John.

That night I was pretty fucked up. I wasn't on the floor or anything, but I was slurring my words. I could feel the third Valium kicking in, and I couldn't hold my head up, but John had his hands wrapped around the back of my skull so I didn't have to worry about that.

Then he was kissing my neck, and with my lips free I murmured, "I want you."

"I want you too, baby," he whispered back, working his way back up to my cheek.

"No," I said, rolling my head around to look him in the eyes. "I really want you. I want you right now."

"I know," he whispered into my ear, and my spine shivered. "But let's save that for a special day."

"All right," I mumbled, my eyes fluttering closed. It was hard to argue with him when my earlobe was between his teeth. He was playing with me and I was completely pliable.

When I got into bed that night, I still had the craziest raging erection. I tried pleasing myself but I was too fucked up to move my arm, so I ended up lazily lying there, touching myself and thinking about him until I fell asleep.

I woke up with a pretty good hangover, but I blinked it away as I popped a Valium and downed a glass of water. Then I checked my phone, and my heart did a little flip when I read the waiting text from John.

Happy Birthday, baby, go look outside.

Happy birthday? Had I really forgotten? I checked the date on my phone and sure enough, it read May 10. Fucking Valium. You can lose days on this stuff, I thought to myself. Then my heart started racing again as I thought about the text.

Go look outside? Why? What had he done? I stumbled around my room trying to get my bathrobe on. Once I had it loosely around my shoulders, I ran downstairs. The house was empty. That was typical. Sometimes I felt like I was the only one that lived there.

I ran into the courtyard. The morning sun wasn't over the roof of the villa yet, and the stones were a cold on my bare feet. I was shivering and high in my bathrobe, but I didn't care about the stunned look from the gate guard. I was too excited.

I looked around outside the gates of the compound and spotted a tan-colored basket tucked behind one of the trees with a card and a bottle of champagne beneath a big red bow. My heart backflipped.

I tried to tuck the basket under my bathrobe as I went back into the compound, looking even stranger than I had before. When I got inside, I put the basket down on the kitchen counter and opened the card. All it said was "Happy Birthday." Under that was an address, and the words, "My house, eight o'clock."

I jumped up and down in the kitchen, excited beyond belief that someone had planned a birthday surprise for me. I popped open the champagne and drank right out of the bottle, spilling a bunch down my chest and soaking my bathrobe. I giggled with happiness.

Then it hit me. This was my first birthday without my mom. A dark presence swept over me, and I felt tears racing down my cheeks and dripping onto my bare feet. I stood there holding onto that champagne with my right hand while my left gently wiped the drops away. I robotically moved to the dishwasher. It was empty, but I turned it on as I sank down on the floor next to it with my back against the cabinets.

I placed the bottle on the floor next to me and closed my eyes as the dishwasher ran through its cycle. I tried my best to stop thinking about my mom, but I couldn't. Every time I tried, I felt guilty. Thoughts and regrets raced through my exhausted brain, but everything came to a halt as the dishwasher made the loudest noise and then died.

I stood up and stared at the dishwasher. I wasn't sure what had happened and what caused it to stop. I tried turning it on again, but to no avail.

"Mom?" I squeaked out quietly. "Are you here?" The dishwasher didn't answer. The kitchen was deathly silent. Was I going crazy? There must have been a logical explanation for what happened, but to me it was a sign. It felt like my mom was telling me to stop being sad and start enjoying my special day.

I couldn't help it, but I started remembering my past birthdays. I'd wake up to my mom gently kissing me on my forehead.

"Happy birthday!" She would say, handing me my first gift. I would sit in bed and open it with a goofy smile, then the maids would serve us breakfast. The ritual was so simple, and yet it was everything. But today, she wasn't there. Nobody was.

My dad was out of town. I don't know if he even knew it was my birthday. Without my mom, there was no one to whip my family into celebration mode, so I don't think he remembered.

I spent some time that morning looking through our old photo albums. I sorted through my favorite pictures of my mom. I made a little pile of them and flipped through, over and over, taking small sips of the champagne.

I took the bottle out to the pool and hung my legs over the side, bouncing ripples together. I didn't know what to do with my day. I had the night to look forward to, but the day kept lingering. I saw my two younger cousins and uncle walking across the courtyard. They gave half a wave. I doubt they knew it was my birthday either.

I spent the rest of the day daydreaming about what my birthday would have been like if she had still been here. I wouldn't have cared if she had shown up empty-handed. All I wanted was to hug my mom and tell her how much I loved and missed her. *Was I ever going to be happy again?* I thought, unconsciously swallowing another Valium, trying to suppress those thoughts and contain myself.

I started getting ready at around six o'clock. I went through fifteen different outfits before I ended up in a white button-down, some denim shorts, and a pair of black flip-flops. Robert shot me a Happy Birthday text, and that made me smile. Someone had remembered. I texted him back and told him about Jo'n. Robert said that he couldn't wait to meet him. That made me smile too.

After checking myself in the mirror for what felt like the hundredth time, I got into my car and sped off to meet John. I had never been to his house, so I wasn't sure if I was in the right place. It was the correct address, but the house was intimidating. It was traditional, but huge and imposing. If my compound was quiet and sophisticated, this compound was fortified and domineering.

There was nobody at the gate, so I buzzed the button and waited. The gates automatically opened. That startled me, but I figured I had to be in the right place, so I drove into the courtyard. I saw John's car, breathed a sigh of relief, and parked next to it.

"Hey, baby," he called out, catching me off guard as I climbed out of my car. "Happy birthday."

"Hey yourself," I called back, smiling at him. He was leaning casually against the doorjamb like the cool guy he was, his thumbs resting on his belt. "This is your house?"

"Yeah, my dad's," he said, walking up to me and giving me a kiss. "You want to come in?"

"Yeah," I said, grinning up at him. "I do."

He led me into the villa, and the entryway opened up into a huge garden of jasmine bushes. The capital was full of them, but here they had been trimmed and cultivated. The little white flowers stood out against the old walls, and the space felt magical.

We went through the walled-off garden then he brought me through a large, jet-black door. The house greeted me with a massive, luxurious living room, with white and beige marble floors, and deep red burgundy curtains that draped down to the black trim. The place felt dark and cold. It was elegant, but off-putting.

"Is there anybody here?" I asked, looking around. Every door was painted black, and every curtain was that deep shade of red. I could tell that all of the furniture had been set up just as it was meant to be, and that nothing ever moved. I wouldn't be surprised if nobody ever sat on those sofas.

"No, my dad arranges travel stuff. High class, big conferences, stuff like that," John said, shrugging. "I don't really know exactly what he does. But my mom always goes with him. So it's just us."

"It's nice," I said, not wanting to tell him his house looked like a vampire's residence.

"Come on, it's less creepy upstairs," he said, chuckling.

The upstairs was carpeted, but the hallways had those same red curtains and black trim. It was weird, but I wasn't going to look too far into it. I was just happy to be with John, so I pushed my hesitancy aside.

When we got to his door, he turned and said, "Okay, close your eyes."

"My eyes?"

"Just close them."

"All right, fine."

I heard the door click open, he guided me forward a few steps, then the door shut behind us. Then he said, "All right, open them."

His bed was covered in rose petals, and a "Happy Birthday" banner hung between his bed posts. I could hardly breathe. Nobody had ever paid so much attention to me or gone out of their way to do something like this. It was an overt and corny romantic move, but it worked.

I turned around to look at him, and he kissed me, then put both his hands flat across my chest and gently laid me down on the bed. One of the rose petals pressed against my cheek. He turned over to his desk against the wall and hit a button on some kind of gadget.

"What was that?" I asked, leaning my head up a little bit.

"My fucking speaker decided to stop working when I need it most," he complained, frowning at the little box.

"I don't need music," I said softly.

"Good," he said, grinning back at me. "I don't either."

Slowly and deliberately, he exaggerated undoing each button on his shirt as he took it off, walking up to the foot of the bed. I sucked in my breath. He was like some Roman statue, chiseled and perfect. I felt my lust and passion rising, but nervousness as well. I didn't know what I was doing. Nobody does, the first time around. Then he climbed on top of me, running his nose along the center of my shirt until it landed next to mine.

"I love you, baby," he whispered.

"I love you, too," I said back, not questioning it for a second as I looked into his piercing, dominant eyes.

He started kissing me, and I became aroused in a matter of seconds, writhing up against his perfect body, drinking in the smell of his cologne. I could feel him against me, and I shuddered with anticipation.

He began working down my neck, undoing my shirt, kissing my chest and nipples, sending me into minor spasms of sensation as he kept going, dancing around my belly button, then further.

As the button on my pants came undone, the waistband relaxed around my hips, and I let out an excited gasp. I was throbbing as he lifted the band of my underwear, and slowly slipped it all away. Then his tongue and lips were exploring every inch of my body, and I was lost to the endless physical and emotional tidal waves of sensation overtaking me.

Everything was moving in slow motion, and every sensation was accentuated. His bare chest against mine, I ran my fingers down the muscular ridges of his back. His kisses were gentle, yet full of fire, and his hips matched that energy as they moved back and forth. It wasn't the way I had imagined it, but it was better! I felt loved and protected. He wanted me.

The nervousness had gone away, and I floated in some strange, blissful place where nothing could hurt me. Someone cared about me, and someone desired me. It was all I had ever wanted. This was my new life, and I had already fallen in love with it.

Chapter Five

JUST LIKE THAT, SUMMER came. I had been dreading it before I met John. My friends were coming home from their universities for a few months. They would all be happy and I would be in the same place, lurking around my compound. I had been dreading seeing all their cheerful faces and hearing their condescending quips about my future.

Now everything was different. I embraced each ray of sun, jumping out of my bed every morning with an extra hop as I popped open that day's dose of Valium. I knew that each day, at some point, I would see John, and that was more than enough to get me out of bed.

John was busy during the day helping his dad run the family business. He still managed to keep in touch with me through texts and quick phone calls. Almost every night we would link up, usually stopping by the cafe for a while and then going to his dad's company's office to make love. It felt like a never-ending day of benzodiazepines and really good sex. As a nineteen-year-old, I thought I was having the time of my life.

June 3, 2005, was an important day because I was going to be reunited with my best friend! I was feeling extra motivated when I woke up, and I danced around my room like I had when everything was great and my mom was still alive. I glanced between my window and my closet, trying to figure out just how hot it was going to be. I finally chose an outfit and gave myself a wink in the mirror as I adjusted the collar on my light-blue polo shirt. I was looking good. I was feeling good.

I didn't know whether it was those magical pills or not, but I was finally becoming happy again.

It took me a while to find my car keys. John didn't let me drive. Every time we hung out, he picked me up. I hadn't been in a real relationship like this before, and so I didn't see how weird that was. It was starting to become a minor issue as I was tied to wherever John went. Plus, family and staff around the compound were beginning to notice the black Audi that picked me up at the front gate in the evenings. Saying it was a friend would only work so much longer.

Either way, it took me forever to find my keys. Once I had them, I threw on my sunglasses and hit the road, idly shuffling through my CD collection as I sank back in my seat. It felt good to drive my own car, especially with the summer sun filtering down on me through the windshield. My car still had that new car smell. It didn't take long to get to the airport, and I arrived a good half an hour early, so I sat in my car blasting Britney and *NSYNC, drumming my fingers on the steering wheel.

I kept checking my watch. I knew it was going to take him a little while to get through customs and baggage claim, but I was anxious and didn't want to sit around waiting anymore, so I started driving the loops of the pickup zone, relentlessly scanning the crowd. I drove around eight times before I saw him, and I broke into a big smile as I shot off a friendly honk and swung up to the curb.

"There he is!" I shouted, cranking the parking brake and jumping out of the car.

"Louie!" Robert called back, kicking his luggage out of his way to give me a big hug.

"Damn, Robert!" I said, pulling back and looking up at him. "When did you get so buff?!"

"I know right?" he said, chuckling. "America, man, you have to be buff to get any action."

"Come on, let's get out of here," I replied, grabbing one of his bags and hauling it into my trunk.

"Please!" He answered, loading his other bag. We got in and pulled away with the windows down, letting the warm breeze blast back our hair as we merged onto the highway.

"So, how is America?" I asked, glancing over to him as he ducked down between his knees to light a cigarette. He was wearing aviators and had a few streaks of blonde dye in his dark hair. His tight T-shirt boasted his newfound muscles. "You look like a goddamn movie star!"

"Everyone looks like a movie star in the States, man," he replied, resting his arm on the door. "They party so hard, it's crazy."

"In Texas?!" I asked, thinking to myself that I hadn't heard a single good thing about that state.

"Everywhere," he said, nodding his head and taking a long drag of his after-flight cigarette. "We went to Miami for spring break. Man, they really know how to do it down there. You gotta come out there, you gotta see what it's all about."

"I'll get out there," I said, feeling a strange pang of anxiety. The United States seemed so far away. I hadn't seriously thought about going back since my dad had pulled me out of school.

"You have to!" Robert said, thumping his hand against the top of the car door. "What's up with you, man? Still seeing that guy? What's his name?"

"John," I said, feeling my anxiety vanish as quickly as it had appeared. "Yeah, I am."

"Few months now, huh?" Robert said.

"A couple of months. He's great."

"I'm excited to meet him," Robert said, flashing a grin. "Look at you, got yourself a boyfriend."

"Yeah, look at me," I laughed back. "I can't believe it either. What about you?"

"I have a boyfriend and two girlfriends," Robert said, leaning his head back against the headrest.

"Shut up!"

"I do."

"No, you don't."

"All right, I don't," he said, and we both cracked up as I made my way toward Robert's house.

I dropped him off and said hi to his mom and the rest of the family, but I didn't stay long since I was feeling kind of droopy from the Valium and I didn't want her worrying about anything. Robert and I agreed to hang out that night with John, and I headed home.

I had been excited to show Robert the cafe, to show him my new life, but since he had gotten in the car the excitement had dimmed. He was more confident and different than he had been a year ago, talking about spring break in Miami and the way they partied. I was starting to worry that what I had found in the Kingdom wouldn't be enough for my old friend, Mr. American movie star. When I got home, I took another pill and passed out for a few hours. It was easier to sleep through the day than to bounce my leg around the house, waiting for the sun to set.

John picked me up around eight thirty. I caught a side eye from one of the new maids as I crossed the courtyard and slipped through the front gate. As soon as I shut the door he leaned over and gave me a big kiss, which I wanted to hold forever, but instead I yanked my head away.

"Not right here," I laughed a little, trying to be playful so I wouldn't piss him off.

"Come on," he said, rolling his eyes. "I have tinted windows."

I leaned over and gave him another kiss, and that seemed to be enough because he started driving off down the tall, winding street.

"You picked your friend up today?" John asked, pulling out another cigarette with his teeth. I didn't find that move very cool anymore. He was always smoking.

"Yeah, my friend Robert."

"He was in the States, right? For school?"

"Yeah, in Texas."

"I've never been to Texas," John remarked.

"Me neither."

We sat in a few moments of silence as we drove, but my worries from earlier kept nagging at me. Eventually I said, "He's kind of different now."

"Different how?"

"I don't know, he's like," I paused to chew my words a bit, then said, "he's like you now."

"Like me?"

"You know, cool and stuff," I said, glancing over to him, anxiously waiting for his reaction.

"You think I'm cool?" John teased, giving me a friendly elbow jab.

"Seriously though," I said, shifting in my seat. "I want to do something cool with him."

"Cool like how?"

"Like a party, or something," I said, shrugging my shoulders. "I don't want him to get bored."

"A friend of mine is having a big party in a few weeks," John said, stubbing out his cigarette and reaching for another one. "You want to go?"

"Will it be cool?" I returned his teasing a little bit, shooting him a sly look as I leaned against the car door.

"So fucking cool," he answered, giving me a big smile.

"All right," I said. "Let's do that."

"Cool," John said, nodding twice.

I gave Robert the address of the café, and he met us there a little later. I was nervous when he walked in, wanting everything to work out. I didn't need Omar weirding him out by saying some dumb shit like he was prone to do.

We did a quick round of introductions, and Omar immediately said, "Another pretty boy, John? Where do you find these guys?" I was horrified, but Robert laughed it off and sat down. We had some beers and some small talk. It was all, generally speaking, a fun night, and I felt dumb for having such reservations about Robert being too cool for me. He was my best friend, and ten months in Texas wasn't going to change that.

We all had a lot of fun together over the next few weeks. We went out constantly, stayed up late, and got all sorts of fucked up. For the first half of the summer, I was never sure what day it was. It wasn't important. All that mattered was what time John was picking me up, where we were meeting Robert, and how many pills I had left in my container.

The big party was on the night of July 7, 2005, and it was going to take place at a warehouse. I had never been to a warehouse party, and I was excited. I didn't know what to expect, and it was a little intimidating. I felt like I had a lot riding on that party. I wanted to show Robert a good time, but I also wanted to impress John. The party seemed like a big step down that road.

That day, I had a lot of time to kill before John picked me up in the evening, and I loafed around the house, cleaning things that didn't need to be cleaned. My sudden onset of OCD had relaxed since the first few months after my mom died, but it still persisted.

I was cleaning the kitchen again, but I got held up thinking about my mom as I polished the handle of the dishwasher. It had been a little while since she popped into my head, and it sent me reeling. I suddenly felt bad that I hadn't been to her grave in so long, and I decided to remedy that immediately. I got dressed and took off to visit my mom.

I chewed on my favorite pill driving to the cemetery, glancing casually at the spot where I crashed as I passed it. It seemed like so long ago, even though it had been less than seven months. When I got to the cemetery, I parked in my usual spot on the side of the winding road. My mom's grave was at the top of a hill, with a big monument on top of it. The whole thing dominated the view, but as I got out of my car and looked up, it wasn't there.

Confused, I looked around, blinking, trying to figure out where I was. Surely I had just parked in the wrong place. I hadn't been here for a while. I was strung out but determined that all I had to do was look for the monument and head in that direction.

I spun around five times and didn't see it. I was getting irritated with myself. How could I be this lost? I got back into the car and started driving loops of the cemetery, scanning every direction, and time and time again I returned to the same spot I had started in with no luck.

On the fourth time around, I got back out of the car. It was where I always parked. I was sure of it. That crooked little tree nearby was a landmark I recognized. But her monument was missing. I started marching up the hill, my heart racing, my panic rising. What the fuck was going on? Did it get damaged? Is it being fixed? Why would nobody tell me?

When I got to the top of the hill, I almost passed out. The place where she had been buried was now a twisted mess of disturbed earth, a huge patch of dirt in the middle of the groomed grass. She was gone!

I stood there for what felt like an eternity. I couldn't make any sense of it. Where had she gone? I started crying as I stood there, my hands shaking and tingling. The longer I cried the more I broke down, until I was kicking and clawing at the dirt, sobbing and screaming, and calling out for her.

After a while I sat back on my heels, my shorts and hands were smeared with dirt, and I looked around, gasping for air. I saw one of the groundskeepers standing nearby, leaning on his rake, watching me.

"You are her son?" He said, standing up straight and leaning his rake against a tree.

"What the fuck happened?!" I asked, trying to wipe my tears away and smearing more dirt on my face in the process. "Where is she?"

"They moved her," he said, his eyes softening. "Over there," and he pointed down the slope to a divot of grass pressed up against the fence.

"They? Who exactly? Why?" Nothing made sense. My brain was like a dumb dog chasing its tail, going around and around to no avail.

"I don't know," he said with a shrug. "Cheaper plot, maybe, sometimes families do that."

"Families," I repeated, struggling to straighten my sunglasses and compose myself. Now it made sense.

"Yes," he said, nodding, "Families can move the plots."

"Families," I said again. I turned and started running down the hill toward where he pointed.

It was an awful spot. The ground sloped up just a little bit at the fence, creating a little gully sort of thing at the base of the hill. The damp ground beneath my feet told me that when it rained, this area flooded, and the fence cast a weird shadow on everything. Mom didn't deserve this place.

I stood there in silence, looking at her new spot. Horrible guilt descended as I wondered if I could have prevented this had I been paying more attention. It felt as if it was all my fault, and that thought devastated me.

"I'm sorry I haven't been around," I said to her finally, finding the nerve to speak. "I'm sorry they put you down here." She didn't respond. She never did, but for some reason I had imagined she would in that moment. "I'll get it fixed," I said, choking up. "I promise."

My family had moved her? A cheaper plot? I knew my fucking uncle was behind it and it wasn't because of needing a cheaper plot. Even months after she had died, he was still clawing at her, trying to rip down her memory.

I was trembling with livid anger when I got back to my car. I turned the key and the radio clicked on. I punched at it, trying to turn it off, and cracked the plastic volume dial.

I don't remember driving home, only that I kept hitting my hands on the steering wheel over and over. I ripped into the compound and immediately saw that nobody was there. All the cars were gone. The place was silent.

I was at a loss with no one to scream at. All I could do was fume and curse as I walked into my house, kicking at the doorframe. I stomped around the kitchen, my fists clenched and my teeth grinding.

What little I had left of her had been desecrated and it tore me to pieces. I felt isolated, even more removed from my family than before. They hadn't told me they were moving her. Were they ever going to?

"Fuck them!" I screamed, pounding my fist against the kitchen counter. I threw a couple of pills of Valium on the counter, grabbed a whiskey glass, and smashed them into powder. I scooped the dust off the counter, into the glass, and filled it with scotch. I didn't like the stuff, but it would get the job done.

I took a huge gulp, forcing it down at the expense of my comfort. My throat and stomach burned as I gagged, heaving for air as I leaned on the counter.

I climbed up the stairs and slowly walked toward my room, hysterically crying. Looking down at my hands, I saw how dirty I had gotten them. I sat on the floor of the shower as long as I could, until my fingers were prunes and the air a huge fog of steam. What Valium and scotch I had gotten down sank heavy in my stomach, sinking into the lining and making me dizzy in the heat.

My phone was on the floor, and I saw it buzz with a text through the glass. It was John. Then I remembered the party. How was I supposed to go to a party? The thought was absurd. I was going to throw up. I let the vomit dribble off my lower lip onto the shower floor. I had to stand up. I had to go to the party. I dragged myself out of the shower and started trying to collect myself.

After I brushed my teeth, I shoveled down a little cold rice from the fridge and got dressed. Then I took some more Valium and sat on the couch, waiting in hollow stillness. Once again, I felt hopeless and lost. A well opened in front of me, deep, dark, and enthralling. It wanted me to jump in, to swim in the blackness. I stared from the couch for a long time, looking down into that unfamiliar, magnetic black hole.

My phone brought me back to reality with a text from John. He was on his way. I was numb, swimming in a cloud of anger and nothingness, loosely bound together by the threads of Valium. When I stood, I realized how fucked up I was, and I gave a little laugh as I stumbled and caught myself on the arm of the couch. Maybe the party would be fun.

Everything was strange as I walked across the courtyard. I glanced over to my uncle's house. The lights were still off. I hated them. I hated that place. I hated that whole branch of my family. The night had come, and the shadows danced in front of me as I took small, shuffling steps toward the main gate. It seemed so far away, and walking had become difficult.

I was leaning against the gate bars when he pulled up, one of the metal rods uncomfortably pressed up against my cheek, but the discomfort was better than moving. I struggled through the little side door and dropped into his passenger seat with a tremendous thud.

"Hey, baby," he said it in the exact same way he always did.

"Hey," I mumbled, letting my head flop back against the headrest.

"You all right?" he asked, looking me up and down.

"Fine," I said, sighing. "Let's go to the party."

"Okay," he said, clicking his tongue. "Whatever you say."

"Where's Robert?" I asked, glancing around the car. "I thought he was riding with us."

"Omar is picking him up," John said, turning his eyes back to the road as he pulled away.

"Omar?" I said back, frowning. "Why?"

"He just is," John said, dismissively. I swear I saw him roll his eyes.

We drove to one of the industrial districts. I don't know how long the drive was. I had my head pressed up against the window, and I was drooling. I was a mess.

John could see how fucked up I was when we got out of the car. I was swaying all over the place and disoriented. This huge building shot up from the blacktop in front of us, like a giant dimensionless wall. It was dark, and I couldn't hear anything.

"Are we here?" I asked, my hips popping forward as I swayed.

"Yeah," he said, looking over me again. "You started early, huh?"

"It's a party, isn't it?" I shot back.

"Just watch yourself," he said, shaking his head. "I can't babysit you all night."

"I don't need a damn babysitter," I said, spitting. The saliva dragged out into a long dribble, and I had to yank it free of my lips.

"Jesus," he said. "Come on."

We went to a small door tucked away at one of the building's corners. John gave his leather jacket a little snap, ran his fingers through his hair, and then rapped the door in a series of rapid knocks that were some kind of secret code. A knock came back, and John did another one, and the metal door creaked open.

A wall of light, noise, and bustling energy hit me, a pure shot of adrenaline to my slurred state, and I perked up at the whirling disco balls hanging from the lofted ceiling.

I inched inside behind John, trying not to trip over my own feet. There was something happening everywhere I looked, and it was overwhelming. People were all around me, wearing tight shirts and party clothes, holding drinks and cigarettes, laughing and shouting with one another.

There was a dance floor farther back. I could hear the pulsing beat and see the blur of hands in the air. The warehouse seemed to stretch forever in front of me, ending in darkness marked with the perfect lines of shelves. I had imagined something shabby and run down, but this place was polished and clean. There was a bar, and a small stage for the DJ.

I was amazed by how many people were there. I didn't know that many gay people lived in the Kingdom, let alone the capital, and here they all were, having a great time. I started feeling confident, briefly forgetting about the trauma of the afternoon as I followed John through the crowd.

"Hey, guys!" I heard Robert call out as we walked up to the bar. "You made it!"

"One of us at least," John said, exchanging greetings with his small squad of friends as I waddled up behind him.

"You all right, Louie?" Robert asked, raising his voice above the blasting music. We were pretty far from the dance floor, but it was still incredibly loud.

"He's just having a better time than anyone else!" Omar's offensive voice came into earshot, and I squinted in confusion as he came up and draped one of his arms around Robert's shoulders. "Aren't you, Louie?"

"What?" I asked, blinking to get a clearer view. I must have looked like some drunken owl flinching at shadows on a barn wall.

"What do you want to drink?" John asked, yelling above the din.

"Does he need one?" David asked, playing with the straw in his drink.

"Fuck off," I muttered, lazily waving my hand his direction.

"I like this Louie," Omar shouted. "This Louie has balls!"

"A drink!" I shouted back over the base. "I want a drink!"

"Here," John said, thrusting a cup into my hands. "Just drink that." I could tell he was pissed off at me, but I didn't care about anything in that moment. All I could think about was the messy mound of disturbed dirt.

"Are you having fun?" I asked, leaning toward Robert. I didn't understand why Omar had his arm around him. I hated that.

"Yeah this party is rockin', man!" Robert yelled, his voice thick with enthusiasm.

I didn't know what I was drinking, but I could taste alcohol, so I sucked it down and made John get me another one. I was way too intoxicated to be talking to a bartender. At least I could recognize that.

Eventually, John sat me down on a couch somewhere by the busy bar and went off with his friends and Robert. I wanted to follow them but my legs were too heavy, and the couch was keeping me there. I lay my head back on the cushion and sipped at my fourth or fifth drink, I was not sure which. Hell, it could have been my fifteenth for all I knew.

I don't know how long I sat there but at some point, this handsome guy, probably in his late thirties, sat down next to me and asked, "Are you alone?"

I looked over to him, cocking my head and squinting. He was dressed nicer than a lot of the guys around, like he was a forty-year-old dad on vacation and was still trying to keep up appearances. He had some nice jeans on, rolled up at the cuff, a crisp button-down, and a sports jacket. He had a kind face with rich brown eyes and a well-groomed beard, and his voice was soothing like the soft rumble of distant thunder. As far as I was concerned right then, he was fucking perfect.

"Right now I am," I said, sloshing my words together as my head fell forward.

"Ah," he said, folding his hands on his knee and nodding. "But you did not come here alone."

"I guess not," I mumbled, clutching my drink with both hands.

"If you don't mind me saying," he began, looking over to me with kindness in his eyes, "you seem to be struggling."

"I'm fucking fine," I retorted, my head rolling forward without my instruction.

"Very well," he said, standing up. "If ever you're not alone, feel free to give me a call," and he handed me a business card. I remember looking up at him, wondering if he was real. Who gives a guy his business card at the capital's largest underground gay party?

I crumpled it in my palm and shoved it into my left pocket. Then I started looking around for John or Robert. I saw David making out with some guy over by the bar, but they weren't over there.

It took about everything I had to get off that couch, but once I was standing I felt renewed energy. I started wading through the mass of people, looking for them, but I couldn't sort anything out. I would look one way, look another, and forget where I had just looked a moment before.

Finally, I tore myself out of the center of the party, and leaned up against one of the shelves, completely exhausted. The second wind had faded as fast as it had come. I looked down the length of the shelves, into the darkness of the warehouse, and I swore I heard Robert's voice floating out of the blackness.

I started inching down the aisle, one hand gripping the shelf for support and the other clutching my dwindling drink. The further I went, the more certain I was that I could hear them, all three of them. What the fuck were they doing back there?

"John?" I called out.

"Louie? Is that you?" I heard Robert answer, and then I saw them, just at the edge of the party lights.

The three of them were huddled around one of the waist-height shelves. Omar was crouching down shifting something around on top

75

of the boxes. John turned around to look at me, and I could see he was pissed.

"I told you to wait on the couch," he said, almost growling.

"What are you doing?" I asked, stumbling a little bit and spilling a splash of my drink on the floor.

"Fucking coke, man!" Omar spat back at me with a cackle, "what the fuck do you think?" and he leaned down to the pile of powder he had been arranging into lines and took a big one down with a hefty snort. "Take that shit," he said, handing the rolled-up bill over to Robert.

Robert bent over and did two lines back-to-back, then swabbed the box with his pinky finger and stuck it in his mouth. He knew what he was doing.

"Fuck you, Omar," John snapped, and then he turned back to me and said, "Just go wait for me in the car, Louie, I won't be long."

"What the fuck?" I ignored him, looking straight at Robert. "What the fuck are you doing?"

"Some fucking coke, man, chill out, your cousin brought us some!" He said, passing the bill back to Omar. "It ain't shit compared to what we got in the States, man, I'll tell you what."

"My cousin?" I echoed.

"Yeah, man," he said back. Then Omar bent down to do another line, and Robert's fingers danced over the back of his neck, rubbing at the base of his hair.

"Just go wait in the car," John said again. He was using his serious voice. Usually that voice scared me into doing whatever he said, but right then it had the opposite effect.

"Fuck you!" I yelled, tossing my cup at him. It only made it about a third of the way before landing with a disappointing splash. "What the fuck!"

"Louie—" John growled at me, but I cut him off.

"Fuck you!"

"Fuck you then!" he shouted back. "Get the fuck out of here if you don't like it!"

I turned away, starting to cry. Nothing made sense. Everything was upside down. People were everywhere, bumping into me and shoving as I waded through the dance floor. Lights and sound swirled and crushed around me as people jumped up and down. Everything was spinning. I felt sick.

Was it Nathan? Cocaine? What the fuck? Cocaine was the reason I had been yanked out of school in Santa Barbara. It was the reason my family had shunned me, and, according to my uncle, the reason my mom had killed herself. I felt betrayed and claustrophobic as I tried to wedge my way through the crowd, reaching out for the door, gasping for air, just trying to get outside. Then I made it. I was outside. I was free. That strong summer breeze threw back my hair as I slogged another leg forward through that dark, industrial lot.

A pair of headlights came up behind me. I thought it was John, and I was getting ready to scream at him for taking my friend away from me, for treating me like a pet, for doing cocaine. He knew what that drug meant to me. But as the car pulled up beside me, I saw the handsome, business card man from before, leaning pensively over the steering wheel.

"Are you all right, young man?" he kindly asked, looking up at my crooked stance, lit up by the moon.

"It's you," I murmured back, twisting my hips around to look at him.

"Would you like a ride home?" he asked, pulling his car to a complete stop beside me.

"That'd be nice," I said, glancing back over my shoulder to see if John had followed me out of the warehouse. He hadn't. I stumbled around to the passenger seat, and he opened it up for me from the inside. I flopped down into the seat, looked over at him, and said, "Now I'm alone," and we took off.

Chapter Six

IT WAS SUPPOSED TO be a great day. It was supposed to be a fun night. I had been looking forward to the party for weeks, and it had all gone horribly wrong in only a few minutes. The party was supposed to be a liberating experience, but instead of enjoying it, I had gotten into a big fight with my best friend and my boyfriend. Now I was sitting in some stranger's car. It was not the way I had envisioned the evening turning out.

It was quiet in the car as we drove, pulling away from the industrial lot and leaving the party behind us. My head was rolling around in the seat with each turn. I couldn't see straight. I wasn't all that sure about what was happening, but I felt safe in the car with that man.

My phone was already buzzing like crazy in my pocket. It was John, calling me over and over again. I didn't care, and though it took me a while to find the volume buttons with my swirling vision, I silenced it and crudely stuffed it back into my pocket.

"Are your friends worried about you?" the man asked, glancing my way as he flicked on his turn signal and pulled onto the main road.

"I doubt it," I said, leaning my head against the car window.

"It seems like they are."

"They can fuck off," I replied, letting out a long sigh.

"Rough night, huh?" he said, throwing out a light chuckle, maybe trying to lighten the mood.

"Rough life, more like," I replied.

"I think we can all relate to that," he said back, sending a warm smile my way. His presence was soothing, and I could feel myself relaxing in the seat, the cool glass of the window up against my cheek, calming me down. Maybe things were going to be all right.

Then my anger came flooding back as quickly as it had subsided. In truth, I felt neglected, as if I had become an afterthought to Robert and John. With John, maybe I always had been, but with Robert, it really hurt. I had known him most of my life. He was my brother, as much as my best friend.

My brain was in complete chaos as I thought about it more and more, letting the silence envelope the car as I stewed. I just wanted to forget the whole night, to wake up the next day and turn my back on everything that had happened. Just when I thought I was happy, finally and truly happy, it had all come crashing down. Again. There were a few tears gathering in my eyes, and I felt terribly embarrassed on top of everything. Crying again, in a stranger's car.

I tried shoving my hand into my pocket for my Valium, but I was still inebriated and I couldn't reach it. I ended up popping my hips up in the seat, trying to fish into my pockets, and miserably fumbling with the pills.

They rattled around like a bag of Skittles when I finally pulled them out. Then the child-safety cap became a trial of its own.

"Having trouble?" he asked, looking over at me after changing lanes.

"Fucking cap," I muttered back, trying with my jellyfish fingers to force it open.

"What is it?"

"Valium."

"You take a lot of those?" he asked, and there was kindness in his voice that I wanted to latch onto.

"I guess," I said, trying to shrug it off. I didn't need a lecture right then.

"Why?" he said, and the simplicity of the question baffled me.

"I don't know," I replied, hearing the hollowness of my own voice. Sure, I knew why I took them. I took them to forget about my mom, to help myself ignore my uncle and his family, and of course, there was John with his clockwork deliveries. I felt myself starting to cry again. I rubbed my eyes with my sleeve in a clumsy, fumbling motion, and my watchband left a weird red impression on my cheek.

"If you don't want to take them anymore," he said, looking straight into my eyes, "then I can help you."

"Why do you care?" I lashed out, the tears coming again in full force. "Who the fuck are you?"

"I know who you are," he said.

"Who doesn't?" I sniffled back.

"My name is Benjamin. You don't know me, but I knew your mother," he went on.

"You did?"

"We worked together, sometimes," he said, nodding his head methodically. "She told me a lot about you. She was very proud of you, you know."

I couldn't hold it in any longer. I was sobbing, my tears cascading. John and Robert didn't matter anymore as I envisioned that empty pile of dirt in the cemetery.

"It's just all too much," I sobbed, clutching my face in my shaking hands. "I'm not big enough for all of it."

"Then just let it out," he said, extending a hand to my shoulder. "Be free of it."

"My whole dad's side of the family," I continued. "They just don't care! They don't care!"

"And what about her side? Do they care?"

"I guess, I mean, I don't know," I cried.

"Maybe you should talk to them," he said. "At least to find out? You may find that they care more than you know."

"You think?" I sniveled, catching a few tears with my wrist.

"You could call them tomorrow, find out for yourself."

"Tomorrow?"

"Why wait?" he replied, giving me a friendly shrug.

We sat and talked in the car for a long time, pulled over on the side of the highway. I told him everything there was to tell, pouring it out between my heaving, tearful breaths. When I finished talking, he simply took my hand, and said, "You're going to be okay, Louie."

When he dropped me off, I climbed out of his car and a huge blast of wind hit me from behind, tossing my hair around and flapping my shirt against my skin. It felt so good to feel that wind, and it gave me a surge of hope. I was going to be all right. I didn't know why, but I was certain of it.

I knew I was hungover before I opened my eyes the next morning. It was horrible. I woke up to the sound of my phone buzzing on the bed next to me. Each vibration sent a clanging chorus through my ears, rattling my brain against the walls of my skull.

I squashed a pillow over my head and reached out blindly for the phone, eventually pulling it to my ear. I didn't have to check the screen to know it was John. He had been calling me all night and bombarding me with texts. I hadn't looked at any of them, but I knew what they would say.

"Hello?" I said, my voice was weak and cracking between my parched lips.

"Louie! What the fuck!" John's booming voice came through the speaker. "What the fuck was—"

I hung up the phone. I didn't want to hear his shit. He instantly started calling me again, so I popped the battery out of the back and tossed it across my room.

It took me a long while to get going, but after a shower and some food, I was at least looking like a proper person again. Eventually, I put my phone back together and turned it on. I glanced over some of the text messages from the night before. Robert was calling me a baby, telling me to grow up, and John was just screaming at me for abandoning him. I put my phone on silent, deleted about forty texts, and walked out to my car.

Benjamin had been right. If my uncle and cousins didn't care, then why should I waste my time thinking about them at all? I was going to see my grandma, my mom's mom. I knew she cared, and if I could talk to anyone about the grave, it was her.

My mom's sister was over at my grandparent's house a lot, so I figured I would text her rather than making my grandma use a cell phone. I sent her a quick text, asking if it was okay to stop by, and that I had some important stuff to talk about. I was extremely anxious as I stood by the car and waited for her reply. I knew they had all been brainwashed against me, that my mom took her own life because of my failings. I didn't know how any kind of interaction would go. Soon enough, she texted back, excited to see me, and told me to come by my grandma's house that afternoon.

I felt less nervous after reading her text than I had been earlier that morning, but I was still uneasy about seeing them as I got into my car and started driving to their house. The sun felt nice coming through my windows, and I drove along at a leisurely pace. I hadn't thought about John since he had screamed into my ear earlier, and it felt freeing, especially behind the wheel of my own car.

My grandparents' house was a mansion. They didn't have a compound like we did, but they made up for it in the sheer grandeur of their home. My grandpa had been in oil and gas in the seventies and eighties and had a lot more money than anyone on my dad's side.

The house itself was set back behind a magnificent lawn, dominated by the elegant ten-foot-high fountain in the center of the circular drive. A tall, white-bricked wall ringed the property, with neat rows of groomed cypress trees running along every inch of the perimeter, so that it was impossible to see the house from outside the imposing black gates.

My anxiety took over every inch of me as I pulled into the drive. I hadn't talked to them in months, not since the funeral. They had been brainwashed with all the rest into thinking my then-fake drug spiral and "expulsion" from school was the reason for my mom's suicide.

My mom's sister was there on the front step, and we made eye contact through my windshield as I parked. I felt my anxiety surge even more as I turned off the car and she hurried over to meet me, her bracelets jingling with each step.

"Louie!" she cried out, and as I shut my door behind me and she took me into a fierce hug, grasping the back of my head and kissing my cheek. "It's so good to see you. Come inside, come."

"It's good to see you too, auntie," I said, trying to hold back the tears I could already feel coming.

"Your grandmother is inside," she said, tucking her arm into mine. "She will be very happy you are here," and she led me up the marble stairs into the foyer, which could have been a small house on its own.

My mom's sister was quite the character. She had a powerful personality that often took up the whole room, but nobody seemed to mind. People adored her, as they had my mother. The two were similar in many ways, but instead of charity work, my aunt had pursued her own business career. Forbes had noted her on their "two hundred most powerful women in the Middle East" list, and if one spent some time with her, it was easy to see how she had gotten there.

My grandma was overjoyed to see me, and I felt foolish for all the anxiety I had felt, and for staying away so long as she cried and hugged me. Apologies were flying in every direction from everybody in the room, and by the end of the tear festival, we were all feeling close once more. Benjamin had been right. These were the people I needed to talk to, and the rest of them could go to hell.

Then I told them about my mom's grave, and my aunt's face changed into one of steely resolve with a firm jaw and fire in her eyes.

"What do you mean they moved her?" she asked, blinking twice. I saw her whole back straighten and her shoulders rise up, like she was getting ready to pounce on some poor gazelle.

"My uncle," I said, "he had her moved." I wasn't entirely sure this was the truth. But who else could it be? I knew it in my gut more than anything.

"Where did he move her to?" my aunt asked. Her fingers were drilling against the arm of the chair, her manicured nails clicking on the wicker in a menacing rhythm.

"Down by the fence," I said. "In the little gulch."

"Come on, Louie," she said, snapping up from her seat. "Let's go."

"Where are we going?" I asked, trying to keep up with her as she marched toward the door. Her strides were long, and each time her feet came down on the marble floor her heels echoed through the huge house, getting louder and louder with every step as her rage seemed to boil up inside.

"Where do you think?" she asked. "To make this right. That bastard. He's always hated us, you know, always. Can't stand that we're richer than he is. He's pathetic," she ranted, pulling her car keys off a hook by the front door. "Like it's his fucking birthright or something! Unbelievable!"

I could hardly get a word in edgewise as she kept on cursing him. I wasn't sure what was going to happen, but I wasn't about to miss it, so I got into her passenger seat while she turned the keys in her Lexus.

"Can you believe him? The audacity of that man! What a pig!" She didn't stop complaining about him the whole time we were in the car, and it was a bit of a drive, even at her breakneck speed. I ate up every word. I had never heard my uncle derided in such a way. Even though I had thought the same things plenty of times, it felt so good to hear them out loud, and to know that I wasn't alone in all of this suppressed sadness and anger.

We came roaring up my winding road, and nearly rear-ended my brother as he was slowly rolling in through the front gate of the compound. My aunt immediately began laying on the car horn, blasting it nonstop at my brother as he pulled into the courtyard.

I could see the confusion on his face as he got out of the car, looking at my aunt and me with this blank, puzzled stare. He opened his mouth to say something, but before he got a word in my aunt had burst out of her door and commenced shrieking at him.

"What did you do?!" she called out, pointing at him. "Don't you care? How dare you! How could you move her? Shame!"

"Auntie?" he said, still blinking, trying to figure out why she was screaming at him "What happened?"

"Don't play dumb!" she hissed, striding right up to him. I got out of the car slowly after her, unsure of how all this was going to play out. My brother was starting to look more terrified than confused the longer she shouted, and I began feeling bad for him.

"I don't know what's going on, auntie," he said, raising his hands up in a mock surrender. "What are you talking about? What did I do?"

"Have you been to visit your mother lately?" she challenged him, sticking her finger right in his face.

"No, I—"

"So you don't know anything about her being moved?" she pressed, grinding her heel into the stone courtyard.

"Moved? What?" my brother balked. It was very clear to me that he really didn't know what was going on.

"Unbelievable," she said, shaking her head. "I'm sorry honey," and she gave him a quick hug, and I could see him looking at me over her shoulder with great, big what-the-fuck-is-going-on eyes. "Now come on."

When I caught up with them, she took us both by the hand, one on each side, and pulled us toward my uncle's house, her heels coming down hard on the stones and the sound echoing off the compound walls.

The big double doors that led into their kitchen was open, letting in the breeze. Nathan was standing in the doorway looking terrified with an open mouth and a pale face. No doubt he had heard the shouting and poked his head out to take a look.

"Go to your room," she commanded him as we reached the door. For half a breath it looked like he was going to protest, but her iron glare sent him packing up the stairs with his tail between his legs. That felt so good to see! For a second I even thought of telling my aunt about what he did to me during the funeral. Then I heard my uncle's voice coming down the hallway, and I tensed, awaiting the storm.

"Miranda," he said, walking into the kitchen, scratching the back of his head. "What on earth is going on? Why are you shouting?"

"You!" she hissed, ready to spit venom from her fangs. "You have no right to speak to me!"

"Miranda—" he tried interrupting her, but she wouldn't let him get a word in before she began her righteous tirade.

"How dare you! Monster! Who do you think you are! On what authority!" They weren't so much questions as they were statements. "You think you can move my sister! How could you think that? Are you really that dumb? What world do you live in where that is okay? Hm? In what world?!"

"What on earth—" my uncle's wife came into the room just then, looking around wildly.

"Don't you say a word, you bitch!" my aunt roared at her. "Sit down and shut up! It's all your fault isn't it? He's too stupid to do any of this. It's all you! You evil bitch!"

"This is outrageous!" my uncle's wife yelled back. "You need to leave, Miranda, now!"

"I am not going anywhere," my aunt said, standing her ground. Standing in her broad, power stance, she looked like the Colossus of Rhodes while she issued her declarations.

"You think you can just make my sister go away. You always hated her. You always hated me. Why? Because she was more than you could ever be! She was loved! She was good! And you, you are just a sad, power-hungry woman with a husband who can't stand the fact that his little brother has more money than he does. I will not hear any more from you! Shut up!"

"What is this about?!" my uncle bellowed, throwing his hands up in exasperation.

"The grave, you idiot!" my aunt screamed back. "You moved her grave! Without telling anyone! Without permission! It is not your decision to make!"

"I don't know what you are talking about, woman!" my uncle shouted back, pounding his fist against the counter.

"Don't deny it, you snake," she pressed back, narrowing her eyes in anger. "That is even lower of you. And don't you dare raise your voice to me! I am the one doing the shouting!"

"It was me!" my uncle's wife barked out, and the room fell silent as all eyes turned her way. "I moved her. She has been dragging the family's name down enough with her suicide, we don't need her on top of the hill like a national hero! People will never stop talking about her! Let her be forgotten! Do you know how much damage she—"

"You are a spiteful bitch! You know that?" My aunt cut her off. "Never presume authority again, or I will destroy you and your hateful little family."

My aunt turned to leave, grabbing me by the hand, when my uncle's wife spoke out in some kind of last-ditch attempt at a rebuttal, saying, "you have some nerve, coming into our home—"

"Me?!" my aunt scoffed, turning to face them one last time. "I am not the one meddling in other people's affairs now, am I? I will see her moved back to where she belongs. Have a shitty afternoon," and just like that, we left.

I had never felt as jubilant as I did walking out of their kitchen, hand in hand with my aunt. Seeing her rain down the insults and accusations I had harbored for months had been liberating, and I walked through the courtyard with a new bounce in my heels. I couldn't quite believe what I had just witnessed, but it felt so good to see my uncle and his wife squirm. I hated them, and I realized then that they hated me too. There were no more illusions or games. The line had been drawn in the sand, and we all knew where we stood.

"Come on, Louie," she said. "I'll take you back to your car."

I looked over my shoulder as I got into her car, and saw my brother standing there awkwardly in the courtyard. His shoulders were slumped, and he was looking back and forth between our house and my uncle's with an emotionless gaze. Our eyes met for a second before I sat down on the seat, and I could see the conflict on his face. He had never done anything wrong in their eyes, not the way I had, and he had never lived with their constant animosity. I gave him a shrug, and I closed the car door behind me.

While we drove, my aunt fired up a cigarette with the car lighter and let a long stream of smoke out the window after a huge drag. Then she looked over at me and said, "I'm so sorry you have to deal with those assholes, Louie."

"It's okay," I said, propping my elbow up on the window. "I got used to it a long time ago."

"It's not okay," she said, shaking her head and taking another hefty drag of her cigarette. "They should know better."

"They're jealous," I said back. "They always have been. Man! That was so awesome, seeing you yelling at them like that."

"They deserve a lot more than just shouting," she replied, biting down on her lower lip. She flicked her ash out of the window and said, "Listen, Louie."

"Yeah?"

"If they fuck with you again, anything, little or big, you come to me. Okay, sweetie?"

"All right," I said, grinning slightly. "I will."

"Good," she said, flashing me a little smile. "We have to look out for one another, you hear me?"

"I hear you, auntie," I said. I felt an incredible tide of validation at that moment. It's hard to describe just how liberating it was to know that I wasn't alone in all of that bullshit, that I had a confidant, a friend who I could rely on, who would back me up against my uncle's antics, and remember my mother for who she had been.

We got back to my grandparents' house and she asked if I wanted to come in for coffee or tea, but I told her I had to get going. She gave me a big hug and a few kisses on both cheeks before ruffling my hair and sending me on my way.

I drove the long way home, not terribly excited to face whatever fallout might be waiting for me at the compound. But I knew whatever it was, I could handle it. This was a new chapter, one of confidence and self-assurance, and I wasn't going to be bowled over anymore. Not by anyone.

When I got home, most of the cars were gone except for my dad's and my uncle's. I parked in the courtyard, and walked tentatively into my house, turning on the lights as I went. My dad wasn't there, so I figured he was next door, talking with my uncle. I smiled a little as I thought about how uncomfortable their conversation must be.

I settled in at the kitchen counter and pulled my phone out of my pocket. I hadn't looked at it all day, not since I silenced it, and I wasn't looking forward to seeing all the texts from John. I was over him. When we had gotten together, he had made me feel like the luckiest, specialist guy in the whole world. Now I felt like his prisoner.

There were at least twenty-five unread texts, and a handful of missed calls. Instead of looking at any of them, I typed a message out, reading: *I don't want to do this anymore. Please don't text or call me. I need to be alone.*

I got his reply instantly. *You'll regret this, Louie. I am not finished with you.*

I frowned, and put my phone through its factory reset, clearing all my contacts and text logs. I could get back the numbers I needed, and I didn't want to manually sort through all of these angry texts. He wasn't important anymore.

I looked up at the sound of the front door opening, and saw my dad and uncle walking in. My uncle looked sheepish, and my dad looked sour. I didn't want to talk with either of them, but there they were.

"Louie," my dad said, walking up to the counter and standing across from me. "Your uncle has something to say to you."

"Louie," my uncle began, walking up beside my dad. When they stood next to each other, you could really tell that they were brothers, the only major difference being that my uncle was stouter with more wrinkle creases on his forehead, and my dad had a bigger mustache.

"What do you want?"

"I want to apologize," he said. "For my wife's behavior. She should not have done that."

"Is that it?" I asked, looking up at him with a cynical glare.

"Yes," he said back, giving me a brisk nod that accentuated his double chin. "Good night."

It was the worst, most fake, and soulless apology I had ever heard, but apparently, for him, it was enough, because after that he turned and went back out the front door. I watched him go, taking a small triumph in imagining the discomfort he must have felt for the whole of that two-sentence exchange.

"Now it is behind us," my father said, clapping his hands once as if a party were about to start.

"Is it really, Dad?" I asked, looking into his eyes.

"Louie," he said, letting out a big sigh. "I know how much you hurt. But you cannot go on like this."

"Go on like what?" I protested, folding my arms across my chest.

"You know," he said, looking at me with intense judgement. I had little to no respect for my father by then, but for some reason that look still gave me a chill, and some disconnected part of me wanted to appeal to him. "You stay out all night and you don't go to school."

"I was going to school," I said, returning his hard look with one of my own, trying to fight back. "In California, remember? But you took me out."

"That is also in the past," he growled back, raising his voice just a touch. I could tell I was irritating him, and I loved it.

"That's not how life works!" I spat back, finally letting my emotions swell. "Things don't just stop mattering after they happen!"

"That is exactly how life works!" he bellowed, and his voice seemed to fill up the whole house, bouncing off every wall, every window, and every piece of furniture. "And I am sorry if you don't like it, but you have to accept reality! What happens if you never go back to school?"

"I inherit your money," I said, pushing back. "That's what happens."

"You will not," he said, his fist curling into a ball as it rested on the counter. "I will see to it. Without a degree, you are without direction, without purpose, and that will destroy you. I have seen it before, I see it now in my brother's children, and it saddens me to see it in you. How have we come to this, my son? I do not wish this for either of us."

"I know," I replied softly.

"You can hate me all you want," he said. "You can hate my brother, you can hate your cousins, hate whoever you want, whatever you want, I don't care. But you have to go back to college, here in the Kingdom. That is the deal."

"Okay," I said, feeling strangely weak. He had taken so much of my confident energy away in just a few minutes, but I knew he was right. I had done nothing for the past few months but take Valium and hook up with John, and it didn't take a genius to see that wasn't going to lead me anywhere. "I'll go back to school."

"Thank you," he said, flattening his fist out on the counter. "Good night," and grabbing a bottle of scotch from the kitchen counter he disappeared into his office, shutting the door behind him.

When I got upstairs, I flopped onto my bed, trying to make sense of everything that had happened in the space of a day. It was a lot to process, and I was still feeling mad at John and Robert for the night before.

In a panic I realized I hadn't taken any Valium for a few hours, and I rapidly became horribly anxious. I had been fine without it, but the second it popped into my head I needed some right then and there.

I frantically started searching my clothes, trying to find my shorts from the night before, confident the Valium was still in the left-side pocket. I knew they were there, and I needed them. I needed them immediately.

I tore at my shorts like a wild animal, but I couldn't hear them rattling. They had to be there, where else could they be? Finally, I found the pocket opening, and I shoved my hand down inside, grasping until my hand closed on Benjamin's crinkled up business card.

As I pulled out the card, I saw the pills sitting on my dresser where I had set them down earlier that morning. I felt foolish for how I had clawed through my laundry like an addict. Was I one? I hadn't considered it until that moment, but I began to feel a creeping shame overtake me.

I sat on the edge of my bed and flattened out Benjamin's business card. I entered his number into my phone and shot off a simple text reading, *Hey, it's Louie.*

I sat there, waiting for him to reply, glancing between my phone and the Valium on my dresser, feeling the intensity of my craving until the phone's vibration startled me so badly I almost fell off the bed.

Hey, Louie, how are you? He replied. I smiled and typed out a response.

Been better. You?

I'm okay. You want to talk about it?

IDK.

I'm volunteering with the Red Cross on Monday night. Do you want to come along? It is more fun than you think.

I read the text a few times to make sure I had gotten it right. It was such a foreign thought to me. My mother had done a ton of volunteering, and sometimes brought me along, but the thought of seeking it out on my own was strange and unfamiliar. It was intimidating, but also inviting. The thought of something entirely new seemed like a good fit. This was another chapter in my life, and I wasn't going to waste it.

That sounds good, I answered, and I smiled to myself as I chewed half a pill and fell asleep.

Chapter Seven

THERE WERE THREE BIG changes in my life that summer. The first was Benjamin. I started seeing him frequently around the end of July, and it was entirely different from every moment I had spent with John.

It was hard to believe how fast everything could flip, first one way, and then the other. I felt like my life had been following the twisting path of a snake, arching back and forth with flicks of its tail, but now at last it sat basking motionless in the warmth of the sun.

I had been increasingly nervous about meeting Benjamin at the Red Cross volunteering night, and had thought about cancelling a few times, but it turned out I had a good time and was glad I had gone. Everyone around me was nice, genuine, and interested in what each other said. It felt refreshing to be there and spend the time with him.

It wasn't long after that we were seeing each other properly. We would go out a lot to elegant cafes, nice wine bars, and that was where we spent most of our time. We sat for hours, just sipping coffees or enjoying glasses of wine, and talking about various subjects. He had such a trove of information living inside of his head, and it was impressive how he could spout off facts about almost anything, casually working them into the conversation. Normally I hated when people did that, like they were smarter than everyone else, but he was soft-spoken and kind, and he could get away with it.

Benjamin was different from John in many ways. He preferred wine to beer. He didn't smoke and pursued a healthier lifestyle. He also preferred to stay home and read books or watch foreign films. His physique was superior to John's. I hadn't seen him shirtless, yet, but I was able to feel his abs under his clothes whenever we cuddled on his sofa. Even though his work kept him busy, he still found the time for daily workouts and sustaining good relationships with friends and family.

He was taller than me, not by much, but when we stood next to each other it was pretty noticeable. I loved how put together he was. One of the first things I always noticed about someone was their nails, because if they were well taken care of it meant the person took themselves seriously, at least that's how I saw it. Ben's nails were perfect. He was clean shaven—I don't think I ever even saw him with a five o'clock shadow—and he always smelled great. Whatever cologne he wore, it really worked for him. It was a real manly smell, which I guess matched his age at thirty-four. The age difference didn't bother me though, it never really had.

He was a great cook too, which was something else I really liked about him. Sometimes I would go over to his house and he would fix a fancy dinner, and we would spend a few hours at the table munching it all down and laughing together.

The second thing that changed that summer was that I started going back to school. I thought a lot about the talk I had with my dad, and I realized that if I really wanted to have a new life, then I had to change everything, not just the guy I was dating. School was a great place to start, and when I returned, I found I had missed it more than I imagined.

It was the oldest public university in the Kingdom, about a half-hour drive from our compound in the Heights. It had these grand old buildings and monuments all over its campus, with a big symmetrical courtyard in the center. Behind the historic fixtures, new buildings were rising up with reflective walls of windows, bouncing the bright sun back onto the old rooftops.

Cranes littered the campus and construction happened constantly, but I didn't mind it at all. I liked the energy—all the people going about their work as I sat listing to snatches of their conversations during their cigarette breaks. At school I felt like I was a part of something. It was a stark difference to the stale stagnation of our silent compound, and I loved it.

I made a few friends around campus, mostly with people from my engineering program, and we started hanging out here and there in our free time. It was as if I had hit pause on my entire life, subbed out all the bad characters and set pieces, and then resumed. A small part of my mind whispered that I was a phony and had abandoned John, that I was a bad person for trying to wash it all away. I convinced myself that keeping busy kept those thoughts buried deep under my consciousness, so I stayed as busy as I could.

I had always been a good student. It was one of the reasons my mom had been so proud of me, and one of the reasons my uncle and his wife hated me. The only real reason I had been expelled from my last university was because I stopped attending my classes, but when I applied myself, I started excelling and succeeding.

The third thing that changed that summer is that I started seeing a therapist. It wasn't my idea, but a condition for my dad to pay for school. At first, I was pretty resistant to it and felt apprehensive about opening up to a complete stranger, but I started warming to the experience within a few visits. It felt nice to be listened to, and it made me feel appreciated somehow.

I told the therapist all about my "friend" John, the Valium, my falling out with Robert, my new "friendship" with Benjamin, the grief of my mom's loss, how her death just didn't make any sense, and how much I despised my uncle's family, especially how Nathan touched me and kissed me. I didn't tell him that I was gay though. I was still in the Kingdom, and I wasn't sure how that would go over. If I had learned anything about growing up gay, the lesson was: better to be safe than sorry.

I think the therapist knew I was holding something back, that was his job after all, but he never pressed me on it, and that was more than fine with me. I was off Valium entirely at that point, and the therapist prescribed me some anti-depressants, but I was pretty sure they weren't doing anything.

I remember telling Benjamin about the therapist. The moment stood out to me because it summarized the difference between him and John. We were in a restaurant at an expensive downtown hotel, having some coffee around lunchtime. He had on this light-brown shirt, recently ironed, and he was casually sipping at the brim of his coffee cup, the steam wafting up to gently bat against his cheeks.

"What's on your mind?" He asked, glancing over the ceramic rim.

"What?" I replied as I regained eye contact with him.

"You seem distracted." He responded, tilting his head gently to the right.

"I guess," I replied, looking down into the dark ripples of my drink, watching the rogue drips leave great streaks across the sides of the shockingly white cup.

"Do you want to talk about it?" he asked, carefully setting down his coffee. The clink of cups against saucers echoed through the entire room, cutting through all the casual chitchat.

"I started seeing a therapist," I said eventually, flicking my eyes back up to catch his reaction.

"That's good," he said, reaching for his cup again.

"Good?"

"It seems like something that could help you," he went on. "I don't mean to presume, but there is certainly no shame or harm in it."

"I wasn't sure what you were going to say," I said, breathing a sigh of relief. It seemed unreasonable that I had been so worried about telling him.

"Why?" he asked, leaning back in his chair a little.

"It's dumb," I said, shaking my head.

"What?"

"I just felt like you would be mad," I said. "I don't think John would have liked it."

"I just want whatever is best," he replied. "I think the therapist will be good for you."

I looked at him for a long time after he said that, wrapping my head around the new and seemingly healthy relationship I was in. It all felt too good to be true, and yet I was really living it. It was like a dream.

Sometimes Benjamin and I would go on double dates with some of his doctor friends. They were always so well-dressed I found myself trying to match them in order to impress Benjamin. I wanted him to think I was good enough for his world, and I wanted his friends to like me. Unlike John and his crew of miscreants, Benjamin's friends were people I actually enjoyed talking to, and they seemed to enjoy talking to me.

On the whole, as the summer progressed, I had never felt better about anything. My mom was back on top of the hill, and I made an effort to visit her at least twice a week. It was as if I had taken a large detour into a confusing storm cloud of drugs and sex, but now I had rediscovered the road that would take me into my future.

I was optimistic about almost everything, but every now and then something small would happen that, in my mind, seemed to threaten what I had been building.

I started seeing John's car around town. At first, I dismissed it as someone driving the same car, which was entirely possible, and the only irritation it caused me was thinking about John for a few minutes before getting on with my day.

But as the summer kept going, I kept seeing it and I started to get paranoid. I would squint at it, trying to make out any distinctive marks that would tell me outright if it was John's car or not. It was always a little too far away, or driving too fast, for me to get a good look. Its phantom lingered in the back of my mind, prodding at my paranoia and slowly rising anxiety.

My therapist thought I was making a big deal out of nothing, that I was freaking myself out and imagining the car, and prescribed me some anti-anxiety medication. I thought that was complete bullshit, and seeds of doubt planted in my mind. Maybe this therapist had been full of shit this whole time. Maybe I shouldn't be telling him anything. Then again, I couldn't tell him the whole story. From his point of view, I probably did sound crazy.

Benjamin thought I was overreacting too. He said plenty of people had those cars, and that black was the most popular color. He told me I didn't have anything to worry about, and for a little while I believed him.

One night the car was stopped at a red light across from the restaurant Benjamin and I were dining in. I saw John's silhouette through the cracked window, the thin line of cigarette smoke creeping out of the gap.

I was terrified. John had not been content to leave me alone, and he could come for me at any moment. But was I being ridiculous? It was a popular area. He could simply be driving through, and it might not have been him every other time I spotted that car.

Why was I so scared of him? He had some sort of controlling aura that I couldn't shake, and it clawed at me when I saw him in his car. He had that dark, magnetic energy that I couldn't entirely set aside, and I thought of his last ominous text: *You're going to regret this, Louie.*

I shivered in my seat, staring through the window, waiting for the light to turn green. It was taking its sweet time, and I wanted to shout at the electrical wires, to rattle them into action, anything to get that car away from the restaurant window.

Finally, the light changed, and he tore off down the street in his typical breakneck style of driving. I let out a long sigh, closing my eyes for a minute, letting my heartbeat calm down. I hated how he had that effect on me, and I didn't know why I couldn't get away from it.

"Are you all right?" Benjamin asked, setting down his coffee again.

"Fine," I said, blinking my eyes open. "I'm fine." I wanted to yell, to scream and point, to expose John and show Benjamin that I wasn't making things up, but I couldn't. I was stuck, frozen and clammy, my heart thumping away with a thundering horror.

"Are you sure? You're pale," he said, leaning in over the table.

"I'm all right," I said, sitting back in my chair with a big breath as I forced myself to smile. "What were we talking about?"

"Your school," he said, straightening his posture. "Do you like it?"

"Right," I said, bringing myself back to the present. "My school."

"Are you sure you're all right?"

"I'm fine, really," I insisted, looking down again at my coffee for a minute before meeting his gaze again and continuing. "It's okay, I mean, it's not UCSB back in California. Still, I'm meeting and making new friends."

"Good, that's good," Benjamin said, "Just give it time and everything will turn out great."

After that night, I was always on the lookout for John's car, and the more I looked, the more I saw it. What really freaked me out was seeing his car in my neighborhood since I knew he lived across town in that weird, creepy mansion. He was there for me, there was nothing else that made sense, and it made my skin crawl.

Yet it seemed to me that there was nothing I could do about it. I couldn't go to the police, because then there would be questions about our relationship. I couldn't go to my family for the exact same reason, just like I couldn't go to my new friends, and I couldn't go to Robert since I thought he was "on John's side."

I could only go to Benjamin, and he thought I was making something out of nothing. "It's a big city, but it's a small community," he would say. It was incredibly isolating to live with that anxiety, expecting to see John's car around any corner, wondering what he would say or do if he ever climbed out of the driver's seat. Just as fast as my blissful new life had begun, it was corrupted by this constant fear of confrontation.

Things started to properly collapse a few weeks later. I was in the kitchen with my brother, which was somewhat rare those days since we kept such different lives. I was busy with school and he was busy helping dad with the family business. He also had his own friends, and since I was pretty consumed with schoolwork and Benjamin, we were hardly ever in the same room. That day was different for whatever reason, and we were making sandwiches for lunch.

"Are you going to come to the card game this week?" he asked, spreading mustard on his sandwich roll.

"I don't know," I said, looking over to him from the fridge. "Why should I?"

"You went two weeks ago, it was fun wasn't it?" he said back, tapping the knife against the mustard jar and tossing it casually into the sink. I cringed as I watched stray mustard splatter against the wall of the sink and the tile backsplash.

"I wouldn't call it fun," I said, stepping over to the sink. "Cards are fun, but I can't stand being at the table with those dumbasses."

"I don't know why you hate them so much," my brother said with a casual shrug. "They're our cousins, we should be friends."

"It doesn't matter," I said, shaking my head while I carefully wiped the mustard from the wall. "They all hate me over there."

"You know, I think they care about you more than you think," my brother said, rifling through slices of cheese.

"How do you figure that?" I asked, rolling my eyes while I rinsed the mustard knife clean and slid it into the dishwasher.

"I was over there yesterday," he said, "I heard auntie Rhonda talking to someone about you on the phone. She sounded interested, not like she was shit talking."

"Talking to someone?" I asked, feeling a pang of anxiety welling up out of nowhere. "Who was she talking to?"

"I don't know," he said, shrugging, "Some doctor."

"What doctor?" I asked, whirling about on my heels to stare him in the face. "What were they talking about? Tell me!"

"Hey, calm down, man," he said, raising up his hands in a mock surrender. "Chill, chill. She said his name, what was it, uh, Niles? Giles?"

"Dr. Lyles?" I asked. "Was that the name she said?"

"Yeah, that's it," he said, his eyes lighting up with the memory. "Who's that?"

"It doesn't matter," I muttered back, my fists clenching at my sides. "You sure that was who she was talking to?"

"Yeah, she was just asking after you, you know?"

"Yeah fuckin' right," I growled, "I gotta go."

Dr. Lyles. My fucking therapist. He was talking to my uncle's wife. I knew it was too good to be true, all of it. It was all some fucking trick, like I was on the Truman Show, stuck in my little oblivious bubble.

I was pissed. I could feel anger bubbling over my anxiety, taking hold of my core and forcing me out the door. I had an appointment with Dr. Lyles that afternoon, but I didn't want to wait until then to confront him. I wanted to throw him against the wall and scream into his face, just so he really knew how mad I was. Of course he was talking to her. Of course it was all part of her plan to get me out of the picture. Of course I couldn't trust anybody. Everything was fucked.

I drove around for a couple of hours before my appointment, idly switching lanes and taking random exits. I couldn't think about anything for more than a minute, my mind was such a whirlpool. Driving made sense. At that moment, it was the only thing that made sense. There were rules. People, for the most part, followed the rules, and everyone got where they were going. Simple. Easy. Efficient.

I finally screeched into the parking garage under Dr. Lyle's building. I was breathing heavily as I marched into the elevator, hitting the twenty-fourth-floor button so hard that I jammed my thumb, and my mood only got worse.

The elevator ride took forever. I was tapping my feet, and even though the AC was blasting, I had sweat forming in my armpits and on my temples. When the door finally dinged open I nearly knocked over some poor guy with a bunch of boxes on a dolly, and I could tell by the glance he gave me that I looked something frightful, all worked up.

Dr. Lyle's office was a stale space with a great view, like he thought that would make up for the bland furniture and walls. "Louie, come in, how are you?" he asked, rising from his chair as I came into the room.

"I'm fucking upset," I said, planting myself squarely in the middle of the room.

"Why don't you take a seat?" he asked, gesturing to the sofa. "We can talk about what's going on. Here, I'll shut the door."

"So you can tell my uncle's wife everything?" I asked, cocking my head and narrowing my eyes.

"I beg your pardon?" he asked, freezing mid-motion.

"I know you've been telling her everything!" I shouted at him. "What the fuck!"

"Louie, let's take a breath, shall we?" he said, inching toward his desk.

"You're just some hired spy, huh?" I asked, throwing up my arms. "And I'm supposed to trust you?"

"Louie—"

"Saying my name over and over isn't going to help!" I shouted, feeling the strain on my throat from the volume. I wasn't sure if I had ever shouted so loud.

"Louie—"

"Go fuck yourself!" I spat at him. I could have stood there and yelled for the full hour, screaming about everything, but I didn't want to say anything else to him. He wasn't worth the breath, and it would all get back to her in the end. It was bullshit.

I turned and stormed out of the office, streaming down the hallway like a flaming meteor. That time around, I could have stood in the elevator forever, not wanting to deal with everything on the other side of those sliding doors.

But still they opened, and still I had to trudge through the parking garage. As I walked to my car and fished in my shorts for my keys, the startling blast of a car alarm from across the garage made me jump, and my keys went clattering onto the concrete.

I looked around, trying to see where the alarm was coming from, but I couldn't make it out, and then it stopped just as fast as it had started. I picked up my keys and started feeling creeped out. What if that had been John? It was probably just someone fumbling with their keys, but what if it was John?

Now my anger was turning back into anxiety as I started up my car and swiftly pulled out of the parking garage. My heart was blasting away in my chest, and I looked every direction for his car. It had to be somewhere. He had to be following me. I could feel his pervasive gaze from somewhere, bearing down on me.

But I couldn't see it. He wasn't there. I was a mess, and I hated it. The one person I was supposed to be able to tell everything to was a plant for my uncle's wife. My boyfriend thought I was crazy. I was alone, and it hurt so badly. Everything was fucked.

I merged onto the highway, headed home, just wanting to crawl into bed, and in my side mirror I saw John's Audi merging in behind me.

Chapter Eight

I T WAS JOHN'S CAR all right, there was no mistaking his silhouette in
my rearview mirror, the cigarette hanging out of the corner of his
mouth and his left arm lounging lazily out of the driver's side window.
My pupils dilated, my palms were clamming up, my limbs were growing
stiff, and my heart was shouting at me in my chest, screaming in loud,
rhythmic thumps of fear. Before I knew it I was swerving out of my lane,
getting honked at left and right, because I couldn't take my eyes off of
the car behind me.

I jerked the car back into my lane, my palms leaving disgusting
splotches of sweat on the steering wheel. He was right behind me,
adding his horn to the chorus of angry drivers as I freaked out more and
more, trying to keep the car straight and unable to. I was rattled. He was
coming for me, and I didn't know what to do.

I had been terrified at the thought of this moment—when he
escalated from following to confrontation. Now that moment was here.
He was bearing down on me, his front bumper edging closer and closer,
edging over to the left, and then to the right. Every time I looked in my
mirror, he was somewhere else, blaring away on his horn, chasing me
down the highway.

I thought I was going to die. I didn't know if he was trying to kill
me or not, but the way I was driving I was sure I was going to die. For
the life of me, I couldn't keep the car straight, my hands and arms were
shaking. A truck, slamming on his horn, hurled past me on the right,

and the enormous sound startled me. I jerked the wheel hard, and my whole car went with it, cutting into the left lane and prompting another bout of horn blasts.

John sped up and slid in behind me, nudging his bumper up to the back of my car, like a viper rearing back to strike. I had to get off the highway, I had to escape, but I was walled in by cars flying past, and caught between John's aggressive tailgating and a large box truck in front of me.

There was an exit coming up, I could see the sign down the road a bit, and I knew I had to take it. I started moving right, but John was there, slashing his car back into the right lane and cutting me off.

"Shit!" I yelled into my steering wheel, slamming my fist against the dash, then my foot onto the brake as I looked at the truck's brake lights in front of me. As I slowed, John sped ahead and I lost sight of him around the box truck. Was I safe?

It was now or never, so I twisted my wheel and gunned it across the right two lanes, shooting toward the upcoming exit. Just as I began turning off the highway, John's car appeared again behind me, and I nearly passed out from my escalating panic attack. The light at the end of the ramp was red, but I didn't care. I had to get away. I was going to die.

I didn't look either way at the intersection. I just put my foot down on the gas, clenched the wheel with both hands, and screamed out at the top of my lungs as I plunged through the red light with John's car screeching to a stop behind me.

I heard horns all around me, but I only looked straight ahead, and before I realized what I had really done I was through the intersection, banging a fast right turn down a side street, and gasping for breath as I came to a stop behind an idling delivery truck.

"Fuck!" I screamed to myself, slamming both of my hands against the wheel once more. The incident was catching up with me, the craziness of it all. Had he been trying to kill me, or was he just scaring me? Either way, I was freaked out, sweat soaked my shirt collar and under my arms.

I sat behind the truck for ten or fifteen minutes, just trying to get myself together. I felt like a pile of pieces in my seat, and I couldn't get them to fit into place again. I wasn't a person, just a clustered ball of nerves and fear and relief that the incident was over.

I knew I had to get home. I couldn't sit there forever, but the thought of driving my car was making my head spin even more. "You gotta get home," I told myself. "You gotta drive."

In the end, it was fear that got me moving. I was scared that John was nearby, just circling the little block I was on, and eventually he would close in. I wasn't going to let that happen, so wiping the thick beads of sweat from my forehead I clicked the shifter into first and pulled away.

On the drive home I scanned everywhere for John's car, but I never saw him. He had vanished into the city. A small part of me wanted to catch a glimpse of his car, just so I would know where he was, but I pulled through my front gate without any such sighting.

I must have looked crazy clambering out of my car in a hurry, my clothes disheveled from my streaks of sweat and practically sprinting to my room. When I got there, I slammed the door behind me, locked it, and collapsed into a loose collection of limbs on my floor, trying to take deep, steady breaths. It was over, I was safe, but still I felt threatened. I couldn't escape him, no matter what I did, and I hated it.

Ever since I started seeing his car around, I had been worried that something like that would happen, yet the thought of an actual confrontation was a foreign one. I couldn't have fathomed that he would have done something like try and run me off the road, or at least try and scare me. Why was he doing this? We had only been together for a few months, and we hadn't done much with our time except get me addicted to Valium, have sex, and go out. What was it about me? What was it about him?

I wanted to talk to Benjamin about it, but I felt like I couldn't because he had been so dismissive of John before. How was he going to react to a crazy story like this one? Would he even believe me? In the space of an afternoon, everything in my life that I thought I had figured out was falling apart. Again.

I was crushed with defeat. Just when I started to get things back on track, someone would yank the carpet out from under me and I would fall back on my ass, bruising my tailbone and awkwardly limping for weeks.

My therapist couldn't be trusted, my ex was threatening and following me, and my boyfriend thought I was making stuff up. It was all fucked, and all I could do was lie on my floor and cry. I missed my mom so much right then, I felt physically crushed, like there was a fifty-pound weight sitting on my back, pinning me to the floor.

I lay there until the weight was gone, I think it was at least an hour, and then took a long shower. I felt so lonely I wanted to reach out to Robert, but I knew he was still mad at me. My new school friends wouldn't understand anything, so I couldn't go to them. The one person I could talk to was Joseph. Even though we hadn't hung out since I got together with John, I had always trusted him, and I knew he was someone I could rely on.

After rustling my hair with a towel, I picked up my cell, and shot Joseph a text. *Want to grab a beer or something?* I was halfway through getting dressed when his reply buzzed through. *Sure, where at?*

We met at a little bar outside of the city center. I got there early and grabbed a table way in the back corner of the space, giving me a view of the whole restaurant with quick access to the emergency exit. If I even thought I saw John, I was going to bolt.

I broke into a big smile when I saw Joseph. He walked in the door with the same joyous bounce he always had in his step, mitigated by his serious brow and strong jawline. After glancing around, he spotted me and gave me a friendly wave as he sauntered over.

"Hey, man!" he said, reaching out his arms for a hug. "It's been too long!"

"Hey, Joseph," I said back, rising for his hug then slinking back into my seat. "How have you been?"

"Shit, man, fine I guess, just working with my dad when I'm not busy with my classes and school," Joseph said, resting one of his legs on the opposite knee. "What about you? I haven't heard from you in a little while. Everything good?"

"Not really," I said, shrugging off the seriousness with a little nervous chuckle.

He gave me a quizzical squint as he lit up a cigarette, laid his lighter on the table, and asked, "What's going on, dude?"

It took me three beers worth of time to lay it all out for Joseph. I babbled on and on while he sat there pensively, nodding a little bit and prodding me on with a question here and there.

"So, I don't know what to do," I concluded, sipping down the rest of my beer.

"Louie, that's scary as shit," Joseph said, with deadly seriousness in his eyes.

"Yeah, I know, that's what I've been trying to tell Benjamin," I said.

"You know where John lives?" he said, setting down his glass with a sinister thud.

"Sure, but—"

"I'm going to fuck this guy up, Louie," Joseph said with a scary, steely resolve.

"No, no, I can handle it," I protested. The thought of Joseph confronting John terrified me. Joseph was tough, but John was dangerous, and I didn't want to pull Joseph into things any more than I already had. "I just don't know what to do about Benjamin."

Joseph let out a long sigh, blowing his cigarette smoke through his nose. He looked at me for a second, squinting a bit, then seemed to resign himself to my wishes and replied, "Well, what do you want to do?" he asked, waving over another round.

"I don't know, that's the problem," I answered.

"No, you don't know what to do," he replied, unfolding his leg and putting the other one up. "I think you know what you want to do."

"And what's that?"

"Oh, come on, Louie," Joseph said. "You can't be too hard on yourself. You beat yourself up, you know that?"

"Yeah, I guess," I said softly.

"Go and talk to Benjamin," Joseph said, sticking out his chin. "You got nothing to worry about with him. You like him, right?"

"Yeah."

"So don't run away from him just because he was wrong about something," Joseph bounced back. "You see what I'm saying?"

"Yeah, I do," I said, looking down as the server swapped out our empty glasses for brimming ones. "Thanks."

"For what?" Joseph said, looking confused while he raised up his fourth glass of beer.

"For listening," I said back, looking up at him.

"Fuck, man," he said, gesturing with his beer for a little cheers. "That's why I'm here. I care about you, and I'm here if you need my help."

We hung out for a few more hours, got some dinner at a little shawarma place we liked, and called it a night. I was pretty tipsy and sluggish by the time we were done, and as I drove home, I felt the day's excitement catching up to me. By the time I pulled into our front gate, it was all I could do to keep my eyes open, and in stark contrast to my hurried exit earlier that day I dragged myself across the courtyard and up to my bedroom.

When I fell into my bed, I checked my phone one more time and saw a text from Benjamin.

Lunch tomorrow?

I smiled while I read it, and sent back, *Absolutely.*

The next day while we were eating sandwiches I told him about my therapist and the car chase with John. Just like Joseph, he took everything super well and listened patiently. I remember being surprised when he apologized for not taking me seriously. He made me feel heard and valued, and in my life that feeling only came along once in a while.

"You sound like you could use some time away," he said, wiping his chin with the neatly folded napkin.

"Time away?"

"A vacation," he said, giving me a brisk nod. "Get out of the city for a weekend."

"And go where?" I asked.

"What about the sea?"

"The sea?"

"Sure, it's beautiful, relaxing. The air is good for you."

"I can't just take a vacation. I have school," I replied.

"When's your last class for the week?" he asked, taking a small sip of his coffee.

"Thursday afternoon. I get out at three."

"And your first class?"

"Sunday."

"Well, there you have it," he said, giving me a kind smile. "We will leave Thursday evening."

"We?" I laughed back. "It's a nice thought, but I can't."

"Why not?" he asked, cocking his head to the right. "You told me yourself you never study."

"That's true," I said, smiling back at him. "You're serious, aren't you?"

"Quite serious," he said, setting down his coffee cup, still smiling. "Would you like that?"

"Yeah, I would," I said. I thought about it for a few more seconds, then said, "Let's go to the sea."

I packed a small duffel bag with my swimsuit and some summer clothes and brought it to school with me that Thursday. My dad was in London on business, my brother wasn't home, and the maids were nowhere to be found, so I didn't tell anyone where I was going. I figured if they were worried, they would text or call. It wasn't unusual for us to go days without seeing each other, so I didn't think any more about it.

School, which usually went by quickly, took forever that day. The longer the day went, the more I realized how excited I was for the trip. I had never gone on any sort of vacation with someone other than my family or my childhood friends, and I was daydreaming of the sheer freedom I was about to experience.

When classes finished I damn near ran down the grand old hallways, ducking around the big coned-off construction areas, and leapt into Benjamin's waiting car.

"You ready?" he asked, helping shift my duffel bag to the back seat.

"Let's get out of here," I said back. I leaned over, gave him a kiss, and we took off.

It was about a four-hour drive to the sea, and when we got there we cut south down the coast for another hour, finally reaching a secluded resort perched between the shore and a huge cluster of smooth, bright boulders.

It was dark by the time we arrived, so we decided to save the beach for the next day and get some dinner at the hotel restaurant. The whole place was fabulous and elegant, with big gold-leafed pillars shooting out of the marble floors, holding up the high, ornate ceilings.

The restaurant had thick, dark-green tablecloths and was practically empty. We took a seat next to the floor-to-ceiling windows, and Benjamin ordered a bottle of wine. I didn't know jack about wine, and he would try and teach me about it when he ordered, but I never really absorbed any of it.

"It's a shame it's so dark," Benjamin said, trying to make out the shoreline through the bright indoor reflection of the restaurant. "The view will be beautiful in the morning."

"This is a nice place," I said, raising up my wine glass for a toast.

"It is, isn't it?" he remarked in his usual, dignified manner. "Kind of the company to put us up somewhere so nice, isn't it?"

"The company?" I asked, blinking at him blankly.

"Most business trips aren't this enjoyable," he said, sending me a sly wink as the server slowly worked their way over.

"Business," I affirmed. I hated that we couldn't be there publicly as a couple, but if a weekend away cost the price of two hotel rooms instead of one then we would pay it.

As I ordered fish, I admitted it felt foolish not eating fish on the seashore, and Benjamin chuckled at me for it. We went through two bottles of wine and way too much food just for the fun of it before trudging upstairs, clutching our stomachs in the elevator, pronouncing our guts as much as we could and cracking ourselves up.

We got up to the rooms and checked down the hallway before we snuck in the same door, throwing the privacy hanger on the doorknob. The room was huge, with the same massive windows as downstairs across the whole wall. The entryway was marble, and then the room opened up into a large carpeted observatory that in the daylight surely had an impeccable view of the sea.

Benjamin had a funny sway in his step from the wine, and he danced himself over to the mini bar with a few snaps of his fingers. I was still laughing from the elevator, and his antics only made me laugh harder as I collapsed down onto the couch, wiping moisture out of my eye before it turned into a tear.

"You want some more?" he asked, inspecting a small bottle of wine from the minibar.

"Yeah," I said, trying to calm down my hilarity. "Just a little."

"What's a little?" he said back with a proud puff of his cheeks, yanking the corkscrew out of the bottle with an echoing pop. He tipped the bottle over and poured a huge portion into one of the empty glasses.

"That's a lot," I said, struggling a little bit to get off the couch.

"No," he said, trying to pull his face into a serious mask. "This is a lot." And he poured the rest of the bottle into his own glass. Together we looked at the two wine glasses and their unproportioned servings, looked up at each other, and started laughing again.

I saw him drink wine all the time, but I had never seen him so loose. He wasn't wasted or inebriated, but he definitely had the sway of someone with more than a few glasses in him. It was so different from being with John. When he and I would go out, we would both drive ourselves into the furthest reaches of intoxication that we could find. By the end of the night, at least one of us was shitfaced. Benjamin wasn't like that. He was jovial and boisterous. I thought it was very cute, and I steered myself around the edge of the bar counter.

"What are you doing?" he said with a smirk.

"What do you think?" I said back, laying my arms over his shoulders.

"Well—"

I interrupted him with a kiss, sliding my arms down from his shoulders to his arms. Then he seized me by the waist and pulled me in tight, pressing his lips firmly against mine, and I gave out a little laugh.

We swayed over to the bed, kissing and chuckling, moving our hands up and down each other's backs and arms, until the back of my knees hit the edge of the bed and I tumbled backward onto it.

I fumbled with the buttons on his shirt, finally getting them free and reaching down the length of his bare shoulder, pushing the shirt away while his hand gently moved down my torso. It got hotter and heavier by the second, both of us driving at one another with unrestricted passion. Then as the last piece of clothing came away, and he hovered above me, I found our eyes drifting together.

Looking into his eyes, something strange happened that I could not then account for. I suddenly felt awkward, almost as if I had been caught doing something wrong. I clenched my eyes shut as his hot breath brushed against my neck, and things were normal again.

I kept my eyes shut as our tongues danced over each other and we twisted the sheets into a clustered knot, yanking them from their corners, moving in between tight grapples and sensitive embraces. We kept at it as long as we could, until the sky was growing a shade brighter and we collapsed into a deep satisfying sleep amidst the mess we had made of the pillows.

When I finally pulled myself out of bed the next morning, I was struck by the light of the day, and I winced through the bright rays as I searched around for my underwear. I got up and walked to the window, rubbing the little crumbs from the corner of my eyes, and drank in the view.

The sea was a vast myriad of shimmering caps, shifting back and forth. The waves lapped gently against the crusted white shores, and the sky was bright blue. I had seen the sea plenty of times, but never from all the way up here. It was shining and striking, and right then there was nowhere else in the world I wanted to be.

"You're up," Benjamin groaned, rolling away from the sun.

"How are you feeling?" I joked, kicking a stray pillow out of my way as I turned back around.

"Like an old man," he complained, pulling himself up against the headboard. "What should we do with the day?"

"Get some breakfast," I answered confidently.

The rest of the weekend was beautiful. We did nothing but sip on wine, swim in the sea, and snack on cheese and crackers in between our huge meals. The sun shone down on my face as I lay on the coarse sand. Behind me, the red and white rock landscape crawled up toward white wisps of cloud. It was peaceful, and for an entire day, I didn't think about John or my crazy family.

The first time we went down to the beach, I had a flash of anxiety. I hated swimming. I found bodies of saltwater pretty gross, and was terrified of nasty seaweed getting stuck to my body as I swam. But I wanted to impress Benjamin. I didn't want him to think I was high maintenance, and that I wouldn't do things he liked just because I didn't, and I wanted to share the moment with him.

Still, I paused on shore as the waves lapped against my ankles. Benjamin dove in headfirst, sending out sparkling droplets that dazzled in the bright sun. He popped his head up from the waves, and he shook the water from his face with a gleeful expression.

"Come on in!" he called back to me.

"Shit," I muttered under my breath, then replied, "Coming!" I had to do it. I sucked in a huge breath, took a few big strides, and dove in after him.

That night, we sat on the beach, looking out at the water as it reflected the moon, shattered into luminous pieces by the shifting surf. I looked out across the sea and saw the flickering lights of the Israeli coast on the far side. Suddenly, I broke into a light bout of laughter.

"What's so funny?" Benjamin asked.

"You can see Israel from here," I answered.

"Yes," he said with a little chuckle. "Why's that funny?"

"I was just thinking about this guy," I said.

"A guy?" he replied, raising his eyebrows.

"Not like that," I said back. "I was talking to this guy from Israel online once, and he flew over to have coffee with me and my friend. But when we met him, he was the ugliest guy I think I had ever seen. I couldn't say anything. I just looked at him with a dumb face," I said, letting my laughter subside a bit. "I was so embarrassed."

"You are terrible," he joked back, and we shared a long laugh in the moonlight.

I existed in a state of relaxation and joy for those few days. It was probably the best business trip anyone had ever taken in the Kingdom, and I drank in every minute of it. Before we left, I gave my unused room a toss over, trying to make it look like someone had actually spent some time there.

Everything felt surreal as we checked out of the hotel. Some part of me didn't think that I actually had to go back to the city, that we would leave the hotel and go somewhere else just as fun and secluded. My phone had been dead since we arrived, so I plugged it into Benjamin's charger that he had hooked up to his cigarette lighter.

I leaned my head on the window and looked out at the landscape as we pulled away until my phone gave a little buzz and I looked down. There were a handful of voicemails from my dad, but they were all two seconds long and didn't tell me anything. There were also some texts from my brother bugging out about where I was, so I begrudgingly responded that I was headed home.

I felt my mood plummet with every kilometer farther down the road. I knew my dad would have something to say about me disappearing, as if he had the right. The fear of the shit storm that was waiting for me grew more and more intense as the capital's skyline came into sight.

I looked at the tall buildings standing out among the clusters of four and five story apartments. I could see my neighborhood on one of the city's hills, and I hated the fact that I had to go back.

Traffic got thicker as we reached the city, and we slowed while we wound through downtown. I started feeling claustrophobic, looking around at the cars crawling past us, expecting John to show up at any moment. Just like that, my anxiety was back. I was home, in the real world, trapped in the confines of this Kingdom. My phone lit up with a text from my brother.

You better get home, dude, Dad's pissed.

"Shit," I said.

"What's that?" Benjamin asked, looking over at me.

"Nothing," I said, frowning. "Just take me home."

Chapter Nine

MY FRONT DOOR WAS an ominous obelisk looming over me as I crossed the courtyard, my heels slapping against the stone with each hesitant step. I knew my dad was waiting for me. The weekend had been the best trip of my life, and all that built-up happiness was draining away into crushing anxiety.

He was waiting in the kitchen, I could see him standing there from the door, resting his palms flat on the countertop with a glass of scotch, a finger's reach away from his right hand.

"I'm back," I announced, clicking the door shut behind me. The afternoon sun streamed in through the windows, and the lingering dust in the room appeared like a faint trace of some invisible wall. I walked through it, dropping my duffel bag on the couch as I went past.

"You're back," he echoed, letting the words out with a slow sigh as he nudged his scotch with his knuckle. The ice cubes clinked together, and the sound of it was louder than my tentative footsteps down the hallway.

"I saw you called me," I said, entering the kitchen. I decided it was best to get ahead of it, just to get his freak out over with so I could go slink away to my room, text Benjamin or Joseph, and go to sleep.

"I did," he replied, nodding once as his finger uncurled and hooked out for his scotch. The ice cubes clattered again, and the sound was practically deafening. "Several times."

"Yeah, I saw that," I said, reaching the counter across from him.

"Didn't feel like calling back?"

"Well, I was on my way home," I said back, "So I figured it could wait."

"So your phone was off?" he asked, lifting the glass up to his lips, but he just held it there like he was enjoying the smell.

"So?"

"What if I needed to reach you? I didn't know where you were," he said, the sternness creeping into his voice.

"So?" I said, shrugging.

"So?" he replied incredulously, making a little flourish with his scotch, his only prop available. "In what world is that all right?"

"What's the big deal?" I shot back, letting my voice rise. "You're gone for weeks sometimes."

"I'm not you, am I?" he shouted back, escalating his voice to a full boom.

"What's that supposed to mean?" I screamed, slamming my palm against the counter with a savage slap.

"Oh, come on, Louie," he scoffed. "You know what it means."

"No, I don't think so," I said back hotly. "You tell me."

"Don't do this," he growled. "Why won't you just be normal, huh? Why do you have to push back? You're not supposed to!"

"Supposed to?" I gawked. "Not supposed to? Who do you think you are?"

"I am your father!" he bellowed, his voice bouncing off the walls like some dreaded rubber ball. "You want to do this? Fine, let's do it. Let's clear all the bullshit away and lay it all out there."

"Let's!" I shot back.

"You are my property!" he roared back, growing two inches taller and leaning in over the counter. "You are supposed to do as you're told, not run around, dragging the family name through the dirt, having breakdowns, using drugs! You're a disgrace!"

"Fuck you!" I shouted back. "I don't care!"

"That's your problem, Louie!" he responded, making another poking move with his scotch. "You don't care! About our family! About anything! Don't you know who we are? Don't you know people talk about us? You're important, Louie, whether you like it or not, so fucking act like it! You can't go off and disappear!"

"I didn't ask for any of this!" I lamented.

"Well, tough luck!" he spat back, slapping his glass down so hard I thought it would break. "Because that doesn't matter! I have tried with you, God help me, Louie, I have tried, but you won't listen. Well, I hope you can understand me this time. You are never to pull such a stunt again, do you hear me? Do you? The next time you go off the grid, I will have public security find you. If you're not in the country, I'll call in a favor and have the goddamn Mossad root you out! And they will! You cannot escape this! This is what you are! Who we are! Stop fucking with it! Why is that so hard? Now shut your fucking mouth before you think about saying something else, absorb what I'm saying to you, and fuck off!"

I should have told him to fuck off right back, I should have stormed out, smashed some glasses, made a scene. Instead I shrunk back into my shell like I always did, my tail between my legs and my ego evaporated.

I couldn't fight back. The will just wasn't there. It was a brutal moment in which I cemented for myself a feeling of weakness that would ultimately ruin the next few years of my life. I was trapped, a possession, and like an overly disciplined dog I slunk away into a monotonous routine, all the while looking over my shoulder as I harbored unrelenting fear and anxiety. It was exhausting, it was shameful, and I demeaned myself little by little until there wasn't much left.

He won. I lost. Fuck it. I went upstairs, dejected, and lay in bed staring at the ceiling. I realized that I just had to wait. Wait for school to be over, and wait to start my own life. I thought I already had, but I had only fooled myself into believing I had autonomy. It was time to bunker down and simply exist.

I focused on school. I tried distracting myself with my new friends, but they weren't much help. We would go to the mall and hang around the food court, slowly sipping soda, or we would visit six different stores idly buying sunglasses. Sometimes we would hang out at a hookah bar or go shopping for new clothes. It wasn't an exciting life, but it was what it was.

Benjamin and I would see each other about once or twice a week, sometimes every other week. Anything more would look suspicious, and since he wasn't my age I couldn't write him off as a friend. It sucked because I had a ton of free time and couldn't really do anything with it.

Robert was pretty much at arm's length from then on. With the summer almost over, he went back to the United States for school, and we didn't make any real effort to talk or reconnect. By then it was a fading friendship. That truly sucked. I had known him almost my whole life. How did we become like this?

I reached out to his mom, and we had coffee a few times. It was good to catch up with her, but I couldn't talk to her about what was going on. I didn't want to throw Robert under the bus by talking about the gay warehouse party and cocaine, so we mostly just chatted about school. Still, it was good to see her. She had always been nice to me, and it was affirming to get a little positive reinforcement, even if it was just about my engineering degree.

Just like that the summer wound down, and then it was over. I hadn't seen John around since the incident on the highway, and I was starting to feel a bit more relaxed. I was still a mess of nerves all the time, but it wasn't quite as bad.

Then, in November, the bombs went off. I had gotten home from school and retreated into my room like I usually did, fiddling with my phone and talking to Benjamin. A few hours went by, and I was thinking about getting something to eat when I heard three, deep booms echo through the evening air. I didn't think anything of it at the time since they were pretty distant. It could have been a delivery truck or something. Then, a few minutes later, a heavy, hammering knock rocked my door.

"Louie!" my brother shouted.

"What?" I asked, sitting up quickly as he opened the door.

"Good, you're here," he said, letting out a big breath.

"What are you talking about?" I asked, hopping off the bed.

"We got attacked," he said, shaking his head.

"What?" I said again, trying to figure out what he meant. "What do you mean?"

"Fucking terrorists, man," he said, rubbing the back of his head. "They blew up downtown."

"What?" I said once more, blinking at him.

"Come on," he said, "It's on TV."

I followed him downstairs in a weird trance, and silently sat down on the couch as the news blared away on the television. "We're just getting preliminary reports now, but it appears there has been a series of explosions among several of the city's most prominent hotels. At this time, we do not know the number of people killed or injured, but preliminary reports are coming in from eyewitnesses describing at least five bodies so far at the Grand Hyatt—"

"Fuck," I muttered, finding my place on the couch without looking.

"Yeah, man," my brother said. "It's fucked up."

Three big hotels had been bombed simultaneously, and utter chaos had followed. The news crews on the ground didn't seem to understand what was happening, they were just running around, videotaping the carnage, cluttered rubble, and the emergency personnel trying to pull people out of partially collapsed buildings.

I shook my head as we watched, not knowing if I should say something, or what, if anything, I could say. I guess my brother felt the same way because we both just sat there, shaking our heads in silence.

It went on all night. We must have fallen asleep at some point because we both woke up on the big sectional, our feet crammed together into the corner joint and our drool leaving mirrored patches on either end of the cushions.

The TV was still on, and it was all the same news as far as I could tell. The reporters were still saying that nobody had claimed responsibility and that the death toll exceeded fifty. There were over a hundred people in the hospitals, and the whole city was in some kind of lockdown.

Usually I could see a lot of the city traffic from the kitchen window, or anywhere on the second floor. That day, as I dragged myself into the kitchen to grab a Pepsi Light and looked down on the valley, I didn't see anything moving. Everything was eerily still.

Apparently, one of the hotels was hosting a wedding reception with a bunch of nobility present, and they had been hit pretty hard. Both the groom and the bride's fathers died in the explosion. The news told us we had to stay put, that the only people allowed on the streets were the police and the security forces.

My dad was nowhere to be found, as usual, so my brother and I spent the whole day idly watching the news, saying a few "fucks" and "Christs" here and there as the TV played on. They said the king was on a trip to Kazakhstan, and that he was flying back as soon as he could. Like I gave a fuck about the king.

They ran some broadcasts from the US, and their President was bumbling on about keeping the Kingdom safe, talking about support from the White House. God he was an idiot, him and his fucking ears, his big nose, and his dumb dynasty. It was like that for days.

Eventually the news picked a suspect, this guy named Zarqawi. He was from the Kingdom originally, had a huge tribal family who controlled a large area in the Kingdom, but he had been sentenced to death a year ago for the murder of a government official in his front yard. Of course, the Kingdom didn't have him in custody, but they tried and sentenced him all the same along with a handful of others. The US wanted him too, for everything related to his activity in Iraq, so it became a real media circus. His extended family took out full-page ads in the paper denouncing him.

Everything was complete chaos for about a month. My classes were shut down for two weeks, and when they started again, campus was eerily quiet. People wouldn't look at each other, they kept their heads down, glancing only from their peripherals. It was spooky living in fear like that, waiting for a new high-profile venue to erupt in fire and sirens.

Yet it never came, and eventually things started evening out. They weren't normal, I'm not sure they ever were again, but they got better than that paralytic month of fear. Then the holidays came around. I remembered how awful Christmas the year before had been, and I was determined not to relive it. I spent most of December that year at my Grandma's house with my grandparents and my aunt. It was nice, nicer than my house, and I decided then that I would spend every Christmas with them, rather than with my dad.

The bombings were a constant topic of conversation, of thought, of paranoia, even after things settled down. People were going back to work and back to school, but the attacks were still on everyone's mind, even if they were hiding in the background.

My aunt had some good advice. She told me that the only way to feel normal was to do normal things, like go out to the mall with my friends. So that's what I did.

It was February, and a really shitty way to start 2006. I was out with a few friends from school, trying to feel normal. As I pulled into the parking garage, I could have sworn I saw John's car flashing past in the rearview. I got all clammy and weird while I tried to park, and my friend gave me an odd look, but I played it off like I was claustrophobic.

"Oh, I never knew that," my friend said.

"Yeah, it's not that bad," I answered. "It just acts up sometimes."

"I get that," he said back, and to my great relief, that was that.

We did our usual mall thing, walking between the designer stores and picking at fries in the food court. It was boring, but it was simple and mundane, and it made sense. I remember looking around at everyone else there and thinking that we were all trying to feel like the world was normal.

I think we killed a few hours wandering around, but eventually we parted ways on our way back down to the parking garage. One of my friends was riding with me, so we headed down a couple more stories to my car.

We walked down the row, and my anxiety rose again the closer we got to my dormant taillights. It was all wrong, even the air I was breathing was tainted with the residue of John's proximity. I had seen him. He was here. He was coming for me.

I stopped in my tracks as I got halfway around the trunk toward the driver's side. My friend was walking to the passenger's side, waiting for me to unlock it, but I couldn't move. There was a light coming from my dashboard, this hollow red color, blinking a little slower than a turn signal. I couldn't hear any kind of clicking or ticking, but I could see the red blinking. It wasn't part of my car. It wasn't supposed to be there.

"Stop!" I shouted, and my friend jumped in alarm.

"What?"

"Look," I said, pointing to the dash. "You see that light?"

"Yeah, isn't that your car alarm?"

"No," I said, taking a step back from the car. "That's not supposed to be there."

"Fuck!" he yelped, scrambling back to where I was. "What the hell, dude?"

"I don't know," I answered, feeling my arms starting to shake.

"We gotta call someone," he said, shaking his head vigorously. "Dude, it could be a bomb."

"What the fuck? A bomb?" I balked, jumping back from the car.

Someone was walking nearby us when he said it, and they dropped their shopping bags and screamed, "Bomb!" After that the whole parking garage was flooded with security forces wearing body armor and sporting sleek submachine guns. One of the officials had me and my friend over to the side, questioning us and taking notes on his little paper pad, which looked funny in the hands of a guy wearing full, bulky body armor.

"And you're sure this light wasn't there before?" he asked for the eighth time.

It took hours, and the whole time I was a panicked mess. They swept the outside of the car with sensors before the tactical team broke into it. I offered them the key but they said it wasn't safe since the trigger could be in the lock. I didn't think that was likely, since I had only been away from the car for a few hours, but still they did what they did.

Then the man in the huge, puffy bomb suit crawled in there and started carefully fishing around. He was in there for a few hours. Meanwhile, the entire mall had been evacuated. People were lined up on the sidewalks a couple blocks away, standing in ranks behind the news vans and the police barricades. It was a complete nightmare, and I wished it would end.

My breath was short, my hands were shaking, and my feet were sore as I stood there for the time it took them to conduct their search. Different people kept coming up to me, asking the same questions.

Eventually, the guy in the bomb suit got out of the car and had a long talk with the note-taking man. They went back and forth with shrugging and head shaking, then the notebook man went around talking to the guys with guns. Before I knew it they were all packing up, shuffling back to their vans and cruisers.

"What's going on?" I asked, taking a few steps toward the guy with the notebook. "Did you find it?"

"There's nothing there," he said, giving me a horrible scowl. "You've wasted a lot of time and manpower here. You have anything else to say?"

"What are you talking about?" I stammered. "That can't be right."

"Look, kid, we swept it eight times. There's nothing there."

"But I saw—"

"There's no bomb," he grunted back, scrunching up his nose just before he coughed. "Go home."

"But—"

"It's over kid, just go home," he snapped, flipped his notebook shut, and walked away. I was standing there in complete confusion when another officer leaned over and said, "You might want to wait a little bit before you drive away, let the news vans clear out."

"Okay," I mumbled back, passively watching the clusterfuck of panic I had caused slowly dissipate around me.

"Hey, Louie, I'm gonna grab a car," my friend said, inching away from me.

"Yeah, all right," I replied.

"See you."

"Yeah, see you," and he was gone.

Why couldn't I do anything right? I couldn't even go to the mall like someone my age was supposed to without everything going to complete shit. I couldn't bear the thought of climbing into my car and driving away like nothing had happened. How could I? The embarrassment was too much. Had I really just made the whole thing up?

I had seen that light blinking. I knew it wasn't part of my car. Had it been a reflection from across the garage? A trick of stray sunlight? No, we were underground, I had seen it, I knew what I saw. But then again, maybe I didn't.

I stared at my car for a while before getting in, wondering if I was truly crazy. Was I losing my mind? The bomb squad had turned my car inside out, and as I sat on the seat I felt the cushion flattening out underneath me.

I turned the keys and heard the familiar rumble of my car's engine. Letting out a long breath, I threw it into reverse and backed out of the space. All I knew was that I had to get home. At least there, I could hide in my room, curl up in my bed, and pretend as if none of this had ever happened.

Driving around one of the concrete pillars, I turned toward the exit. The light of the early evening lit up the huge rectangular exit like a beacon. If I could make it through that then I was home free, and I could leave this stupid parking garage behind forever.

I rolled my window down to let the warm breeze wash over me as I drove up the exit ramp. The air felt like the only thing in the world that wasn't out to get me. The whole place was silent, save the sound of my tires slowly rolling over smooth pavement. Creeping up the exit ramp, I stopped for a minute, my hands tight around the rim of the steering wheel. I just wanted to sit and breathe for a minute before I got on the busy roads.

Then I heard the click. In the Kingdom you hear that sound everywhere, any time of day. People are always smoking, sometimes lighting their next cigarette with their last, but anywhere you are you hear those little clicks of a Bic lighter, of the thumb sliding over the metal gear and then slamming down on the plastic gas release. But the parking garage was empty. It had been evacuated.

I looked left out my window and there he was, leaning up against the smooth white wall with one foot propped up behind him like he was on a movie poster. His cigarette dripped thick, fresh smoke, swirling down around his pressed collar and then drifting up past his jaw.

He had sunglasses on, and I could see my own dumb reflection in their mirrored lenses through the tendrils of smoke. My jaw was hanging open and there was complete shock in my eyes. He flashed a quick smile my way, and from his belt he flashed an red laser pointer straight at me. That little blinking light danced over my dashboard, and my anxiety exploded into sheer terror. I slammed on the gas and rocketed forward.

"Stop!" the ticket man shouted, waving his arms wildly. I hit the brakes crudely as I looked forward and stopped just short of plowing through the parking gate. When I glanced back to where John had been standing, he was gone, leaving only a thin trail of smoke in his wake.

I stammered my way out of the parking garage, mumbling an apology to the booth operator. He said something back but it was just a weird whining in my ears. The whole world had the volume turned down. I had my hands on the wheel in a rigid position, my elbows locked and my knuckles white from their iron grip on the leather.

As I drove through the city, I scrunched up my cheeks, trying to prevent myself from crying as long as I could. Eventually the tears started pouring down my face, dribbling down over my quivering chin and raining onto my shirt and pants.

"Fuck!" I screamed into my steering wheel, letting the tears cascade into sobs. "Fuck fuck fuck fuck!" I couldn't escape. John was everywhere, lurking around all the corners and under all the bridges, and now I was sure that he was going to ruin my life. Nowhere was safe, nowhere except my room. I was almost home.

I sat in the courtyard for a bit, frantically wiping my eyes to conceal the fact I had been bawling alone in my car. Then I sucked in a deep breath, and scurried as quick as I could through the house, but before I could get up the stairs, I heard my dad's voice from the kitchen.

"Louie, is that you?"

"Yeah," I called back, moving through the living room.

"I just got off the phone with the Prime Minister!" he shouted, marching down the hall toward me. "What the hell did you do?"

"Nothing," I mumbled, and quickened my pace, I got up a few steps before he rounded the corner into view.

"Nothing! That's all you have to say? They evacuated the whole mall, Louie!"

I just kept going. I didn't have the energy to fight him, not then. As I shut my bedroom door behind me, his shouting became muffled, and I collapsed onto my bed.

Lying there, I pulled my knees up into the fetal position and clutched one of my pillows. I felt manipulated, like I was a toy that John was playing with, and just like when we had been dating, I felt an utter lack of agency and self-worth. I was nothing. Just a pawn.

Still in a ball, I pulled out my phone and wiped fresh tears away on my pillow. I typed out a text to Benjamin, asking him if he would pick me up and go for a drink or two. Before I was finished writing the text, my phone buzzed with an incoming message. I smiled, thinking Benjamin had texted me just as I was texting him, and then I opened it.

Heard you suck cock. How much?

I flung it across the room, and it bounced off the wall and onto my light-blue upholstered chair with all the durability of a Nokia flip phone.

"What the fuck!" I lamented, crawling further into my shell. I watched my phone from across the room, shuddering with fear every time it vibrated. Nowhere was safe, not even my room, and fear and anxiety took over every cell of my being, leaving a puddle of unhinged tears and impending doom.

Chapter Ten

THE MORNINGS WERE ALWAYS a fresh start, at least until I remembered whatever I was distraught about from the previous day. That morning I had about four minutes of calm before it all came crashing down. After I used the bathroom and washed my face I reached for my phone, but it wasn't on my nightstand.

Frowning, I started ruffling through my bed, flipping my pillows over and pulling my blankets back. I must have fallen asleep with it, but I couldn't find it, and I got more and more frustrated the longer I pawed at the bedding. Where the hell did it go?

Then, like remembering the last few moments of a dream, I recalled hurling my phone across the room. My frown deepened as I looked over to the wall, and my eyes traced down from the tiny blemish my phone had created in the paint, and there it was, laying on the floor.

Half of me didn't want to pick it up. Yesterday had been fucked beyond belief, and I didn't want to face whatever digital shitstorm awaited me on that little screen. I thought about the text that had come through late in the night: *Heard you suck cock, how much?* What the fuck was that about?

The other half of me didn't believe it. I had probably made it up, just a weird snippet of a dream that resulted from the previous day's enormous amount of stress. I walked over to my phone like it was a bomb I had to defuse, locking my eyes on its tiny exterior display.

I stood over it, staring down, wondering what hell I would find there, and the phone buzzed against my big toe.

I crouched down and flipped it open, blinking as my eyes adjusted from the morning light to the bright little box and the little letters all crammed together. When I looked at the screen, I couldn't believe what I was seeing. It took a few more passes for me to absorb it. My inbox was full of messages, all from random numbers, and each one said pretty much the same thing as the first text.

My weight rolled back from the balls of my feet to my heels as I slumped against my wall, dropping the phone back onto the carpet. None of it made sense, and my head was starting to spin, trying to work it all out, and I couldn't. I felt sick, a deep churning in my stomach, far down, and the flutter of anxiety in the top of my chest.

"Go away," I said to my phone, nudging it with my foot. "Stop it." It answered back with a little buzz. I didn't want to look at it, so I climbed into the shower and stood there for a long time, kicking little ripples of water toward the drain and watching them bounce back against the tiled wall.

I had school that day, and after school I would probably meet Benjamin for a snack and a drink. Then I'd come home, crawl into bed, and fall asleep. The whole day was mapped out, and the day after it, and the one after that. I didn't want to do any of it. I didn't even want to be in the shower. But I didn't want to get out, because that would mean facing everything else in the world. It was sickening, and dark, and I would have cried if I could have mustered the sheer emotion required.

It was unusually hot that day, and the sun crushed me as I walked to my car. We had a whole covered parking area, but I always parked out in the courtyard so I could keep my mom's parking spot open. Everyone on the compound was mad about it, always telling me how my car was in the way, but I didn't care. I wasn't going to park in her spot. A part of me desperately needed to believe that she was coming back, that she was on a very long vacation and one day she would show up. That spot needed to remain vacant. That vacation needed to come to an end.

When I got to my car, I felt my stomach sink. I hadn't noticed it the day before, probably due to the emotional wreck I was at the time, but looking at my car in the daylight I saw a big ugly scratch on the driver's side door.

"Damn it," I muttered, tracing the scratch with my finger. No doubt the bomb squad had scuffed it with some big piece of equipment. All I could do was hope my dad never noticed, it was just another thing he would scream at me about, or my brother would laugh at. I had heard him the night before, walking down the hall, talking on his phone, laughing and saying something about the mall. I couldn't blame him. From his eyes it was a funny story I guess. With a drawn-out sigh, I got into the car.

The seats were hot and sticky when I sat down, the air stale and suffocating, but I closed the vents and kept the windows up, baking in the sweltering heat just because it wasn't what I normally did. I thought I had found a new routine, but I had been fooling myself. I was just as much of a mess as I had always been, and all I could do was slog through it.

The texts stopped coming in that afternoon. Wherever my number had been, it wasn't there anymore. I had to chalk it up to coincidence because I couldn't find any other explanation. It was probably a few thirteen-year-olds in their parents' basement, bouncing random numbers around the internet for a laugh. Someday they would figure out how unamusing it all was, but until then I was just happy the texts had stopped.

Time started slipping past again as I got back to school and tried forgetting about the mall. School became an escape from everything else. I never wanted an engineering degree. In California I was going into premed, but my dad decided the world had enough surgeons. Engineering, though, well that was a smart play. Just like that, my path was laid out in front of me.

Grumpy as I had been starting the coursework, I found myself slowly growing to like it. School had always been easy for me, unlike my cousins, and university wasn't that much harder than high school. People would complain about staying up for hours at night, studying and writing research papers, but it never took me that long.

Either way, I ended up liking my classes. I liked the way everything worked when the numbers lined up, how all the tiny pieces of something had to be just so. In the chaotic shitstorm of my life, the careful planning and precise measurements made sense, and it was comforting when I got it right, time and time again.

I think my high marks in school were the only things that kept my dad off my back after the mall incident. He had gotten hell for it from the prime minister, and I had to hear about that for a while, but eventually it faded into the background as my grades for the first semester rolled around.

I hardly ever saw anybody at home. I tried to arrange my time so that I was out all day, and only went back home to take my shoes off and fall asleep. That seemed to suit my dad just fine, and my brother was always off with his friends.

My afternoons were for my school friends. I was also seeing my old high school friends more frequently, but usually on the weekends. Reconnecting with some of them gave me a comforting feeling, like they existed in a world where all this bullshit hadn't happened, and we could just laugh about growing up. Every time we hung out, I felt lighter, and I liked it.

School days were for school friends. When classes finished, we would go out for coffee or drinks, sometimes spending a few hours at a hookah bar. I didn't smoke cigarettes, but I enjoyed puffing on a hookah tube and letting huge billows of smoke drift up toward the ceiling. I liked the low light and relaxed environment, the comfortable couches, and the soft hum of conversation swirling through separate pockets of artificial aromas.

After an afternoon hangout, I would usually meet up with Benjamin for some food. Most of the time it wasn't a full dinner, just some stuff to pick at between a few glasses of wine. I kept a nice buzz on from the moment I got out of class until I fell asleep. I knew it was maybe too much, but I rationalized it by telling myself it was better than binging on Valium. There were still times I craved those pills, and the chance to curl up into a ball of nothingness, but alcohol got me by.

There were a good few weeks after the mall incident where I didn't see John's car at all. A piece of me wanted to believe that he was done, that the whole mall thing was his grand goodbye, some spectacular sendoff, one last huge headfuck. But a bigger part of me wasn't that naive. I knew he was going to show up again and again, here and there, until he got what he wanted. What that was, I had no idea.

Sure enough, I caught sight of him in March, driving in lazy circles around the campus parking lot as I walked to my car one afternoon. I stood there in the lot, looking at him through his windshield from across the rows, but I couldn't make out his face through the reflection of the sun and the swirl of his cigarette smoke.

"What now?" I called out through the empty lot at his headlights. "Huh? I'm right fucking here!" I didn't know what I wanted out of that exchange. Maybe I wanted to show him that I wasn't afraid anymore, even though I was. Maybe I was just bored out of my mind with the routine I had built and wanted to see what would happen.

I felt anticipation building inside me, my blood getting hot and my cheeks tingling. "What now?" I shouted at his car again. "What are you going to do? Huh?" I screamed, throwing my hands up in the air. "Come the fuck on!"

I was heaving and sweating, standing there in the bright sun, my arms slowly sinking down from above my head, blinking through the glint on his windshield. I was trying not to feel the fear bubbling up through the anger and outrage at this fucking guy who imposed himself on every aspect of my life.

Then he flicked his cigarette butt out of the driver's window, pulled a slow U-turn, and rolled away through the parking lot. Watching him drive away, I was devastated. I wanted him gone, of course, but in that moment I wanted something to happen. I didn't know what, just something, some sort of resolution to all his craziness. Instead he left, and I stood, again, dripping sweat, drenched in fear, anxiety, and anger—and just as stuck as I had been an hour ago.

"Fuck you!" I bellowed after him, my legs beginning to wobble. Voice faltering, I repeated to myself, "Fuck you." I got into my car and cried, mumbling, "Fucking worthless," as I wiped away tears. I drove home, drank half a fifth of whiskey, and fell asleep.

A couple weeks later, I was out with my school friends. We were having coffee at a hookah bar after class, throwing light jokes around when my phone started spazzing out in my pocket.

I thought it was my dad at first, having found some new thing to harass me over, but when I pulled my phone out I saw a handful of texts from numbers I didn't recognize. I frowned as I flipped my phone open, and then slammed it shut as soon as I read the first text.

This the blowjob guy? Got your number from a friend.

I could feel myself getting pale as my chronic anxiety cried out for attention inside my chest, and I crammed my phone back into my pocket as fast as I could.

"You okay, Louie?" my friend asked, gesturing toward me with the hose. "You look shook."

"Yeah," I said, shaking my head. "Yeah, I'm fine."

"You look like you just ran over a cat or something," he said back.

"Yeah, on your bicycle," another one added, breathing out a big cloud.

"Damn, that's gross, dude," the first one said, shaking his head.

"You okay, though?"

"Yeah," I said, "I told you, I'm fine."

"Too much nicotine probably," my friend added. "See, Louie, that's why you should smoke cigarettes."

"That's a really compelling argument," I replied, trying to push the text out of my mind.

"Oh shit! Guess who's popular?" my other friend said, grinning as he looked down at his laptop.

"Not you, dumbass," friend one laughed back.

"Check it out, man," friend two argued, pointing at his laptop. "Just got three more friend requests."

"From who?" friend one scoffed. "You're already friends with everybody who's got Facebook."

"Check out these chicks, dude," friend two refuted, passing over the laptop.

"Oh shit," friend one said, raising his eyebrows as he peered at the laptop. "They are bangin'! Check it out, Louie," and he tossed me the laptop.

"Watch it! That's my laptop!" friend two complained.

I looked down at the screen. This was part of blending in. "Yeah, they're all hot," I said, handing friend two back his laptop. "Who are they?"

"Who knows, who cares," he said, adjusting on the couch and diving back into his laptop. "But maybe we can get together, you know?"

"Why are you just accepting people you don't know?" I asked, feeling more texts flood in and tapping my leg to try and hide the vibrations.

"Duh, dude, because they're hot," he replied, rolling his eyes like it was the stupidest question in the world.

"That's the best reason," friend one agreed through a field of hookah smoke.

"That's super stupid," I said, twitching as my phone vibrated again. "It could literally be anybody."

"Yeah, or it could be this hot chick," he said back, rolling his eyes again.

My phone buzzed again, and I snapped. Standing up quickly I said, "I gotta go guys."

"Later, dude," friend two said.

"Watch out for cats," friend one said.

"Fuck off," I laughed back, trying to shrug off my spiking anxiety as I hurried out of the hookah bar.

My phone kept buzzing, text after text with each step I took down the sidewalk. Eventually I couldn't take it, and I stopped in the middle of the sidewalk, pulled out my phone, and screamed, "Stop it!" right at its little front display. A few people walking past gave me some strange looks, but I couldn't be bothered by them.

Then the texts stopped. Just like the first time, except way more had shown up over a far shorter period of time. These days I would assume it was some bot, but back then there was no real explanation, only confusion, anger, and fear.

I crouched on the sidewalk and started deleting them one at a time, trying not to read them, but doing it anyways.

Trying to make a friend...
Is 100 enough...
Can you suck my dick...
U booked on Friday...
I'm at the Regency Palace...
Can we do more than oral...

I started getting hit with waves of these texts about twice a month. I felt like an island bombarded by monstrous tsunami waves that came without warning. Sometimes they lasted for hours, sometimes for ten minutes, sometimes for two days. I kept my phone on silent all the time, checking it constantly to see if a flood had started. I stopped texting my friends, and Benjamin, because I was too afraid to use my phone, expecting a wave to start halfway through a conversation.

It got so bad that I had to change my number, and that kept the attacks at bay for a while. I gave my new number to my close friends, to my family, and to Robert's mom. I thought that bought me safety, but three weeks after I changed it, the texts started coming back in larger numbers than ever before. When those first texts came in after a few weeks of peace, I almost had a complete breakdown.

It was imprisoning to be in constant fear of random bombardments of harassment, and I started drinking more than I had been, just to relax. Since I wasn't seeing a therapist anymore I didn't have any anti-anxiety medication, and I was really getting to like liquor. I had never been big on it before, but the more I drank it, the more I liked it. Even the lights were brighter when I was drunk.

I told my dad I was still going to therapy. I figured he couldn't call me on it, because the only way he would know would be by my uncle's wife telling him that she had bribed the good doctor for information. So far, that was working in my favor.

I thought Benjamin would have gotten bored of me by then, I don't know why, I just assumed it was going to happen. I remember being shocked when I realized he was completely content with our routine of lunches, dinners, and some weekends away. It seemed like he could live that way forever, and that scared me. I was on the run, trying to escape John's meticulous stalking, and whatever phantoms haunted my phone. Sitting still was getting harder and harder.

We were out to dinner one night, picking at some chicken and sipping at some wine. We weren't talking about anything, just eating, and the soft noises of the restaurant began squeezing me. Hardly anybody was talking, nobody was moving, it was all just ice cubes clinking and dishes moving. It was suffocating.

I wanted to run, to tear the tables apart and send the water pitchers crashing, to yank the chandelier from the ceiling and fling it as far as I could just to hear all the crystal droplets shatter against the marble floors in some spectacular sound bite, to scramble out the emergency exit, and stow away on a cargo truck headed for somewhere very far away.

"You're almost halfway through your term, aren't you?" Benjamin asked, setting down his chicken in favor of his wine. "How's it going?"

"Fine," I said back. "It's really easy."

I started getting those random Facebook friend requests too, a little while after the text attacks became regular. I got one every week at first, then two, then eventually one a day. They always showed up around ten o'clock in the morning, which I thought was weird, but I ignored them anyway, so I didn't give it too much thought.

I didn't tell Benjamin about the texts or the friend requests. I probably should have, he would have had something to say, but I didn't. After the therapist, I felt like I had to shoulder everything myself, like I was the only one who could understand it. So that's what I did.

I carried all this shit around everywhere I went, shrinking and shrinking until I felt I wasn't really a person. I was a thing that went about his business and waited for another round of infuriating bullshit to roll around the corner. I lived like that until my birthday came in May, and then everything exploded.

When I opened my eyes that morning, I had forgotten it was my birthday. Every day was the same, so there wasn't a reason for me to think differently. I expected my phone to be full of bullshit, I always did. When it wasn't, I got a brief feeling of relief like standing under a tropical waterfall.

Looking at my phone that morning, I only had one new text in my inbox. I frowned as I read the number over. I didn't have it saved, but I recognized it from somewhere. Then, as I opened it, I remembered where I knew it from.

Happy birthday baby. Go look outside.

It was the same text I had gotten a year ago, that same day, from the same guy. I didn't want to play along with John's bullshit antics, but I also couldn't ignore whatever he might have left outside the house. Someone was going to find it eventually, even if it wasn't me.

It was in the same spot, tucked at the base of a little tree. Instead of a box, there was a bright red envelope. I tucked it into my shirt and went back to my room in a hurry, trying not to attract any birthday attention before I was ready for it.

I sat down on the edge of my bed and opened the envelope. I pulled out a small card, and it looked identical to the card he gave me exactly one year ago on my nineteenth birthday.

Icy fear creeped up my spine as I turned the card over and read the short message inscribed there.

Time to come back, Louie. Happy Birthday!

Chapter Eleven

I USED TO LOVE my birthday more than any other day of the year. When I woke up on my sixth birthday, I was full of joy and excited fascination. It was a wonderful feeling of suspense, knowing that a whole day of fun and happiness had been prepared just for me.

Opening your eyes in the morning is so different when you're a kid. When I was little, I remember having this huge amount of energy right when I sat up, and I would jump out of bed with a big, goofy smile on my face, and race my brother down the hallways to the stairs.

There was an extra reason to run on the morning of my birthday when I was a child, because I knew there would be a fabulous and delicious breakfast waiting for me downstairs. Plus, I knew that I was about to receive my morning present. If my birthday fell on a weekday, we usually did the birthday cake and presents around dinner with the rest of the family, and on the weekend right after, my mom would organize a huge birthday party for me with all of my friends from school. However, every year my mom took me aside and gave me a secret gift in the morning. That was always the best gift I got every year, because she was the only one who really understood me.

When I turned six, I had a pair of footie pajamas that I had spent hours meticulously peeling the rubber traction pads off the bottoms of the feet. The result was a smooth and satisfying slide down the marble hallway, well worth the extra effort of walking around the house.

I stopped my power-slide against the bannister, leaning over it as my feet lifted just half an inch off the floor. Then I heard my mom's voice wafting up from the kitchen, mingling with the sizzling sounds of breakfast.

"Is that you, Louie? You up? Don't you run down those stairs!"

"I'm not!" I called back, taking the last four steps in one leap and landing with an unconcealable thud.

I ramped up for another slide and set off down the hall toward the kitchen, zipping right past my dad's office door where I caught a glimpse of him sitting at his desk, backlit by the windows that overlooked the garden.

"There he is! The birthday boy!" she said as I rocketed into the kitchen. I ran right to her, and she wrapped me in a huge hug like she always did, spinning me around once before letting me drop. "Do you want some breakfast?"

"Yes! Yes!" I babbled back, bobbing my head from side to side and vaulting up into one of the chairs neatly arranged around the kitchen table.

"Why don't you run back upstairs first? Go look in my room," she said, flashing me a smile as she turned back toward the maid making breakfast. "And bring your brother back downstairs with you!"

I leapt down from the chair as fast as I had scrambled up, and shoving off of the kitchen counter I slid back down the hall, twirling around at the bottom of the bannister. I sprinted back up the stairs and made a beeline for the end of the hall, cruising through my parents' bedroom door and bouncing off the foot of their bed.

There was a rectangular gift sitting on my mom's pillow, wrapped in shiny birthday balloon paper. I grabbed it and ran into my room as fast as I could, scooting my little felted feet across the floor.

I sat cross-legged on my bed, holding the present in my lap. It was light, and I could hear the light plastic of a toy box flexing under the wrapper. I tore at the paper, ripping away the corner and exposing a huge swath of the box beneath.

You can always tell what a gift is before the paper is all the way off, but it's not totally real until all the wrapping is gone. Until that moment it's still a magical entity, and even if you can see what it is, it only contributes to the excitement of unwrapping the present.

That morning I knew what it was the second I made the first tear, and I grinned ear to ear as I cleared away the rest. It was a Barbie. I wanted to scream at the top of my lungs, to jump up and down on my bed and throw pillows at my ceiling, but I couldn't do any of that. I knew this was a secret, and it was just for me.

With a big, silly smile on my face I tucked the Barbie under the pillows, straightening my blankets so the maids didn't unearth my prize. I never would have gotten a Barbie if it wasn't for my Mom, and I knew it. She was my lifeline.

I was about to go back downstairs for breakfast, but I stopped myself at the door. I couldn't wait, I was too excited. Turning around I jumped back onto my bed and reached into my pillows, pulling out the Barbie, I had to at least hold it out of the box.

There was tape over the top and the side of the box, and being six I didn't know the best way to tackle that obstacle. So, excitement overwhelming me, I went at it with my fingernails, poking and slicing, doing everything in my six-year-old capacity to get the little lid open.

Finally, I punched through, my fingernail diving through the tape seal, and my thumb struck down against the edge of the cardboard, slicing it open.

The envelope in my hand had blood on it. There was a small, bright paper cut on my thumb, and the blood was trickling out, making a mess of my bathrobe and getting the card all sticky.

For half a second that morning of my twentieth birthday, I forgot all the bullshit. I was just a six-year-old kid overjoyed at his secret Barbie. The second I cut my finger on that stupid envelope it all come running back, pounding on the door, screaming at me to let it inside, and what did I do? I opened the door, and let it walk all over me.

In one hand, I held my phone, with that smug text staring up at me: *Happy Birthday baby. Go look outside.*

In the other hand I held the card, with its short and menacing message taunting me: *Time to come back, Louie. Happy Birthday!*

There was blood all over the card, my robe, my hand, there was no special breakfast, no mom, and no happiness. Just a paper cut and encroaching doom.

I could only do one thing at a time, so the first thing I did was pinch my thumb to stop the bleeding. I sat there and held it, trying to figure out what I was supposed to do next. Then a thought popped in, and it grew and grew in import and menace, dominating every drop of my being. How the hell did he get my new number?

I looked down at my phone, letting the card drop to the floor. There were only a few people who had this number, and John, or any of his dumbass friends, were not among them. So how was this possible? If I could plug the leak, then maybe I could keep the ship from sinking. It wasn't that hard to get a new phone number. I had done it once, I could do it again, but I had to find out where John had gotten it.

My phone made me jump a bit as it started to ring, vibrating loudly in my palm. It was Benjamin, calling to wish me a happy birthday no doubt. I should have been excited to see his name on the little screen, he was my boyfriend after all, but instead I felt that icy fear and panic envelop me.

I couldn't answer, there was no way I could talk to him. If I even heard his voice, I would break down, I knew I would. I would bawl, spit, and cry, and I couldn't deal with that. There was only one thing I could do. I had to find out how John had gotten my number. In that moment, it was the only thing that mattered. My ship was sinking and I had to save it.

Another buzz. Another text. It was John.

Did you find it?

What do you want? I shot back.

You.

I felt sick reading that word. Deep down I knew he was never going to leave me alone, he had demonstrated it time and time again, but now the truth was unavoidable. Then he sent another one.

You have to come back.

Leave me alone. I replied. I wanted to throw my phone across the room and put another chip in the paint, but there was a dark compulsion stopping me, telling me to grip the phone tightly and wait for his answer.

His text came in, but instead of some snarky reply, my phone screen showed the little loading wheel as it processed an incoming image, then loaded it one grueling stripe at a time.

At first, I didn't know what I was looking at. The image was small, and somewhat dark. It looked like a room, and I could make out a bed in the center of the picture. Something was strange though, I felt like I had seen it before.

Then another picture started downloading. I frowned as I watched the progress wheel, unable to put it all together. The image started loading. It was the same picture, the same room, the same bed, only this time I was in the picture, standing in the middle of the frame with a fucking blindfold on.

It was John's room. There were rose petals on the bed. As I processed what was happening he sent another picture, this time with him taking off the blindfold. Then another, and in that one we were naked.

I made a movie. Like the screenshots?

I didn't have a reply, I just sat there on my bed, pale and nauseous, not wanting to exist. John sent me one last picture, but this one wasn't from his room. I saw his hand, holding up a flash drive, but the truly terrifying thing was the background. He was standing in front of an office-building, one of the newer ones downtown. The one that had the name of our company in big, shiny chrome lettering. I got one more text from John.

I'll pick you up at 8. Don't fuck this up.

I felt my stomach buckle under the sickening stress. I did a hurried flop off of my bed, lurched into the bathroom, and barely got the toilet lid up before I started vomiting. I didn't have any food in me, but I was so disturbed and mad and sick about John that I was involuntarily spewing stomach acid all over the place.

It burned my throat and nose, the fumes stung my eyes, my abdomen ached with each prolonged wretch, and my hands shook as I gripped the sides of the toilet. When I was done I wanted to brush my teeth, to shower, but I couldn't pick myself off the floor. I was stuck in my wallowing, and all I wanted was some Valium.

Then my phone started up again from outside the bathroom. People were calling me. It was my birthday. I had to talk to them. I had to act normal. All my problems with John were mine alone. I couldn't tell anyone without exposing my secret life. I had to talk to people, at least my family.

"All right," I said to myself, spitting acidic dribbles from my bottom lip. "All right."

I pulled myself into the shower and sat there on the floor, holding my knees to my chest, letting the hot water pour down on me until my fingers were a wrinkled mess. Then I brushed my teeth four times to get the taste of rotten fire out of my throat. It didn't work.

Benjamin had called again, and my aunt had called once. I had two new voicemails, and a few more unread texts. I knew I had to call them back, at least my aunt since she would have been with my grandma.

When I picked up my phone again I felt that same horrible pit well up in my gut. John's message had been clear, in his calculated ominous way. He had a sex tape of us, from my birthday a year ago, or at least pictures. He knew where my dad's company was, and he would drop off that flash drive without a second thought if I didn't get in his car at eight o'clock. I couldn't think about it, not yet, I had to call my aunt back. One thing at a time.

I hit "call back" on her missed call and held it to my ear. As it rang, the picture of the flash drive kept going through my head, and I kept trying to slap it aside to less and less avail.

"Happy Birthday!" a small chorus shot through the speaker.

"Happy Birthday, sweetie!" I heard my grandma's voice come through in the background.

"Hey, thanks," I said, fighting back the tide of tears.

"Happy Birthday, Louie," My aunt said. "What are you doing today, hm? Any big plans?"

"Plans," I repeated.

"Yeah, what are you doing for your birthday?" she asked. I could hear a few kitchen sounds in the background, and my grandma said, "Pass me that juice there, I can't reach it."

"Yeah okay, hold on a minute," my grandpa replied.

"Louie, can you hear me?" My aunt asked.

I'll pick you up at 8. Don't fuck this up.

The levy broke, and I started bawling. I couldn't even get through one stupid phone call. Fucking idiot. Fucking worthless.

"Louie, what's wrong?" My aunt asked, concern immediately creeping into her voice as I cried and cried into the cell phone. "Louie? What's wrong, honey?"

"I-I-I-I," I heaved, trying to say anything besides the truth. "I just miss my mom," I blurted out. Of course that was true, but it wasn't the reason I was having a complete breakdown over the phone.

"Oh sweetie," she said, letting out a long breath. "We all do."

"I can't-I can't," I blustered, the tears running down my face.

"Do you want to come over here?" she asked softly. "We can have some lunch, a cake, would you like that?"

"I'm sorry," I grunted, trying to wipe my tears off of the phone with my chin, but they just kept coming. "I can't. I-I gotta go."

"Okay, sweetie," she said. "You call if you need to, you hear?"

"Yeah."

"Happy Birthday, Louie."

"Thanks."

"Okay, bye bye now, come by later if you want, all right?"

"Okay, thanks."

"All right, bye honey."

I hung up the phone and let it fall loosely between my fingers into my lap. I wanted to curl up and cry all day, but I still had to talk to Benjamin. My hand shaking, I grabbed up the phone again and flipped it open.

I couldn't do it. I couldn't call him. I was worthless. I was crying. I couldn't talk to him, so I typed out a short text: *Sorry, family breakfast, call you later.*

Okay! Happy Birthday! He buzzed back.

Backing out of his text, I saw I had one from Robert's mom in my inbox. I clicked it open and read: *Happy Birthday, Louie! Hope it's a great one!!!*

As I read her text, a gear clicked into place, and a thought came to me. I wrote back: *Thanks so much! Hey just wondering, did you ever give Robert my new number?*

I was terrified and sweating as I waited for her reply. It was the only thing that made sense, and yet it was soul crushing to think about.

Yes, probably about a month ago.

Thanks! I replied, then I buried my face in my pillows and screamed. Fucking Robert. At least I knew how John had gotten my new number. There was both comfort and sadness in that knowledge. The leak was closed, but my friendship with Robert was over. It mostly had been. But now it was a certainty.

I sat in a pool of my tears and sweat for a while, flopping around like a useless blob of flesh without bones. My phone kept rattling off with various birthday wishes, but I didn't have the energy to look at them anymore. I didn't have the energy to do anything except sniffle and cry, crave Valium, and wish I had never been born.

It would have been easier, I figured, if I had never existed. Not to be dead, or to be somewhere else, just to never have been. I would never have had to worry about anything, and that wouldn't have been so bad, I figured. Or maybe I would have been someone else, someone born on the other side of the world, living happily in a tame Canadian country town. That would have been all right, better than this at least.

At some point, I got up and stripped off my damp clothes, leaving them in a sloppy, stinking pile. I threw on a new pair of underwear and shuffled out onto my balcony. The warm breeze felt unusually cool against my tear-streaked cheeks, drying away the wet.

Laying my hands on the railing, I peered over the side, down to the tiled courtyard below. It wasn't a huge drop, but it wasn't a small one either. I cocked my head as I looked over the edge, and a thought floated by for the first time.

I had never seriously considered killing myself, but in that moment it suddenly seemed a viable alternative to all the bullshit. I could just keep leaning over the rail, further and further, until I slipped and tumbled into oblivion. It wouldn't be that bad, really, just a little turbulence on my flight out of the Kingdom, and then I would be free.

For a moment I was excited about the idea, at the chance to get away from it all, but the longer I looked over the edge, the less sense it made. How far was that drop really? Sure, it was a tall second story, but it wasn't that high. Would I actually die? Or would I just break my legs? Would I fuck it up like I did with everything else and end up paralyzed from the waist down? That was the only way my life could truly get worse, I decided, and so I went back inside. I was so unsure of myself, so depressed and broken, that I didn't even trust myself to commit suicide properly.

Fucking worthless.

I spent the next nine hours feeling like absolute shit. I showered three more times because I kept sweating, cried every time my tear ducts had replenished, and ignored texts and calls from my friends. My dad or my brother never knocked on my door. They were probably out. They probably thought I was out, too. Really, I knew they didn't care. At least my dad didn't, my brother was just living his own life, oblivious to anything outside of it.

John's texts kept coming back, plastering themselves against the wall of my inner eye, commanding me however he saw fit. I felt like I had lost all autonomy, like I wasn't a real person anymore. Every once in a while,

I would look up from my knees and take in my room, and each time it seemed darker and smaller. It was a cell, its four walls pressing down, keeping me right where I was supposed to be.

I kept looking at the scratched spot on the wall from when I had thrown my phone. It seemed like it was getting bigger and bigger the longer I looked, reaching out to swallow me up. After an hour it was all I could see, as if it were screaming, commanding every ounce of my attention, not letting me go.

Around seven I took a short shower and started getting dressed. It took me a while because all my clothes suddenly looked dumb, and I found myself not caring about how I looked. Instead of trying on a few different things, I just stared into my closet for a good ten minutes, moving my eyes over the hanging shirts and the folded pants and not caring about any of it.

Finally, I threw some clothes on and trudged downstairs. I realized I hadn't eaten or drunk anything the whole day, and I immediately became intensely thirsty. I got down to the kitchen and fumbled weakly with the tap, letting the water run over my hand and wrist for a moment before fishing a glass from the dishwasher.

Water never tasted so good, and I nearly collapsed from relief. I drank cup after cup until I was gasping for air and I could hear my stomach sloshing around, then I let out a long burp that felt almost as good as drinking water.

"Woah, nice one," my brother's voice made me jump as he walked into the kitchen. "Happy birthday, man. Where've you been all day?"

"Thanks," I said, putting the glass back into the dishwasher. "I—" but I fell short as my phone buzzed. It was John. I knew before I took it out of my pocket. It had to be.

"You okay? You look like you just saw a ghost," he said with a little laugh.

"Fine," I mumbled, flipping open the phone.

I'm here.

"I gotta go," I said, stuffing the phone back down into my pocket, and casting my eyes downward to avoid eye contact.

"Where're you going?" he asked, turning to watch me march out of the kitchen.

"Out," I answered, locking my eyes on the distant front door.

"All right, man," he called after me. "Happy birthday!" and I walked out the door.

I felt like I was in a tunnel, walking across the courtyard. I couldn't see anything in my peripherals, I couldn't hear the city below, I could only focus on the looming headlights that sat on the far side of the gate. They were so bright, even from the distance, that I had to squint.

The only sound I could hear was the soft rumble of his engine, and the clack of my shoes slapping the stone as I walked, then the creak of the gate as I walked through it.

I could smell his cigarette, and see the thin smoke drifting up out of his window, over the roof of his car, and twisting toward me before the breeze batted it away. He didn't say anything as I approached. He didn't have to.

I reached the car and I heard the click of his doors unlocking. This was it, my last chance to do anything else besides get into that car. I knew in my heart that once I got in, I wouldn't ever get out. But what choice did I have? What life did I have?

I opened the door and got in the car.

Chapter Twelve

"THERE YOU ARE," JOHN said, flicking his eyes around like a snake as I got into the car. "Happy birthday."

I didn't say anything back, I didn't even look at him. I just climbed into the car and kept my face against the window. I was trying to keep my whole body from shaking with fear while my palms clammed up, and I kept my eyes focused away from his. I wanted to scream into his face, to pummel him with my fists, but I was too afraid.

"You ready?" he asked, bouncing his hand all excited on the gear shifter. He was acting like this wasn't all his fucked-up plan, like we were just hanging out. I didn't respond. I felt sick. "Good," he said, "let's go," and we sped off down the hill.

He wore a devilish smile to match his crisp black shirt, and he had a pair of sunglasses resting on his forehead like an insect's extra set of eyes. I could have sworn his tongue was flicking out and in, but I didn't want to look away from the window. I just bit down on my lower lip and watched the other cars that we passed, hoping the people I caught glimpses of were having a better day than me.

"How's school going?" he asked out of nowhere, and I almost looked over to answer reflexively, but instead I bit down harder on my lip. I wanted to lash out, but as enraged as I was, I was also terrified. He had me under some fucked up spell of fear. I didn't say anything back.

"Going good?" he went on, pretending like I was having an actual conversation with him. "Good, that's good," he replied, leaning out over the steering wheel to peek around a corner. "Engineering, right? That's what you're studying. A lot of money there if you do it right, but I guess that doesn't matter to you as long as daddy is here to pick up the tab." he said, revving out into an intersection.

I still hadn't said anything, and I wasn't going to. I hated him, I was squirming as far away from him as I could get, forcing myself into an uncomfortable wedge against the door. I wanted to spit in his face, but I was too afraid of his wrath to do anything.

"All right, that's it," he said, his voice dropping into a growl. John glanced over his right shoulder, and swung his car across a couple lanes, coming to a sudden stop along the curb. As soon as we were stopped, he turned to me and began barking orders.

"We gotta get something straight, all right, Louie?"

I kept looking out the window. I didn't want to look at him.

"Fucking look at me!" he yelled, his hand snapping out and grabbing hold of my chin. He clamped down with his thumb, and it hurt as he yanked my head around to meet his gaze. "You fucking look at me when I'm talking to you, got it?"

"All right, shit, I will!" I fretted, trying to pull away from his grip. It hurt like hell, the way he was pinching my chin, but I couldn't get out of it. I was already pressed as far against the car door as I could get.

"Okay, good," he said, staring me down with his cruel eyes. With his other hand he reached into his shirt pocket and pulled out a small oblong pill. "Now take this."

"What is it?" I asked weakly, my eyes flicking between him and the pill.

"You don't ask fucking questions!" he screamed, and he thrust my head backward, slamming it into the passenger window. "You got that?"

"Yeah," I stuttered, trying to keep the tears out of my eyes. My whole head smarted from the impact, and his grip was still strong as iron on my chin.

"You do what I say, when I say," he went on. "So take the stupid pill."

I did a weak wiggle of a nod, the tears pinching out of the corners of my eyes. He squeezed my cheeks, forcing my mouth open just a bit, and fed me the pill like a dog, watching carefully to see that I swallowed it.

"Good," he said when he was satisfied, and he relaxed his grip a little on my chin. "Rule number two, you're with me, right? Just me. So, I want you to call professor boy toy, set up a meeting, you gotta tell him it's over. You get it? But you gotta do it in person. I have to watch, and make sure you do good. You get it?"

"He—" I tried to protest, but the longer I sat there the faster I felt my will draining away. My eyes were moving past watering, but I didn't have the energy to let loose the tears.

"No fucking arguing, Louie!" he snapped, pinching my chin with two of his fingers. "That was rule number one! Do you get it or don't you? Because that leads us to rule number three."

He let go of my chin and reached down into his pocket, pulling out a little flash drive and tossing it gently into my lap.

"That's your copy," he said. "If you fuck anything up, you know what happens, right?"

I nodded again.

"Now, call Benjamin," he said, sitting back against his driver's side door. "Make it good, you know, you can meet him tomorrow. Let him down easy because we don't want him crawling back, do we? So don't make it all dramatic."

I reached for my phone with my other hand. It was shaking like crazy, and I could barely get my wrist past the lip of my pocket. Then I held it in my hand, looking blankly at the little lit up screen, unable to go further.

"It's all right, Louie," John said softly. "It's for the best," and he gently took the phone out of my hand. "I'll help you."

I saw him scroll through my contacts for a few seconds. He dialed Benjamin's number and handed me back the phone.

"I don't—" I stuttered, "I can't—"

"You can do it," John coaxed, guiding the phone to my ear, and I could hear the ringing on the other end.

"Louie?" Benjamin's voice came through the little speaker, and it sounded so loud in my ear I wanted to wince and cry. "Hey, Happy Birthday."

"Thanks," I replied.

"You want to get together?" he asked, and I had to jam my knuckle into my mouth so I didn't start bawling outright.

"Listen," I said, my voice wavering and cracking. "Listen, we, we uh—" I bit down on my knuckle again, trying to stop myself from breaking down into a messy pile of tears and wailing. For a second, I forgot that John was in the car, but he brought himself back into my view by reaching out and touching my chin again, as if to play the role of the reassuring friend.

"We should meet up tomorrow," I finally said, wanting to wretch and slam my head through the car's windshield.

"Tomorrow? Not tonight? All right, that's fine I guess—"

"I'm sorry, I'm sorry," I repeated, feeling the tears start to make their way down my cheeks. "We have to talk about something."

"Louie, calm down, it's okay tomorrow works fine. Are you all right? Where are you? What are you talking about?" Benjamin asked. I could hear the concern in his voice, the genuine care for my well-being, and the overwhelming goodness of his person shining through the phone.

"I'm sorry, I'm fine, you know, I just miss my mom," I cried. "I'll see you tomorrow."

John took the phone out of my hand. I could hear Benjamin's distant voice saying something on the other end, then John hit the button and the phone went silent.

As the call went dead, I broke down, letting my knuckles fall from my mouth I started bawling my eyes out, the trickle of tears turning into a torrent.

Suddenly John was reaching out his arms in some sort of conciliatory gesture. I wanted to pound his face with my fist until it was stuck against the back of his head, but I couldn't keep my head above water in that emotional whirlpool, and I was sucked into the storm.

"That was great, Louie, you did great," he said, his voice sinister and slithering.

I leaned away from him as he reached out, and cried against the car window, for how long I'm not sure, but long enough for the pill to start working. I got lighter as I cried, and the night outside came on in full.

"That's enough crying," John finally snapped. "Knock it off. Here, take another Xanax," and he plucked another pill from his shirt pocket, forcing it between my lips.

"Xanax?" I mumbled, twitching as the pill clunked down my dry throat.

"It's great, I got a shitload of it," he replied. "You're gonna love it. Now stop fucking crying. That's over now."

By the time I finished crying I was more broken than I had ever been before. Between the new drugs and everything else, I was numb. None of it mattered, I thought. It was all bullshit, and I was just going through the motions. I felt like a child playing on the beach, toiling in the hot sun to compile millions of grains of sand into a standing structure. All I had done to better myself in the past few months had resulted in my proud castle, standing against the breeze. But here came John, that strong inevitable storm, threatening to wash it all away in a matter of seconds.

"Come on," he said. "Let's get out of here."

"Where are we going?" I asked, my head lulling over onto my shoulder.

"No fucking questions, Louie, what did I say?" he snapped. "Christ."

We drove up to one of the big downtown office buildings, and John swung the car down into the parking garage. I was feeling strange from the drugs, and I didn't like it. I didn't like anything about what was happening, especially this dark underground garage. I wanted to ask him where we were, but I didn't want him to shout at me for asking a question. My head still hurt from getting slammed into the car window.

"Come on," he grunted, getting out of the car. I followed him helplessly toward the elevators, my body swaying with each step as I shuffled along. The garage lights were ominously pale, letting off a discomforting whine one could hear when passing directly beneath them.

We went up to the fourteenth floor. At the time I didn't know it, I wasn't even sure where we were, but after returning to that place again and again, its location became concrete in my mind.

We went through an extravagant reception area with nice chairs and a big oval desk, complete with windows that looked out over the downtown cityscape. It was an impressive office, but it felt oppressive and evil in the dark.

He led me into a big corner office off of the reception area, with a huge wooden desk in front of the windows. There were chairs and a couch set out in front of it, and I could tell that whoever sat there was in charge.

"You like it?" John asked, running his hands over my shoulders from behind me. I didn't answer, I felt like it was better not to say anything. I didn't yet understand what was going on. "My dad's new office, it's pretty nice, huh?"

Then he spun me around so we were facing each other, and said, "Happy birthday, baby," before pushing me down to my knees. One of his hands moved from my shoulder to his belt, undoing the clasp. Suddenly I understood what was happening, and fear shot up through my stomach and I protested.

"No, I don't—"

"Shut up!" he seethed, slapping me swiftly across the face. The impact stung and belittled me as he went on, growling, "I own you, little bitch, you got that?"

"I—"

"Shut up!" Another slap. "I own you! Now go on, take it out."

I could see him getting hard under his tight jeans while I blubbered through a few tears. Another slap. He grabbed my hand and moved it to his zipper, running it open and loosening his pants, saying, "That's right, I own you."

With his slapping hand he scooted his waistband down past his ass, letting the jeans fall away to his ankles while his dick rose up to meet me.

"I don't—"

Another slap.

"I own you."

"No—"

Another slap.

"You don't want to make me angry, Louie."

Another slap.

I opened my mouth to complain again, and he stuck his dick in so hard it slammed against the back of my throat, forcing me to gag and reel. Another slap.

"I own you," and his other hand grabbed my hair, dragging me back.

I cried and choked on him for a few minutes, getting slapped across the cheek whenever I tried to break away. My face was bright red, and I shouted in pain by the time he yanked me up by my hair and threw me forward onto the edge of the desk.

I remember the corner of it caught me in the stomach, knocking the wind clear out of me, and I squirmed for air as he tore at my pants, ripping the button off the waistband.

"I fucking own you," he groaned as he forced himself inside. I tried to scream, but I still couldn't breathe, and my voice was a rasping vacuum as I clawed at the flat surface, looking for anything to grab onto.

"Sit fucking still," he grunted, grabbing hold of my hair again and slamming my forehead once into the top of the desk. I saw blinking lights flash across my eyes as the pain bounced around the front of my skull, then he flattened my left cheek against the surface and went to work, thrusting hard, slapping me again and again as I cried. It was no use. I was his prisoner, as good as bound. Eventually he settled into his rhythm, and I stared at the wall, waiting forever for it to be over.

When he was done, he let out a long, grotesque moan, pressing as far forward as he could before pulling out. Everything hurt. My head, my ass, my ribs, my guts. I was out of tears, reduced to a silent shell of a human punching bag.

"Come on," he said with a certain exuberance in his voice. "We gotta get going."

I couldn't move, I was stuck splayed out on that desk, paralyzed from the pain and the trauma.

"Oh, come on," he scoffed, grabbing my shoulder and pulling me upright. "Get your pants on."

He drove me home, stopping just outside the front gate. My hand was on the door before the car had even stopped, but as I reached for it, he clicked on the child locks. I couldn't speak, I just tried the handle again and again, believing that it would open eventually.

"You're not gonna tell anyone about this, are you?" John asked, leaning back in his seat. "Because you know what will happen if you do. Your dad gets that video, your family fucking disowns you. You'll end up on the streets. Or maybe they'll even kill you. You get it? You're mine."

I was still trying the door. I just wanted to get out of the car.

"You hear me?" he roared, thumping his palm against the steering wheel.

"Yeah," I croaked, my voice barely escaping between my cracked lips.

"Good," he said, relaxing his posture. He clicked off the child locks, the door opened, and I tumbled out of the car as fast as I could. Then he zoomed off down the winding street, and I was left alone in the silent stillness of the night.

I trudged through the gate and dragged myself through the courtyard, moving straight toward the pool. I reached my hand down for my phone, and let it clatter loosely onto the pavement as I reached the edge of the water.

Instead of going around, I stepped over the edge, and let myself plunge into the water. Suddenly the whole world fell away, and all I could feel was the cool embrace of the pool, holding me tightly in complete confidence as it soaked into my clothes.

"What the fuck?" I heard my brother's voice coming from the villa as I came up for air. "Louie, are you in the pool?" I didn't answer; I just treaded water. Then I saw him stick his head out of his window overlooking the courtyard, and with a big wave of his arms he called down, "Why are you in the pool with all your clothes on? Fucking crazy, man," then he disappeared back into his room.

The next day I woke up to a text from Benjamin, asking about where to meet up that night. I blinked a few times, rubbing the crusted flakes from my eyes, reading the text over and over. As I read it, the memory of the night before began floating through my mind, almost like the memory of a nightmare. Was it real? Had I imagined all of it? It couldn't have been real, it was all too terrible, too raw and visceral to be real.

Then I tried to move, and pain vibrated through my body, and I knew without a doubt it had all been real. I curled slowly into a ball, shrinking back into my bed, feeling the tears I knew were on their way. I wasn't a person anymore, I was a thing. John had reached into me and yanked out my soul. I felt worthless and ashamed. He had killed me, I was gone, and in my place sat a shivering, sobbing shell, an imposter in my clothes who would live my life for me from then on, moving through the motions but not actually existing.

I stayed in bed crying most of the day until John picked me up and escorted me to my meeting with Benjamin. We sat across from each other at a little table. He could tell something was wrong. I was a wreck, and in no world was I hiding it well. Over his shoulder I could see John sitting at the bar, casually sipping his beer and keeping his eyes fixed on my face.

"What's going on?" Benjamin asked in his gentle voice. "You seem pretty upset. Didn't have a good birthday?"

I felt like a prisoner, sitting there with Benjamin. I was trapped. I couldn't tell him the truth, but I was having a hard time finding a lie. Meanwhile the pressure of John's gaze bore down from across the room, daring me to cross him. I had been defeated in every way, and now I was subject to his will.

"We have to break up," I finally blurted out, casting my eyes down to the tablecloth.

"Louie, what are you talking about?" he asked, leaning forward and reaching his hand across the table. I pulled mine away from his as I tried to stifle my tears. John was still staring, coolly sipping his drink.

"I'm a mess," I blubbered. "It's my mom, I just can't do it anymore," and now I was crying. A waiter, seemingly headed our way, caught sight of my red eyes and quickly went the other way

"Louie, wait a moment," Benjamin objected, trying again to take my hand.

"I'm sorry," I said again, fumbling to stand up. "I'm sorry I gotta go, I'm sorry."

"Louie! Wait!" he called after me, but I was already fumbling through the door, fleeing as fast as I could from the heartbreak behind me. As I went through the door, I caught sight of John from the corner of my eye. He was smiling.

Over the next couple of weeks, John spoon-fed me Xanax until I was properly addicted, way worse than I had ever been with Valium. He picked me up four or five times a week, and we essentially fell into our old routine, except now I wasn't ever present. My body went along wherever John took it, but in my head I was numb and high, never really hearing what people said, and never saying anything myself.

The spring term at my university ended just in time for me to dive headfirst into a new drug habit. If I had still been enrolled in classes, I would have gotten expelled again for absences. Then again, I'd never heard of someone getting expelled from both of the Kingdom's top universities, so maybe there was something there worth exploring. I had always been too smart for school. Everything was so easy. People were fools.

June came around. John and I were out one night with Omar, and they were talking about something in the background. I kept running my thumb over the few little numbers printed onto the glass beer bottle in my hand. There was music playing too, pretty good music honestly, but I don't recall the band, and it's not like it was live, it was just a recording. It didn't matter.

"Did you hear that, Louie?" Omar asked, thumping me on the shoulder with his big ugly hands.

"Hear what?" I asked, pulling my eyes away from the intricacies of the glass bottle I was holding. "What'd you say?"

"He said Robert is coming back next week, from the States," John said, leaning over to explain above the music.

"Oh, cool," I said, uninterested. Nothing mattered.

"He said he's gonna bring some friends for the whole summer or something, like a group of them," Omar chimed in again, leaning into my other ear. "From America! Fun, isn't it?"

"Yeah, fun," I said, nodding in agreement. "Who is it?"

"How the fuck should I know?" Omar laughed back at me. "You're crazy, Louie."

"Mm-hm," I murmured, letting my attention swing back to the beer bottle.

Through the haze of numbing nothing came a pang of jealousy. Why did I have to hear about Robert coming back for the summer from fucking Omar of all people? What did he mean about Robert bringing friends? Who wants to come to the Kingdom for the summer compared to living in America? None of it really made sense, but instead of working it all out I let the rupture fade back into the fog.

One thing about Xanax is that it really fucks with your memory, especially when you mix it with alcohol. There were many mornings when I opened my eyes and had absolutely no memory of the night before. If I tried really hard, I could bring a few pieces back, maybe where we were at the beginning of the night, but mostly the whole night would just be gone.

I started noticing weird bruises when I took showers, these big blue blotchy marks on my ribcage and my thighs. When I asked John about them, he would laugh and tell me about whatever I had bumped into the night before, the stories almost always ending with me laying on the sidewalk. I should have been embarrassed, or at least concerned, but I really didn't care. It was just one of those things.

A little while later I was out with John in the middle of the day, having some coffee. I wasn't really drinking mine, but I was enjoying the feeling of the warm ceramic cup in my hands.

"There they are," John said, glancing over his coffee toward the door. He held up his other hand and gave a stiff wave.

I turned and looked over my shoulder and was surprised to see Robert walking in the door. Clearly, I had forgotten we were meeting him, but who cares, because there he was, and nothing mattered.

"Hey, welcome back," John said, getting halfway out of his chair to give Robert an informal, friendly handshake.

"Thanks, man," he answered, then he cast his eyes down at my slumped frame and said, "Hey, Louie."

"Hey," I croaked back. Most of the time I spent on Xanax I didn't know what to say, and right then was no exception.

"Guys, I want you to meet my friend Adam," Robert said, gesturing to the guy standing next to him.

The sunlight from the high windows was shining right behind them, so I had to squint to make out Adam's features, but I could tell he was a put together sort of guy. I could see he took care of his nails, so I immediately liked him a little bit. Other than that, he had a clean face with a set of calm, thoughtful eyes.

"From the States, right?" John asked, shaking Adam's hand. "I'm John, this is Louie. Where's everybody else? Thought there was a whole group of you."

"Hey, nice to meet you guys," Adam answered. He had a calm, smooth voice, and I wondered if he was a singer in some unknown but actually pretty good band.

"Everyone else is over at my house with my brothers," Robert answered. "Kicking the jetlag, you know?"

"Sure," John said. "So you guys know each other from Texas?"

"We go to school together there, yeah," Adam replied, settling into his seat. "My family is from Lebanon, originally, but I was born and raised in the US."

"Lebanon?" I asked, tilting my head to one side. "That makes sense."

"Sorry?" Adam asked, looking a little taken aback.

"I just mean nobody from America would come here for the summer," I replied, leaning back in my chair a bit. "America is way better."

"Louie hates it here," Robert said with a light little laugh in his voice, poorly masking his irritation.

"No worries, I get it," Adam said, grinning back at me. "You should come to the US then. You'd have a blast."

"Yeah, right, not after my Santa Barbara drama," I said back, feigning a smile. I could feel John's stare on the other side of my head, as if to remind me that I was never going anywhere without him.

"So how long are you in town?" John asked before Adam had the chance to ask about Santa Barbara. He set down his coffee on its little smudged saucer.

"All summer," Adam answered. He broke from the conversation briefly to order coffee, then returned. "Then I'll head back to the States with everybody for school."

"Cool. This will be fun, man," John said, grinning and pretending to be a nice guy. The charade almost made me burst out into ridiculous laughter. "You guys want to go out tonight?"

"Yeah sure that sounds fun, thanks," Adam said.

"Say nine o'clock?" Robert asked.

"Perfect, great," John agreed. "What are you studying?"

The conversation began to drag on into meaningless small talk, and I found myself retreating back into the nothing nebula that my mind inhabited. Everyone's voices started blending after a while, but Adam's kept cutting through the fog. Not only was it a new voice, but it was nice to listen to.

That night we went out to some bars. Everyone had a great time, as far as I knew. I took two Xanax, drank a few beers, and forgot everything. The next day I woke up with two new bruises.

A few weeks later John and I were hanging out a couple nights in a row, and I suddenly got confused. Normally we would at least meet Omar for a beer or two, but it had been days since we had seen anyone in the standard friend group.

I looked up at John and asked, "Where is everybody?"

"What do you mean?" he asked, raising one eyebrow. He was leaning on the cocktail table with one elbow, his whole body at a casual tilt pointing at his poised beer. I wondered if he was always thinking about acting and looking cool, or if he just fell into it naturally.

"We haven't seen anybody else for days," I said, getting myself back on track. "Where's Robert?"

"In Egypt, where do you think?" John said, shaking his head. "Come on, Louie, it's like you're not even there sometimes."

"Egypt?" I balked.

"Yeah, everyone went to Egypt," John said dismissively. "With that Adam guy and all of his friends."

"Everyone?" I asked, blinking a few times.

"Yeah, well, except for us obviously," he said, taking another drink of his beer.

"Why aren't we in Egypt?" I pressed, feeling an asteroid of anxiety trying to enter the nothing nebula, but getting caught in the Xanax clouds.

"Why?" John asked, looking at me with a big blank stare. "Because you weren't invited, dumbass."

"You were?" I said, my lip starting to tremble.

"Well, sure," he replied as if he was trying to brush the whole thing off. "But you know I can't leave you alone, now can I? Don't worry, we'll take our own vacation, would you like that?"

I couldn't say anything in response. I couldn't imagine anything worse than going on a vacation with John. I was paralyzed.

"Where do you want to go? We could go anywhere, really. What about Bulgaria? Bulgaria's fucking beautiful, it's got great beaches."

"Yeah, sure," I mumbled. I was caught between the terror of a trip with John and the hurt of being left out. I had never been so blatantly excluded from anything, and even though I was as high as a kite, it still stung. It was Robert who had made the invitations, and it was Robert who had left me out. Realizing that brought an abrupt end to whatever good feelings I was getting out of the Xanax that night.

When I got up to my room, I pulled out my phone and called Robert, but it just went to a message about him not being in his service area. Fucking Egypt. Eventually I got out my laptop and started browsing Facebook, just to see what I could find.

Sure enough, there were pictures from the trip showing up already. A whole gaggle of people were giving thumbs up with dumb smiles in front of varying archeological sites and beautiful beaches. How long had they been gone? I had no idea. I didn't even know what day it was.

I refreshed the page, hoping to see something new and different, but instead there was another picture posted from Robert's profile. I frowned and opened the chat list. I saw that he was online. I clicked open a chat with him and wrote:

What the hell? Why didn't you invite me to Egypt? I tapped my fingers up and down on the edge of the computer while I watched the little dots hop up and down as he wrote his reply:

Seriously?

You invited everyone else, I wrote.

You're just a negative person now, he wrote. *It's not fun to be around you.*

You don't understand, I wrote. *John is blackmailing me. He fucking raped me.*

Fuck, dude, you really are crazy.

Fuck you, no I'm not. Why don't you care about me anymore? I haven't done anything to deserve this! Especially from you! He's been taking me to his dad's office and rapes me over and over. He also hits me and beats me up. I can't remember every detail because of the fucking Xanax he gives me.

Wow! You know what man, you really are the reason your mom killed herself. Everybody is saying it. Maybe it should've been you instead. You need to get yourself right. Fuck off. Leave me alone.

That was one blow I never expected. It was the deepest of betrayals, the most intimate of back stabbings. I couldn't reply, my body didn't work. I was stuck, a statue of tormenting grief that tore me apart from within. I knew we hadn't been close for a while, but to see such a concrete severance of that friendship and brotherhood destroyed me. In my imagination, Robert was someone I could have always fallen back on. Now that that was gone I was entirely alone. How many blows like this was my sandcastle going to withstand before it crumbled down and disappeared?

That was the official end of our friendship. I clicked out of the chat window and fell backward, slamming my head down against the pillows again and again until I was out of energy. Eventually I sat back up. One thing at a time. Put the computer away. Take a Xanax. Go to sleep. Nothing mattered.

I leaned forward and squinted at the screen. I would have just slammed it shut were it not for the little red notification in the corner up near the web browser's "X." It was a friend request from Adam. I hit accept and shut the computer. Then I fished out another Xanax and cried myself to sleep.

Chapter Thirteen

T HE SUMMER TICKED AWAY like a clock in a classroom, repeating the same cycle day after day. I waited for John, we went somewhere, he raped me, and then I would wait for it to start over the next day. The longer it went on, the less I felt I had any recourse, and the more I became complacent in my horror, like some pathetic, sad slug slowly sliding toward a pile of salt, too high on Xanax to do anything about it.

I became a shadow of my former self, moving through the spaces I was supposed to inhabit without interaction. I wasn't eating, and I could feel myself getting thinner, probably too thin, but I didn't stop to think about it. Instead I just kept withering beneath the trinity of malnutrition, drug abuse, and habitual sexual assault.

I couldn't talk to anybody about any of it. Out of everyone, Joseph was the only person I could have talked to, should have gone to, but I couldn't do it. I couldn't face that brutal reality being laid bare before me, before him, and the fallout that would follow.

John was right about one thing. If my family got that videotape I would be disowned and cast out. Then I would truly have nothing. I would exist as a drifting piece of human trash, being blown between one sewer drain to the other, waiting for the street sweeper to come along and put an end to my misery. I didn't want anything really, but I knew I didn't want that. The thing was, I was pretty much already there, I just didn't know it yet.

The text attacks started slowing down after a little while, which was only a fleeting relief, because they were replaced by increasing Facebook harassment. I couldn't believe how people would accept every friend request that came their way, not considering if they even knew the person or not.

I got request after request from complete strangers. I wasn't even sure if they were all real people, but they all had a few mutual friends with me. A lot of times they would send me a message reading something like: *hey sexy*, or *looking for a hookup?* It was all bullshit, and I ignored it most of the time, but once in a while one would get to me.

One day a fake profile with my mom's name popped up with a friend request. Normally I would just ignore the requests, but the name drew me in. When I went to that profile's wall and saw the status update on the feed, a wave of nausea came over me. My stomach churned as I read the post, and I wanted to throw up but had nothing in my stomach except for Xanax.

I thought the world should know, I killed myself because my husband found out about my Muslim boyfriend. Fuck all of you! RIP!

There was a ringing in my ears as I scrolled through the comments. I should have just left it alone, closed the web browser, but it was like watching a car accident. I couldn't look away. Some part of me wanted to drink it all in.

Shame on you. This is horrible, someone had written under the post.

I have reported this, read another comment. *Fake account.* But the further I read, the more bullshit I unearthed, and I drank it all up.

Is this true?

Such a shame. Knew she was hiding something. Disgraceful.

Whore! Got what was coming.

Haha I bet this is Louie having another breakdown.

LOL totally dude is fucking crazy.

Fuck that guy.

I pushed my laptop away with my toes, folding my arms tightly into my chest, trying to take a full breath. Laying sideways on my bed,

I glanced toward my little balcony, letting the thought of jumping off of it tiptoe back into my mind.

Even if the fall didn't kill me, I would at least break my leg. If I broke it bad enough, I could bleed to death. That was something to consider. But then again, if I was flailing and screaming with a leg gushing blood against the side of the house, someone would certainly find me before I died. I would wake up in the hospital, with nothing but a lot of pain to show for it, and maybe a permanent limp. It really wasn't my best option.

It irritated me that it probably wouldn't work. At first glance it seemed so obvious and easy, but upon reflection it was just another headache. I didn't have the energy to think up any other way to kill myself, so I chewed on a Xanax and let the day slip away.

Around the end of summer I got a call from Robert. I was surprised to see his number on the screen, and a big part of me wanted to let the call ring out, but eventually I answered, if only to make the buzzing stop.

"Hello?" I said, sitting upright on my bed.

"Louie! What the fuck!" Robert spat back, his anger crackling through the phone's distortion.

"What?" I asked, frowning and scrunching up my nose. I had no idea what he was talking about.

"Don't fuck with me Louie!" Robert yelled. "Why did you put that shit online? What are you trying to do? It's bullshit, man, fuck you, goddamn it!"

"Robert, I don't know what you're talking about," I mumbled, rubbing my eyes. I was so sleepy.

"The fuck you don't!" he went on. "You're not taking me down with you, Louie, you understand? Leave me the fuck alone!"

"Robert—" I tried to get another word in but the call went dead. I could imagine his fuming face while he paced around his kitchen, pissed off beyond belief. But about what?

"Ey, Louie," my brother's voice came from the hallway.

"What?"

"Have you seen this?" he asked, coming to stand in the doorway holding his laptop.

"Seen what?"

"This shit about you and Robert," my brother replied, walking up to the bed, and turning his laptop around.

"Christ," I muttered, glancing over the onslaught of aggressive Facebook messages.

It was another random profile, someone I didn't know, presenting their thesis on how I had been sleeping around with Robert and his brothers for years. Now at least Robert's call made sense. I could see that my brother had real concern on his face, but for me this was just par for the course.

"What the hell, man?" he asked. "Did you get these too?"

"Probably," I groaned, flipping open my own computer. "Yeah," I said, opening my messages. "Fucking assholes. Robert just called me, mad as hell."

"Well yeah, aren't you mad?" my brother asked. "Someone is spreading fake shit about you, dude."

"Yup," I said, letting out a big sigh.

"This shit isn't okay, dude," my brother said, shaking his head emphatically. "People spread rumors like crazy. You don't know who's doing this?"

"I have no idea," I answered truthfully.

"I don't get it," he said. "Doesn't it piss you off?"

"Not really, not anymore," I replied, clicking my computer closed again. "Just sort of makes me sad."

I could see the confusion in him as he turned to leave, not understanding me. I found a shred of humor in the fact that my brother thought me being attacked by some secret assailant on the internet was more likely than me being gay. It was too far outside his reality. What a world, I thought, and took some more Xanax.

It wasn't that I didn't care. Every foul smear and attack cut me deeply as I watched my entire support system, small as it was, fall away. People from school didn't want to talk to me anymore. I was just too much chaos. I understood. I probably wouldn't want to listen to my bitching either, or read all that shit online on a daily basis. It was easier to walk away, and so that's what everyone did. I did truly care, but I was out of energy. Even crying took too much work.

Robert went back to the States with all his friends about a week after that. School was going to start soon, and I'm sure he was eager to get out of the Kingdom. The day they left I got a Facebook message from Adam. I almost didn't catch it. I had started mass-deleting my new messages without reading any of them, since they were always trash, but just as I was about to hit delete a new one popped up and I recognized Adam's picture. Curious, I clicked it open.

Hey! It was good to meet you, I'm sorry we didn't get to hang out that much over this summer, I think you're pretty cute. Anyway, if you're ever in the States, hit me up!

I took a pause reading it, it had been so long since I had gotten any kind of message like that, it almost seemed like it was written in a foreign language. I read it two more times, just to make sure it was real, and after the third read I cracked a tiny smile. It felt good. I had forgotten what that felt like. I started writing back.

Hey, it was good to meet you too. You're not so bad looking yourself. I let myself smile a little bit more, catching that first lift a person gets when they do something flirty. My eyebrows raised when I saw him typing back. I hadn't expected that, but it was exciting.

Haha hey thanks. So how long have you and that guy been together? That was unexpected. He got right to it. My smile started turning into a frown. This was the sort of thing John would beat me up for. I had to be careful.

A while I guess, off and on.

Word, I get that. Are you happy with him and stuff?

Yeah of course, I lied. *Look I gotta go, good talking to you.*

You too, hit me up sometime!

My panic levels had been rising with each new line, and I raced to delete the thread as fast as I could. When it was done, I let out a long breath of relief. I realized I had sweat beading on my temples, so I took some Xanax to calm down.

The last weeks of summer flew by. I couldn't tell the days of the week apart, or the time, and suddenly I found myself sitting across from John in a poorly lit bar, made seemingly entirely from concrete.

"School is going to start for you soon, yeah?" John asked, folding his leg up onto his knee in the little metal chair. I hated this bar. Every time you moved your small, yet surprisingly heavy seat would scrape against the concrete floor.

"Next week," I answered, holding my beer close to my lips like a shield.

"You excited?"

"Why?"

"People get excited about that shit," John said, his face souring. "Whatever, listen, we gotta set up some ground rules."

"Ground rules?" I asked. "For what."

"School, dumbass," John scoffed. "There are a lot of people there."

"Yeah, so what?"

"So, you can't forget."

"Forget what?"

"That I own you," he said, his voice suddenly dropping into a sinister snarl. "Here's how it's going to go. I'll pick you up at your house in the morning, take you to school, then I'll come get you after."

"I have my own car—"

"Shut the fuck up," he growled, leaning forward over the red tin table. "You don't drive. I drive. End of story. You got it?"

"Yeah," I said, deflated. "I got it."

"Good," he said, crossing his arms and unfolding his leg. "Let's get out of here."

"I'm not done with my beer," I said, clutching the bottle tighter. Sometimes it was my only way to delay getting in his car.

"Then fucking finish it," he sighed, tapping his shoulder in angst. "You drink so slow it's ridiculous."

Sure enough, John was there every morning bright and early. He made me give him a copy of my class schedule so he knew when I would be done every day, and he was always there to pick me up. It was the same routine as the summer, only with everything condensed into the evening after classes were out.

One morning I was on my way out the door when my dad stopped me in the kitchen, saying, "Louie, hold on a moment."

"Huh?" I asked, caught off guard. He was holding his coffee cup with both hands in front of his belly and had a curious look on his face.

"I noticed you don't drive to school," he said, bobbing his head toward the courtyard.

"Why is that?"

"Oh," I said, blinking. "There's a guy in our neighborhood who goes to the same school. We have the same major, so we have the same schedule basically."

"Is that so?" he asked, lifting his coffee cup to his lips.

"Uh-huh," I mumbled back, feeling my heart race. "See you later."

"Will we see you for cards tonight?" he called after me.

"Maybe," I replied, closing the door behind me. There was no way in hell I was going to play poker with my asshole of an uncle and my cousins, but my dad already knew that.

The day at school was the same as always, but when John picked me up he seemed a bit more cheerful than usual, bouncing a little in his seat.

"Hey, good day?"

"Fine I guess," I said, getting into the car.

"You want a pretzel?" he asked suddenly. "I could really use a fucking pretzel. I've been thinking about it all day."

"A pretzel?" I asked, looking at him blankly, expecting a slap any second.

"Yeah, man, let's go to the mall and get some pretzels, I'm fucking dying for one."

"Okay," I said, confused. "A pretzel sounds good."

"Hell yeah it does," he said, nodding vigorously.

We drove to the mall and pulled into the garage. I hadn't been there since the incident with the tactical teams, and I felt my skin prickle as we rolled down the entry ramp. It wasn't super busy, and there were plenty of spots, but John kept driving down, down to the deepest level where there were no cars at all and parked in the corner. I thought he was going to rape me right there, and I felt my body tensing up, preparing for the bludgeoning shots to my ribs, but he opened his door and hopped out, a big spring in his step.

"Fucking pretzel," I heard him mutter before closing the car door. I felt a wave of relief. I never knew when he was going to strike, and that had been a close call. I knew it would happen again eventually, but where and when were always a mystery.

We walked around the mall for a few minutes with our pretzels, and John kept making this gross, sloppy sound every time he sucked down another bite. Then I stopped, my eyes locked on the person ahead. It was Benjamin, walking with a shopping bag from his favorite store over his arm, probably some fall clothes.

We saw each other. He was looking right at me. I quickly broke my eyes away, turning my gaze downward. I couldn't take it. I felt so ashamed and worthless, as if I had been caught in the act. I could feel him looking at me, his eyes bearing into the top of my skull, and I started to cry, shoving the pretzel sleeve into my face to hide the tears.

"Are you fucking serious?" John hissed into my ear. "Come on, we're leaving." He picked me up by one of my arms and yanked me toward the elevators. "Unbelievable." The elevator doors shut, and the second we were alone he shouted, "What the hell, Louie? Keep it together! Can't even enjoy a fucking pretzel!" and he slapped me hard across the left cheek.

"I'm sorry," I groaned. Another slap.

"Unbelievable," he said again. The doors opened, and we stepped out into the empty garage floor. John's car sat in the corner, the edges obscured by shadows, looking like some kind of phantom, heralding doom. "Get the fuck in."

I got into the seat slowly, pulling the door shut with dread. I knew he was going to hit me for crying, but I still didn't see it coming. The second the door clicked shut his fist came fast, smashing into my jaw, and throwing my head into the car window. Everything was instantly spinning and twinkling, and then his fist came again.

I didn't have time between blows to cry out in protest, or even in pain, it was just a blitz beating, shattering me.

It stopped for a moment, and though I couldn't really see, I managed to croak out, "Stop, I'm sorry—" but then the pain came again from my neck, the fucking vampire that he was. His teeth bit deep into my skin, and I could feel my hot blood running down the front of my shirt. I screamed out, wailing into the empty garage, and he turned me to bite my back. I could hear my skin breaking over the ringing in my ears, and I started yelling again but he slammed my head back against the window once more.

I whimpered as he withdrew, my shirt sticky with blood in both the front and the back, the pain swimming up all around me, and I heard him say, "You bled all over my fucking car, asshole," then his fists came again.

Everything swirled in shades of white and red as my vision failed. Instead of feeling the pain, I started to feel my body shutting down, one function at a time. First it was my eyes, then my ears, and all I could smell was the hot iron of blood streaming out of my nose. I felt the car moving, and John yelling something that I couldn't make out through my fog.

He was repeating himself, over and over, and it was bringing me back around. I could hear him again.

"Louie!" he shouted.

"Huh?" I gargled.

"If you tell the doctors anything, you will fucking die, you understand?"

"Doctors?" I tried to turn my head to look at him but it hurt too bad.

"You understand?" he screamed.

"I got it," I said, letting my eyelids flicker shut again and the ringing take over my ears. Then there were people and lights everywhere, and I was smelling the sterile halls of the hospital.

"Are you with me?" I heard, and I blinked a few times as I adjusted to the shape in front of me.

"I'm here," I wheezed. "Who are you?"

"My name is Dr. Edward," he said in a soothing tone. "I've just been stitching you up."

"Mm-hm," I mumbled, blinking a few more times. It was awfully bright.

"It seems you had quite the fall," he said, setting his clipboard down and drawing the curtain closed around us.

"Yeah," I said, thinking about what John had screamed in the car. "I'm really clumsy."

"I see," the doctor said, flashing me a patient smile. "And the bite marks?"

"Just horsing around, you know," I said, shrugging. My whole head hurt like hell, and the shrug had shot a spasm of pain through my neck. My hand went to the pain, and I found a thick bandage covering the bite wound.

"Horsing around goes too far, then you fall down some stairs, do I have that right?" Dr. Edward asked, sitting down on the little stool beside the hospital bed.

"That's it," I said, nodding. "You got it."

"You know," he began, glancing down to the clipboard. "Louie, this is a safe place, I'm a safe person. A good person. If there's something you want to tell me, you shouldn't feel afraid."

"I just told you," I said, imagining John's rage. "It's like you said the first time. Fell down some stairs."

He looked at me for a few more minutes, then suddenly said, "All right. Someone will be in with your discharge forms in a short while. Now you have a concussion, you know what that means, right?"

"Yeah," I said. "Sort of."

"The nurse will go over it with you," Dr. Edward said, standing. "You take care, Louie, you hear me?"

"Yeah."

"All right," he said, and I could hear him sighing as he left through the curtain.

A couple hours later they released me with some heavy painkillers. John was there to pick me up. I got in the car, still holding the pills in my left hand. I didn't want to look at him or hear his voice, but here I was.

"You say anything?" he asked immediately. I shook my head silently, looking ahead through the windshield. "Good. What're those?" and he took the pain pills out of my palm. "I'm gonna keep these. Here, take Xanax instead," and he placed a brand-new bottle of pills where the painkillers used to be. I sat silent and stoic as he drove me home, and didn't say anything as I got out of the car, but he called after me, saying, "Don't ever be such a bitch again," and then he sped away.

I couldn't feel anything. I was completely numb. I trudged through the gate and stopped in my tracks, surveying the hordes of cars parked outside my uncle's villa. I remembered it was a Thursday. Fucking poker night. It was almost worth laughing about. Just my luck. Nothing mattered. At least they were at my uncles' and I wouldn't have to see anyone as I pulled myself up to my room.

I skirted the edge of the courtyard, staying in the shadow of the compound wall, and crept into my house through the back door. I could hear the laughter and conversation floating from next door, and it made me want to scream. It made me want to die. Nothing mattered. I was fucking worthless.

I got to my room and put the bottle of Xanax on my desk, glancing toward my balcony. I was already so beat up, surely the fall would be just enough to get me over the edge. Then they would all have to clean it up. Fuck 'em.

But then I had a revolutionary idea, an idea that made me feel like a complete idiot for never thinking of it before. I hurried to my dad's office and poured myself a huge glass of scotch. This was going to work perfectly. I was even getting a little excited as I waddled back to my room.

No more John. No more bullshit. No more shithead cousins. No more online rumors. No more pain. No more secrets. I swallowed something like thirty pills of Xanax and drank down all the scotch. I won.

I was surprised how fast it came on. I hadn't been sure how long I would have to wait, and I was walking down the hall to get another glass of scotch when I collapsed. The glass shattered. I couldn't move. I couldn't see. Everything was hot. Then, as far as I knew, I died.

Chapter Fourteen

THE FIRST THING I HEARD was a soft, rhythmic beep somewhere to my right. It was as if I were ascending through quicksand, pulled up by a massive, clanking winch, grinding slowly against the deep, dark trap I had found myself in.

With each great turn of the gear, the wet sand resisted, clinging to my arms and legs, smothering my chest and mouth, but up I went still until I could hear that solemn beep.

I could feel the winch groaning under the stress in the darkness, but that beep grew louder and louder, and something in me decided that I needed to find it. I needed to see it, to hold it, and this black pit of damp sand would not keep me.

The winch protested with a great grinding moan as I began to wriggle and lash upward with my arms, reaching for the cable that pulled me, trying to worm my way out, trying to find that haunting sound, and then suddenly, as if I had broken through some invisible membrane, I shot forth like a clown in a cartoon canon, and left the mud pit behind.

Beep. Beep. Beep. Beep. Click. Whir. Beep. Beep. Beep. Beep. Click. Whir. Beep. Beep. Beep. Beep.

"We've got movement in bed six. Go and find Dr. Edward."

Click. Whir. Beep.

"He's awake?"

"Almost."

"All right let's take a look here."

Beep. Beep. Beep.

"Hey there, Louie, you remember me?" The voice was familiar, but I couldn't place it. I tried to mumble something back, but I wasn't all there yet. "Can you open your eyes for me? That's it, there you are."

After a few moments I started to get a picture of my surroundings through the shifting, blurry shades of white moving all around me. I was in the hospital, that much was clear. I could make out a few solid shapes gathered nearby, and as the doctor flashed a penlight in my eyes I came into full consciousness.

"Dad?" I croaked, blinking a few times to make sure I wasn't hallucinating. He was standing beside the bed in his typical serious fashion, his hands clasped behind his back and his chin downturned.

"It's all right, Louie," he said. "You're okay."

"There he is," Dr. Edward said, sitting back on the little stool beside me. "Welcome back, young man."

"What—" I started to ask, and then I began to remember.

"Easy now, you're in the hospital," Dr. Edward said. "You're going to stay here for a little while, just relax."

"He's awake," my dad said, glancing toward the doctor. "He should go home. He will be more comfortable."

"Home," I mumbled, reaching around for my cell phone. "I want to go home."

"Sir, could you give us just a moment?" Dr. Edward said, turning to my dad. "I would like to talk to Louie privately, just for a minute."

My dad looked me up and down for half a second, then said, "Of course," and slowly paced toward the hallway, glancing back once over his shoulder.

Dr. Edward got up and pulled the curtain closed around the bed, then standing over me he raised his eyebrows a bit and said, "Tough night for you, huh?"

"Yeah," I mumbled back. "I guess so."

"You're lucky, you know," he went on, sitting down again beside the bed. "Your father found you on your side. If you had been on your back, it's unlikely we would be having this conversation."

"Lucky," I echoed, letting my eyes wander up to the ceiling and its pale fluorescents.

"You had thrown up most of your stomach's contents when your father found you," he said, glancing down at his clipboard. "Fortunately, you seem to have avoided taking enough to cause permanent damage." Then he went into his long coat and pulled out the little orange bottle, holding it up for me to see.

"This is quite the Xanax prescription," he said, setting the bottle down on the little table beside the stool. "Except it doesn't have a name on it. Or a pharmacy. Where did it come from, Louie?"

"I, uh, I don't remember," I muttered, casting my eyes sideways at the empty bottle.

"Are you sure?" he asked, raising his eyebrows. "It seems like a lot of Xanax to just show up out of the blue. I gave you pain pills earlier in the day, did you mix them up?"

"Yeah, I…I can't remember," I insisted, shaking my head. I heard the stiff hospital pillow shifting under my head with each little movement. "I was just in pain, I took too many, I just, I don't remember."

"All right, that's fine," he said, taking the bottle and slipping it back into his coat. "That's all right. You remember earlier, what I said? You can trust me, Louie, I'm the guy who helps you, not the other way around. You remember that?"

"Yeah, I remember," I whispered, moving my gaze to the ceiling lights once more.

"Are you sure you can't remember where you got the Xanax?" he asked softly, placing one of his hands on mine.

"Yeah, I'm sure," I said, clenching my jaw a bit. As I did, the pain from my beating came flaring up, and I winced.

"Okay," he whispered back. "Now you sit tight, I want to keep you here for a little while. I'm going to talk with your father."

"Wait," I said, reaching up and grabbing his sleeve. My voice was cracked and pathetic. "Don't, uh, don't tell my dad that, you know, that I was here before."

He looked me up and down, letting out a subtle sigh as he clicked his pen a few times. "If that's what you want, okay," he said, and I felt a huge wave of relief washing over me. "But you can't hide those stitches."

Dr. Edward pushed open the curtain and turned away. I saw my dad looming in the hallway, looking in through one of the wide windows, walking up to the door as the doctor went to meet him. I felt my heart racing as I watched them talking, worrying that the doctor would tell everything. This was it. It was all over now. Then they came back to the bed together, my dad holding his coat over his arm, his chin still turned downward.

"Louie, we've agreed it's best you stay here for a day at least," Dr. Edward said. "I understand you want to get home, but just sit tight. I need to ensure you make a full recovery, do you understand?"

"Yeah," I said, looking between the two of them. "Where is my phone?"

"I'm not sure," Dr. Edward said. "I didn't think you had it with you when you were brought in."

"Did you drive me here?" I asked, glancing up to my dad.

"The ambulance brought you here," Dr. Edward said.

"My phone—" I said again, all the horrific possibilities running through my head. I could imagine John calling and calling, sending text after text. *You fucking answer me. I own you. Fuck you, Louie, pick up the phone or I am going to tell your dad everything!* What would happen if I never replied? Would he just show up? Break in? Drop the flash drive off at my dad's office?

"The chauffeur will bring it by in the morning," my dad said. I could see the clock on the wall behind him, reading 1:06 a.m. "I'm sure it's in your room. Do you want me to stay the night?"

"No," I said with a sigh, shaking my head a bit. "I'm fine, it's just fifteen minutes away, I'll be fine."

"Okay," he said softly, shuffling his feet while he straightened his coat over his arm. "I'll see you tomorrow." As I watched him go, the only thing I could think about was my phone. I had maybe four or five hours to wait until the sun came up and the chauffeur brought my phone over. Was that too long? I wanted to tear out my hair, but I couldn't show panic. John could be outing me to the world any minute, or maybe he already had. I started feeling sick to my stomach as I imagined John slipping the flash drive through a mail slit.

After my dad was gone from view, Dr. Edward sat back down beside me. I groaned a little, not wanting anything to do with him anymore. I just wanted to be out of that bed, back home. I wanted my phone. I wanted to be safe again.

"Louie," he began, folding his hands together. "Listen, if you need to talk about anything, I can listen, and I won't tell anyone."

"Can I just be alone please," I said back, letting my head flop to the other side of the pillow.

"People don't take Xanax for pain, Louie," he said softly.

"It's like you said," I shot back. "I mixed them up."

He let out a short breath from his nose, and asked, "Does this have anything to do with Benjamin?"

My world fell out from under me. The room spun instantly. I couldn't hear anything except for this horrible ringing, and my vision was blurring while my heart raced. I began hyperventilating. "Louie! Stay with me, Louie! Louie!" I could hear him calling my name over and over, cutting through the wailing ring. "Come on, Louie, you're still here. There you go, easy now, big breaths, slow it down, there you go."

I came back around and found that I was sweating profusely all over my face, and that my armpits were soaked.

"Just a small panic attack, nothing to worry about," he said in a comforting tone. "You're safe."

"How—" I choked. "How do you know Benjamin?" Had I been rambling on in my delirium? What had I said? Had I outed myself just through sheer stupidity?

"It's all right, calm down. You're safe, Louie, you hear me?"

"Safe," I said back, the word sounding hollow as it left my cracked lips.

"Benjamin is my friend. Remember? We were all going to go out to dinner together, but then you two ran off to the sea. You remember that?"

"The sea," I said, and I felt tears welling up, mingling with my sticky sweat, and streaking down my face. "I remember."

"You understand?" he said, taking my hand again. "You're safe."

"Don't—" I choked again, my lips quivering. "Don't tell Benjamin about this, please. Any of it. He—"

"I won't," Dr. Edward said, patting my hand lightly before withdrawing from the bedside. "Now you try and get some rest, someone will be in to check on you from time to time. Can you do that for me?"

"Sure," I said, trying to wipe away the tears. "I can do that."

"All right, Louie," he said, hanging the clipboard on the end of the bed. "Take care of yourself," then he switched off the light, and finally left me alone.

That night I dreamed the same thing over and over, waking frequently in fits of shivering sweat. I stood alone in the desert, holding a duffel bag, and standing far away in the distance I could see John. He was laughing as he held up the flash drive, slipping it into an envelope.

But this time, I was screaming at him, yelling for him to stop, that I was leaving the hospital, I was coming back, and I started running toward him. The hot sand burned as I stumbled in the dunes, lugging this heavy duffel bag behind me, feeling the heels of my feet kicking back against it.

There was a fortress in the distance, amid the shifting slices of heat, and when I saw it, I knew that it was mine. Those were my walls, my gates, my towers, my sandstone ramparts. That great bastion of sandstone became clearer and clearer as I ran toward it, but still John was ahead of me, closer than I could ever get.

I could feel his wicked fingers reaching out for the wrought iron door, feel the poison of his touch seeping into the cracks of my fortifications, corrupting the integrity of its construction, eating it away from the inside. I had to stop him, to save myself, but I couldn't catch up.

I stood helpless as John winked out of existence, and my castle collapsed in a great flood of sand, the confines of its stone blocks shattering into millions and millions of coarse, hot grains of sand, swept up in a great breeze. Then all was still, and standing alone in the sand I screamed, crying out to the hot, beating sun, feeling my fortress settle into the nothingness of the desert.

Suddenly, all around me, the sand began shifting, and scorpions began clawing their way to the surface, encircling me, growing closer and larger. But there! There was a rock. A tall rock. If I could climb it, I would be safe.

I hauled the duffel bag to the rock, moving as fast as I could, tripping in the burning sand, feeling the coarse grains scrape against my knees, screaming at the duffel bag to be lighter.

There was a horde of scorpions now, a tidal wave of venom washing toward me as I reached the rock. In a blind panic I clawed at the face of it, trying to pull myself and the duffel bag higher, out of danger. The scorpions clustered around the base of the rock, climbing over one another, trying to get closer, trying to rip me apart and lay eggs in the decaying cavities of my body, and in my fear, I fell.

When the morning came, I was exhausted. Sleep had been torture, and I sat groggily in the hospital bed, rubbing the flakes from my eyes, feeling more spent than I had the night before.

The clock read 7:30. I had no idea when to expect anyone from my family, or when Ron, the chauffeur, would drop off my phone. I panicked immediately, dreading John's rage. I sat there, trying to breathe, running my hands across my face over and over, letting time slip by.

"Dude! What the fuck?" my brother's voice came booming into the small room, and I snapped out of my trance, astonished to see his groomed face bumbling in, his hands raised up in an expression of disbelief. "What the hell happened?" The clock read 8:03.

"Hey," I grunted, sitting up a bit against the uncomfortable pillows. "Fucking stupid accident, I swear," I said, shaking my head to play it up. "I was just trying to kill the pain, and I lost track of how many pills I was taking."

"Come on, Louie!" he gawked. "You gotta be more careful!"

His reaction made me smile just a little. He was so innocent, so naive. I could tell that he believed me, that he was worried about me.

"I'll be more careful," I replied. "I promise."

"Oh!" he said, his eyes lighting up in remembrance. "I got your precious phone," and he pulled it out of his pocket. He gestured to the chips and cracks in the corner with his thumb and remarked, "You gotta stop dropping this thing, dude. One day it'll break for good."

"Holy shit," I gasped, grabbing the phone out of his hands, and immediately looking through my inbox.

"Damn, never saw someone so relieved to get their phone back," my brother mentioned.

I didn't say anything back. There were no new texts from John, no new calls, no nothing. I was safe. All I could do was shut my eyes and rest my head, clutching the phone tightly in my lap. I was safe.

My dad came by a little later and told me I was being released that afternoon. The whole day I kept checking my phone, expecting John to hit me up every passing minute. What would I tell him? Could I keep this a secret? I would certainly try. But he never called, never texted, so I sat in bed all day bouncing my leg, waiting for the storm to break.

A nurse came in around two o'clock with a tray of food. "Are you hungry, sweetie?" she asked, shuffling over to the bedside.

"No," I answered.

"Well, too bad," she replied with a wink. "You have to eat. Doctor's orders." She set the tray down on my lap and pulled off the little plastic dome, revealing some horrible looking slop. Was that supposed to be oatmeal?

"What is that?" I asked, nodding to the plate.

"Does it matter?" she shot back, flashing me a brief smile. "I'll be back in a bit to see that you ate it all."

It was horrible. I made a stupid face with every bite I took like a little kid eating broccoli, but I got it down. Even though it tasted awful, my stomach felt better, and I had a small moment of triumph when I put down the plastic spoon on the empty plate. The clock read 2:34. The door opened.

"I ate all of it," I announced proudly, glancing toward the door, but instead of the nurse, it was John. That small victory shattered as fear gripped my entire body. I couldn't move. I never used to understand the expression "a deer in the headlights." Why wouldn't the deer run away? Why sit there frozen, waiting for death approaching at sixty miles an hour?

Now I understood it. Sometimes, all you can do in the face of impending danger is freeze and wait for it. Fight or flight was a myth. There was a third option: fight, flight, or freeze, and I was frozen.

John shut the door behind him, and walked coolly to the stool beside the bed, taking a seat casually like he was kicking back at a bar. My eyes flicked to the window that faced the hallway, expecting to see my dad or brother walk in at any moment. How was I supposed to explain him? What would I introduce him as? He was a full decade older than I was, it could only look suspicious.

"Don't worry, they're gone," John said, following my gaze to the window. "For now, at least."

"What—"

"I sat out there all morning and afternoon, waiting for your family to leave," he went on, turning his attention back to me. "Don't worry about them."

"How—" I stuttered, feeling my throat dry up. "How did you know I was here?"

"Psh," he scoffed, "come on, Louie. Don't play dumb. I know everything about you." The scorpions were back, climbing up out of the sand. "Now you listen to me," he said, leaning forward until his face was next to my ear. "I'm going to be nice to you for a few days. You relax, get better. But don't you ever pull something like this again. I'm not done with you. You don't get to take the easy way out. I own you."

I felt utterly pathetic. This would never end. He would never let me go. I was powerless, stuck in the quagmire he created. I wanted to cry, to tear out my hair and wail at the sky like the Greek mourners of old. I was alone in the desert, without recourse, surrounded by scorpions.

"Well, is it all down?" the nurse asked, swinging the door wide open. I saw John give a little jump as he pulled back from the bed, and I realized that was the first time I had ever seen him startled in any way.

"Anyways, you get better," John said to me, turning away in a hurry.

"How are we feeling today, Louie?" Dr. Edward's voice came floating in behind the nurse, and John made a little shuffle around him before disappearing down the hall.

"Oh! I am proud of you," the nurse remarked, taking the tray away.

"Who was that?" Dr. Edward asked, bobbing his head in the direction of the hall.

"Just a friend," I said. "Checking in, you know?"

"That's a good friend to have," the nurse remarked, flashing me one more smile before walking out of the room with the empty food tray.

"Does your friend usually make your heart race?" Dr. Edward asked once we were alone.

"What?" I said, trying to blink away the tears that were slowly building.

"Your pulse," Dr. Edward said, gesturing to the beeping machine next to me with his pen. "It's going pretty quick, and you look like you're about to cry. Is everything all right, Louie?"

"I just, I just—" I tried to answer but bit down on my lip, trying to stop the crying, but it was inevitable, and I began sobbing.

"Hey there, it's all right," Dr. Edward said, sitting down on the foot of the bed. "What's the matter, hm?"

"I just miss my mom," I cried out, hugging my legs close to my chest, and burying my teary eyes in my kneecaps. It wasn't a lie. It wasn't the reason I was crying, but it was true. "I just want her to tell me that everything is okay."

"Of course," he said in a soothing voice. "Your friend, was he the one you were horsing around with, you know, before you fell down the stairs?"

I almost said yes, I was caught so off guard, but I found that reserve of strength deep down, bit my tongue, and shook my head. I didn't want to look at him. He knew I was lying. It was obvious.

"Okay," he said softly with that same resignation as the night before. Then he stood up from the bed and said, "You're being discharged in a couple of hours. You sure you'll be all right heading home?"

"I'll be fine," I mustered through my crying. "I'm okay."

"This is my card," he said, laying the small cardstock rectangle on the table beside my bed. "You call me if you ever need to talk, you hear me?" I nodded, barely glancing up at him. "Listen, Louie," he went on, his voice becoming serious. "I can patch you up, but I can't really help you if you don't let me."

"I don't need help," I said back weakly.

"Yes, you do," he said back. "You know how this will end."

"You don't know what you're talking about," I growled, bitterness flooding into my voice. I felt as if I were defending my very existence.

"Call anytime," he concluded, tapping the card with his finger. "Take care of yourself, Louie." Then he straightened his coat, clicked his pen, and left the room.

Ron came and picked me up around four o'clock. We didn't speak, but I saw him looking at me with concern and sympathy from the rearview mirror. I felt pity for him and wondered if other chauffeurs were surrounded by so much chaos and sadness.

When we pulled into the courtyard, I saw my dad's SUV pulled up in front of our villa, with some of the staff loading big pieces of luggage into the trunk. Just like that, he would be off to London or somewhere else in Europe, or wherever it was he went all over the world. But why the SUV? Ron always took him to the airport in the Mercedes. As I got out of the car, I saw my brother walking toward the SUV with a backpack, and I knew something was up.

"What's going on?" I asked, wincing against the bright light that bounced off the surface of the pool.

"We're going to the country," my brother answered. "Dad's idea."

"Why? I have school tomorrow." I asked, confused.

"Family bonding. Dad's idea. School is taken care of, nerd." My brother shot back, slinging his backpack into the trunk. "We're leaving in, like, ten minutes though, so you better get some shit together."

I started walking toward the front door, but each step shot pain through my ribs. I was still in bad shape from my beating, and I would have stumbled myself right into the ground if Ron hadn't caught my arm.

"I'll help you up the stairs, sir," he said, giving me a kind glance as he helped steady me.

"Sir?" I said, giggling. "I'm only twenty years old, Ron. Sir is for old people, you know, like my dad." Ron just looked at me, patted me on my back and smiled.

I got a few CDs together, along with my portable player and headphones. I didn't care about clothes, so I randomly tossed a spare shirt and pair of pants into a bag with my laptop and buckled in for the drive to our country house.

The drive was silent for the most part, save the tinny sound of music bleeding out of my brother's and my headphones. We hadn't been to the country house since my mom died, and it felt strange to look out the window at the familiar scenery that used to mean we were on our way to a great weekend. Now it just felt hollow.

After about forty minutes I got through my first CD and popped out my headphones. We would be there soon enough. I looked up to the front seat and saw my dad's hairy forearm resting on the top of the wheel, just like when I was a little kid.

"Good music?" he asked, glancing back at me through the rearview.

"Yeah, sure," I replied. My brother was drooling against the passenger side window.

"You know, I always liked the Beatles," he said, and I couldn't help but crack a little smile.

"Really?"

"Sure, they can really rock out, huh?"

"Yeah," I said, holding my smile just a moment longer. "I guess so." Then out of the blue he remarked, "That black car has been behind us since we left the capital. Funny when those things happen."

I turned my head slowly, feeling an icy fear creeping into my heart. I could feel the bite wounds in my shoulder. I didn't want to look, to see, but I did, and there he was, cruising right along behind us in that stupid black sports car, baring his teeth like a barracuda stalking its prey.

Chapter Fifteen

DIRT FLEW UP BEHIND us as my dad turned off the main road, obscuring everything in the rear windshield. John's car disappeared in the cloud as tiny rocks bounced up and clattered against the underside of my dad's SUV, each stone ringing loudly in my ears as I scanned the dust behind us in panic. He was gone, just like that. I would have preferred that he followed us all the way to the house, at least that way he wouldn't be keeping me in such paralytic suspense. Now I was helpless, but that wasn't anything new.

The road up the hillside was narrow and winding, and as we climbed up, I kept looking back, trying to catch a glimpse of the phantom I knew was still following me, but he wasn't there. I curled my toes against the balls of my feet inside of my shoes, holding them there as tightly as I could, trying not to show the car my exploding anxiety.

The drive up the hill was a lot shorter than I remembered, and before I knew it, we were pulling up to the big white gate. As a child, the gate was the entrance to a world of adventure and play, but now as I looked up at it, all I could see was an intrusive hunk of metal actively contradicting its surroundings.

My dad reached up to the visor and hit the remote clip, clanking open the gate. Its hinges cried out, and I winced at the sound, again curling my toes. The house at the end of the driveway looked the same as it always had, but to me it seemed a hollow shell of old memories.

A few staff waited for us under the porte-cochere, lined up like they were receiving royalty. I know it made my dad feel important, but it made me feel cornered. I didn't want to look at or speak with anyone, I just wanted to dig a hole, stick my head in it, and suffocate like those surrounded Roman soldiers at Cannae, stranded without hope in the face of impending death.

I jumped in my seat when my door swung open. There was a staff member, who seemed extremely happy, boasting a big goofy smile as he offered his hand to help me out of the car.

"Hello there, sir!" he announced jovially. "Welcome back sir, may I—"

"Louie!" I snapped, blinking twice at the sun streaming in through the open car door. He looked taken aback, worried that he had done something wrong. I felt bad, this guy didn't know any better. He didn't know I was on the verge of a complete and permanent breakdown. "Sorry," I mumbled. "My name is Louie, call me Louie. Please."

"Very good, sir," he said, no doubt reflexively. I could tell he was just glad I wasn't going to shout at him. I slowly swung my legs around and climbed out of the hulking SUV, landing on the granite stone paver with a little hop, and took a long look around the property.

From where I was standing, I could see everything except the trails that led down to the lawn on the other side of the house. The place seemed unchanged, as if it had been frozen in time. The pool furniture under the pergola was still set up exactly the way my mom had arranged it, and I had a sinking feeling that the rest of the house would be the same way. It was like those first few nights in our main house all over again, and I felt the cruel reality of her absence. Now I needed her more than ever. The feeling washed over me again. I was alone.

I finally took a step from where I stood, not paying any attention to where I was going, and collided with a staff member carrying our luggage.

"Sorry, sir!" he exclaimed, fumbling not to drop my brother's backpack.

"No, it's my fault," I said, turning around. "Louie, call me Louie."

"Yes, si—" he caught himself and smiled. "Louie."

I watched the man carry our luggage up toward the house, and another of the staff opened the door for him. I could see past him into the foyer, and my heart sank. Everything was exactly the same, and I didn't want to face that. I took a sharp left and walked past my dad and brother, heading for the pool on the left side of the house.

"Louie, where are you going?" my dad called after me.

"I'm going to sit down under the pergola," I answered, reaching the top of the exterior stairs that wrapped around the house.

"All right, be sure to come up for dinner," he said, and the two of them disappeared into the house.

My heart was loud in my chest, thumping with each step I took down the sunbaked bricks. I reached out to touch the railing, but it was hot from the sun, and I withdrew my hand quickly. Rounding the bottom of the stairs, I stepped onto the expansive lawn, the pool and pergola a little way ahead. Since I couldn't stand being inside the house, this was the best place I could think of to be alone.

I spun one of the big pool chairs around, so its back faced the house, its heavy wooden feet dragging over the stone platform. I didn't want to look up at those windows, and everything they encompassed. As I turned the seat, I caught a glimpse of the blinds being opened in the living room, and for half a second, I could have sworn I saw my mom walking past the glass. But she wasn't there, and I knew it, so I settled into the seat, and let the strong valley breeze blow over me, though I could hardly breathe.

Every moment I shut my eyes I saw John's car in the rearview mirror, zooming down the highway, cigarette hanging lazily from his fingers out the driver's side window. I could imagine his smug, predatory face as he followed us into the countryside, and the more I dwelt on it, the more anxious I became. This place was supposed to be an escape, but it felt far more like a rattrap.

I was sitting there for all of three minutes when my phone buzzed, freaking me out. I nearly threw it into the pool, but my dread overruled my surprise, and I nervously clicked open the unread text. It was John.

I'm outside the gate. Come now.

My heart nearly stopped. The breeze blew into my slack-jawed mouth but didn't fill my lunges. This was the inevitable clash of my two worlds, and it was going to destroy me.

I can't leave right now, please understand. I typed back frantically. My whole body was cold, and all I could feel was the rising beat of my heart, thumping faster and faster. I wanted some fucking Xanax, if only to calm down.

Then I'm coming up to tell your dad everything. You're dead.

No! I shot back, jumping up from the chair so fast I knocked my ankle against one of its legs. I didn't feel the pain because of my adrenaline and anxiety, but it would later become an annoying bruise. *I'll come right down.*

In my panic I hustled back up the stairs, my body screaming to me to stop. I was still beat to shit from when John had put me in the hospital and leaping up multiple stairs brought great jolts of pain through my torso. I tried not to cry, I was so fucking sick of crying, but the tears rolled down anyways as I shuffled my way down the driveway.

I punched in the code on the little side door at the gate, and let it click shut behind me. His car was parked about a hundred feet down the drive, the bright sun reflecting off of its jet-black paint job. The driver's door opened, and he lumbered out like an outlaw from an old John Wayne movie, his hips wide, his clothes black, and his cigarette sending a swirl of smoke around his shoulders.

"What the hell are you doing?" I cried out, flapping my hands at my sides in exasperation. "My dad saw you following us! You can't be here! Why are you doing this?" And my burst of anger subsided into my residual, paralytic fear.

John cocked his head, as if he were listening to me in amusement. After I was done, he stepped coolly up to me, and blew a stream of smoke into my eyes. As I coughed and clenched my eyes shut, he tossed his cigarette aside.

"I told you, Louie," he said. "I own you." Then his hands shot out faster than I could react, and his iron fingers wrapped tightly around my neck, choking me with violent, painful strength. "I will fucking kill you if you ever talk to me like that again, you hear me?" he seethed, tightening his grip further. My vision was going red around the rims, and my lungs were screaming for air. "I will fucking murder you," he growled into my ear, then he suddenly let go, and I fell into the dirt, retching and gasping for oxygen. The dust swirled up around me and clouded my nose, caking my lips as I heaved for air. "Now get the fuck in," he said, sliding back into his car like he had just stopped for gas.

I would have cried more, but I felt as if he had choked all the tears from my eyes, so with my shoulders slumped I went around to the passenger door and got into his hell machine.

We drove for a little while down the country roads, and I watched the sun moving lower as I leaned my head against the window and sniffled. He could have killed me in the road, I thought, and that may have just been easier than all of this. Suddenly the car stopped. I looked around, and saw we were in the middle of nowhere. Maybe he would kill me here, I thought. At least it would all be done with. Then the sound of his zipper broke my fantasy.

"Go on then," he said. "You know what to do."

"I don't—" I started, but he slapped me hard across my bruised jaw, then again on the ear, and the world started ringing.

"Fucking get to it," he huffed. "Don't make me hurt you again."

I turned toward him slowly, shifting in my seat. He was sitting back, stroking his hard dick with one hand, and resting the other on my headrest. I must have taken too long because he slapped me again, and again, and again. My left ear was pounding and humming, and the sound inside my head was like a drill diving into my brain. Eventually he just grabbed the back of my hair, forced my head down, and didn't let go until he was finished.

Afterward, he drove me back to the gate. He grabbed me by the chin, looked into my red puffy eyes, and said, "I'll be back very soon. When I text you, you come right the fuck down here, you get it? You do as I say." I nodded, and silently stumbled out of his car.

His headlights disappeared into the distance as I trudged up the driveway. The lights around the courtyard were lit as the last shreds of sunset faded in the distance, so I went around in the grass to avoid being seen. I didn't want to see or talk to anyone. I didn't want to go into that house, either, but more and more it seemed to me that what I wanted simply didn't matter. It hadn't for a long time. I should have been used to it. I wanted some Xanax.

I took a few big breaths at the front door, reaching tentatively for the handle. I just wanted to get up to my room without being seen, but those hopes disappeared the moment I crossed the threshold.

"Hey, Louie!" my dad called out from the kitchen. "You want a steak? Of course you do, what am I saying." he had a strange levity in his voice, like I hadn't heard from him since I was maybe five or six years old.

"Sure," I called back, trying to pull myself together as fast as possible. I just wanted some goddamn Xanax. "Give me ten minutes, I gotta go to the bathroom."

"We didn't need to know that, bro!" my brother's voice joined the conversation, and I heard my dad chuckle.

I turned on the tap, grabbed a towel, and cried into it, curling up on the floor against the base of the tub. Life was bullshit, and I finally understood fully that I didn't want to be alive anymore. After I cried what tears were left, I washed my face and changed my clothes, put on a fake face, then joined my brother in the living room. Stallone was on the TV, killing a man with his huge knife. My brother loved Rambo.

"You okay, man?" he asked as I settled onto the other side of the couch. "You seem off."

"Yeah, I'm fine," I said, bringing my knees to my chest. "Which one is this?"

"*First Blood*, bro!" he exclaimed, clapping his hands. "He's a hardcore motherfucker, you know?"

"Yeah," I mumbled. "He sure is." I had no fucking idea or clue.

I sat there on the couch, staring blankly at the movie. Part of me could hear my mom and her friends laughing in the living room, swinging their hips just a little bit to Middle Eastern music, clinking their glasses of wine, and enjoying some time away from the capital.

It was around ten o'clock when our dad called us in for dinner. My dad had some scotch, my brother ate enough food for three people, and I poked at the fat running along the edge of the steak. They were laughing and talking, and I was wishing John had killed me in the road.

I looked up from my plate and saw past the table into the kitchen. One of the staff was cleaning up the dishes my dad had made, and I thought of how my mom loved spending time there, helping with the cooking, and asking the staff about their families. Then my dad's heavy scotch glass came down on the table, and the thud brought me back to the sound of my brother's laughter. Someone had just told a joke. I wasn't sure who.

A cell phone started ringing, and I nearly fell out of my chair thinking that John was already back. My hand went to my pocket, but after a few seconds I realized it was my brother's ringtone.

"Hello?" he said, answering it with a puzzled look on his face. My dad let out a sigh, gesturing for him to put the phone away, but my brother's brow furrowed further as he listened to the voice on the other end. "No, Louie is here with us," and both of them started staring at me. "No, he was in the hospital, he hasn't used his laptop in like, what, three days."

"What is going on?" my dad asked, folding his hands together on the table in front of him, pushing his plate away.

"Hey, let me call you back, okay?" my brother said. "All right, yeah, two seconds," and he hung up.

"Who was that?" I asked, fearing the worst.

"That was your friend Christine," my brother said, his face becoming more serious than I had ever seen it. "She said her whole family got Facebook messages saying she got an abortion, but that it was your baby."

"What? Mine?" I gawked. "That's impossible!"

"Yeah, I know," my brother said, shaking his head. "What the fuck?"

"Language!" My dad snapped. Then he turned to look at me and asked, "What is Facebook?"

"It's social media, Dad," my brother said, subtly rolling his eyes. "It's like email, but everyone can see everything."

My brother and I spent the next fifteen minutes explaining how Facebook worked to my dad, and then he asked about the rumors. My brother did most of the talking, telling him how people have been getting fake messages about me for a while now. Occasionally my dad would turn to me and ask, "Is that true?" and I would nod.

He finished his scotch, dried the corners of his mouth with a napkin, and stood up from the table. "I'm going to make a call," he said. "We'll find out where these messages are coming from."

"You can do that?" my brother asked, his eyes wide.

"I can do anything," he replied, picked up his empty glass, and walked out of the room.

After he left, my brother scarfed down what food was still on the table and I went to my room. The Facebook rumors had gotten more frequent, nastier, and I still had no idea where they were coming from. Maybe it was good that my dad knew about it. He had friends in high enough places that maybe he could make them stop. Still, I didn't care too much anymore. The rumors and online harassment didn't seem to matter compared to the monster that stalked my every movement.

I thought of the doctor's words. *You know how this ends.* John was going to kill me, there was no doubt in my mind. I just wished he would hurry up and get it over with, so all this would stop.

I opened my laptop and pulled up Facebook. My inbox was bursting, as per usual, with angry rants from people I once considered friends, or at least friendly acquaintances. In between their fits of rage were more fake profiles, asking if I sucked dick for money. It had all become rather normal, and I didn't linger over any of them as I navigated to Adam's profile. I'm not sure why I messaged him, maybe it was because he was the only person in recent memory who hadn't automatically branded me as a drug-addicted fuckup. I opened a new chat window and wrote: *Hey.*

I lay on my stomach with my chin propped on my hands, staring at the screen, waiting for a reply. But he was in the States, it was the middle of the day there. He was probably in class or throwing a frisbee on the green like a typical American college student. No response. He wasn't even online. After a few minutes I shut my eyes and tried to fall asleep.

Then I heard a new message come in. It was Adam.

Hey yourself!

I'm not sure why I did what I did next. I was so resigned to my inevitable fate, that I didn't believe I could change it. But some part of me didn't want to just vanish, some part of me wanted to be remembered for the person I really was and what I endured. I knew that when John killed me, everyone would believe it was suicide. Between my mom and my stint in the hospital, nobody would think twice.

I didn't want to disappear. I wanted to be dead, I wanted it to be over, but I didn't want John to skate away into the unknown. At least that's why I think I did what I did, but who's to really say? Christ, I wanted some fucking Xanax.

I told Adam everything, starting with the warehouse party and the cocaine. I told him about how Robert had been turned against me, how John would rape and beat me, how he spoon-fed me drugs and blackmailed me to keep me in line, how I was sure my life was nearing its end and I didn't want to be forgotten. I was crying while I wrote the words. I was so fucking sick of crying.

They say that after you get something off your chest, you feel lighter, but I didn't. Instead I felt wretched, sick, and vile. Putting it all out there made it more real than I was ready for. Before that moment, it was just a part of my life that was slowly eating everything else away. Now, vomiting out this tale of abuse, I realized how much it dominated every aspect of my life, that it had eaten everything else up long ago. I existed purely as a plaything of that sadistic vampire of a man, and that I was, in fact, his property.

I lay there waiting for Adam's reply. I had sent him an essay's worth of blood-curdling truth, and I wouldn't have been surprised if he never answered. There was a small piece of me that felt ashamed for telling him everything, and for saddling him with such brutal knowledge. All I wanted was some goddamn Xanax. Then, up popped a response.

I'm so sorry, Louie, he wrote. *You can't go to the police?*

Of course not, you know where we live, I answered. It seemed like a stupid question. How the hell could I go to the police? I'd be outing myself, and then the hurt wouldn't come from John, but everybody else in that Godforsaken Kingdom.

I get it. He wrote back eventually, and I wondered if he did. He had grown up in the States, and all the religious redneck conservatives in the world didn't stack up to the collective disgrace and hate in a rigid Middle Eastern society.

Ugh. This really sucks, and I am very sorry that you're going through this right now. Being forced to quit school in California, your mom's death, your family, your friends turning on you, and now this asshole. You should move out here, get away. The US is safer for us, and he wouldn't follow you here.

He might.

Think about it, you could start fresh.

That's a myth, nobody can do that.

Just think about it. You have a place to crash in Texas.

What, with Robert?

No, with me. Just think about it.

And then what? Be someone else's liability?

No. You'll transfer to UT here in Austin. Away from all that evil.

I don't have any money to my name. This is almost impossible. I need to get my passport and green card from my dad's safe. He took them away back in 2004.

We will figure this out together. I will help you as much as I possibly can. I promise.

Why? Why do you want to help me?

Remember that night I saw you for the first time with Robert and John?

Yes. I do.

I couldn't stop thinking about your eyes. Until this very moment, I knew something was going on. But didn't think it was this bad. I wanna look at your eyes again. In person.

I didn't know how to reply. I had opened up to Adam more than I had with anybody else and he still liked me?! Was this a sick game? Were Robert and John in on this as well? Was I going to get beaten up tomorrow in that dumb Audi from hell? How was I going to know if Adam was really genuine about helping me?

Maybe you should create a secret email or a Facebook account with a fake name and communicate with me there? I don't want you to get in trouble because of me. I don't want John to hurt you.

That was all I needed to see and read. I knew Adam was being honest and not playing any sick games.

That's a really good idea. Let's delete this thread.

Yes, let's. And Louie, promise me that you'll think about moving out here?

I will.

Chapter Sixteen

W<small>E STAYED IN THE</small> country for a few more days. Each minute I spent there, the walls closed in tighter, until the property became a prison, both physically and mentally, binding me with the memories lurking behind every corner, waiting to pounce and mock me. I could hear my childhood laughter, feel the warmth in my chest from the joy and games, and then I felt the glaring absence of any such light in my current life.

I walked through the hallways of the country house, trudging my feet, not really trying to get anywhere in particular. When it was time for a meal, I would pull myself toward the dining room, always arriving last. Once I stopped in front of the bathroom door, looking wistfully down at the reflective marble floors in front of me.

I could hear the footfalls of children, and I almost smiled as I recalled one of our most intense shenanigans. There was a whole horde of us— me, my brother, Robert, and all of his brothers, and our other friends. Our parents had sent us off to the country home early in the morning, saying they would join us after they were done with work for the day. Of course, all of that went in one ear and out the other. All we really knew was that we were alone—except for the staff of course—in this big playground of a house. Suffice to say, we immediately got to work.

Like all little kids, we liked to play war. The game looked different every time we played it, but the principles were always the same. We had to get the other team. What "getting them" meant depended on our surroundings and available weaponry, and on that occasion, we had the whole house and kitchen at our disposal.

The teams were the USA and the UK—they were the countries that fought all the wars after all. Robert and I were the UK, because, well, England had a Queen, and at the time that was much cooler than a President. I was Queen Elizabeth and Robert was Princess Diana. We even grabbed a few pieces of jewelry out of my mom's room upstairs to look more royal.

It was by far the most elaborate and drawn-out game of war we had ever played. The fruit became grenades, the candy became bullets, pillows and loaves of bread were swords, and eggs were our artillery.

"Fire in the hole!" I screamed.

"Roger that! Fire!" Robert shouted back.

We let loose the end of the slingshot, and four large brown eggs shot out, soaring across the living room. They plastered themselves against the back of the red leather couch. My brother poked his head up from behind the couch, surveyed the damage, and shouted out.

"Return fire! Go, go, go!"

Then came a volley of M&M's, bundled in muffin wrappers and sealed with a rubber band. They exploded as they slammed into the floor at our feet, showering us with bright specks of chocolate.

"Retreat!" Robert screamed. "Fall back to Fort Victoria!"

The kitchen counter was our fort, and there we endured a brutal barrage of eggs, pears, and dates.

"Charge!" My brother yelled in an overly dramatic Texan accent. "Come on boys! Fix bayonets! Charge!"

But we were lying in wait with our secret weapon—a full bottle of ketchup, primed and ready for action in close quarters. Into the kitchen they came, and at that moment we stood and unleashed a bright red stream upon our enemies.

They turned to flee back to the living room and we pursued, painting smiley faces on Bill Clinton's back as we chased them all the way outside and down the hill to the edge of the pool. We were about to accept their honorable surrender when one of the staff appeared, flush in the face, fists clenched tightly together.

"What time are your parents going to be here?" she asked as calmly as she could.

"I dunno," I answered, my ketchup gun still aimed at my brother.

"They just said later," my brother added.

"Yeah, later," Robert chimed in. The three of us were very proud of our answers.

"Do you mean later today?" she asked back, and if I had been older, I would have noticed the vein popping out on her left temple.

"Yeah, they said they had to work," one of our friends added.

"Mama said dinnertime," my other friend said. "I think."

The housekeeper looked at us with pale anguish. No doubt she wanted to turn us upside down and spank us, but obviously she couldn't without being fired and sent back to Egypt in a blink of an eye.

One thing she could do though was remind us of our parents' wrath. They were coming later that day, and nothing we could say or do would spare us from the colossal shitstorm if they found the house in its war-torn condition.

In the space of a few moments we turned to complete panic. The scene became like a children's cartoon, all of us running and yelling and trying our best to get the house back in order. We weren't used to cleaning up our own messes, so we weren't very good at it, but the thought of my dad and mom walking in the door while there were lines of ketchup snaking through the hallway and egg yolks drying against the back of the couch was enough to make us try.

Of course the staff did most of the work, but they still stuck sponges in our little hands and ordered us about, and we did the best we could in the space of a few hours to restore the property to the pristine condition that our parents were expecting upon arrival.

Some of the rugs were beyond saving, at least that afternoon, and the staff brought in spares from somewhere, rushing the ketchup- and chocolate-stained articles off the property. It was a mad rush of scrubbing and scolding, but somehow we restored the house to its original condition.

When the cleaning was done, we sat on the kitchen floor laughing, and then the staff posed us in pool chairs with lemonade just as our parents' cars pulled into the driveway. One of the housekeepers gave me a big wink as we heard the car doors shutting in the courtyard and our parents' voices floating out. Those were the good times.

Then I blinked, and the memory was gone. I was alone in the wide hallway, dreading going any further. I was miserable. I wanted to die. But I went to the dinner table and poked at my rice, pretending to eat so nobody would say anything.

After a few more days we packed the car and got ready to leave. I could tell that my brother and dad didn't want to go, that they were enjoying this little vacation from the city. I didn't care where I was. John would find me anywhere, he had shown that time and time again, and I had grown to accept it. Everything was futile. I wished I were dead.

One of the staff shut the trunk, and the rest waved goodbye as we pulled away, my dad drove this big lazy loop around the courtyard to get pointed the right way down the driveway. Out of my window, I could see the ATVs in their covered spot, still blanketed with tarps, and I thought of the rides I would take with Robert all around the property.

I thought about how happy we used to be, blasting Britney Spears while tearing down the dirt trails, and how, after our rides, we would sneak upstairs to give each other facials with my mom's imported products after fixing one another's eyebrows. I thought of the sounds of my brother and his friends floating through the windows from the soccer field as Robert and I did each other up, and my whole being longed for those simpler times.

But that era was gone, and it was not coming back, so I bit my lip and shut my eyes, and endured the ride back to the capital.

"Louie," my dad said as we drove into the city, and I looked up from pressing my head against the window.

"Yeah?"

"That friend of yours," he started, and my heart dropped into the bowels of my stomach as I waited for him to continue. "Who you carpool with," and my anxiety slackened, though it lingered.

"Yeah?"

"Is he still going to pick you up this week? Or should I have Ron drive you?"

"Yeah, he's still going to pick me up," I said weakly. A week ago, I would have felt as if I had dodged a bullet, but now I didn't feel much of anything.

"All right," my dad said. Then, as if it were a thought that just strolled through, he said, "that's a good friend."

I couldn't reply. John was one awful human being. He certainly wasn't a friend. Eventually we were home, and I went up to my room where I could think about jumping off my balcony in peace. As I lie there, idly ruffling my sheets, I thought of the old movies where the imprisoned princess would make a rope out of bed sheets and escape some perilous circumstance. My eyes moved between my sheets and balcony with this new train of thought.

A short drop and a sudden stop. That's what they said in those old Westerns. Hanging might be my best option, one that I had never considered, and one that had been in front of me the entire time. I mulled it over as I fell asleep. There was a lot more to consider before that train pulled away from the station.

I spent that Friday, the day after we got back home, contemplating hanging myself. I hadn't heard from John since that first day in the country, and I would have just as soon been dead before he called me again. But my brother was home, and I couldn't leap off my balcony with him around. It would have destroyed him, and that I couldn't do. He was innocent of everything, and I didn't want to drag him into it. At least, that's what I told myself as I stood on my balcony with a rope of sheets anchored to the baluster. Then on Saturday, a new dam broke, and a wholly different river forced its way into the house.

My aunt had heard about my suicide attempt. How, I wasn't sure, but it wasn't too surprising. News traveled fast among the Kingdom's wealthiest families, and one way or another she had heard the story. I had branded it an accident, but everyone knew that was bullshit.

It wasn't often that our house phone rang, and my first thought was that John had gotten bored of me and was going to spill the beans for fun. I thought of my rope, ready to go at a moment's notice, as I sat in the kitchen and watched my dad answer the phone.

I watched his face contort into anger as he listened, and then he began shouting back, and within a few words I knew it wasn't John.

"How dare you call here!" he shouted, nearly foaming at the mouth. "You are not a part of this family any longer! I forbid you! Forbid you from calling us again. You are not to speak with him, never again, I forbid it!"

He slammed the phone back down on the receiver, angrier than I had ever seen him, and as he turned he saw me sitting at the counter, pointlessly poking at my cereal. He looked flustered, as if I had caught him as a child chucking eggs against the leather couch.

"Who was that?" I asked.

"Nobody," he answered, trying to pull himself together. There was sweat on his temples. I had never seen him sweat, not even during the hot days of July and August. He always seemed composed, collected, a machine of a man, but at that moment he was rattled like a fox that had been caught in a hunting trap.

"Nobody," he said, turning away and reaching for his sunglasses. "I'll see you later." I watched him go, and soon I heard his car burning out of the driveway. The second I heard that, I walked to the phone, disabled the caller ID, and redialed.

"Hello?" the voice on the other end said.

"Auntie!" I exclaimed, recognizing that safety blanket of a voice anywhere I heard it.

"Louie!" she exclaimed. "Sweetie, are you okay? How are you?"

"I'm fine," I said, trying not to burst into tears. "What was all that about?"

"Nothing, honey, nothing," she replied, and I could hear the tears she held back with every breath. "Just, just come see us when you can, all right?"

"I'm on my way," I said back, "is that all right?"

"Sure honey," she said. She was crying now, I could tell. "Come on over."

It took me a few minutes to find my car keys since I hadn't driven in a while, but I eventually got into my Volvo and cruised over to my aunt's house. On the way I passed the place where I had wrecked my mom's car, and I stifled back a few tears.

My aunt was waiting for me on the steps, the way she always did, and I felt a rush of warmth when I saw her. She bustled over to the car as I parked, and the second I emerged from my seat she swamped me with a huge hug. She was already crying as she took me into her embrace, and as I felt her grip around my shoulders tighten, I began to cry as well. I was so sick of crying, but in that moment it felt right, so together we bawled in the driveway.

She took me into the house where we had some tea and talked about everything except my suicide attempt and our family drama, or John. It felt so good to have a moment in life where I could pretend nothing was wrong, and that I was just visiting with my caring aunt.

But nothing good can ever last, and about an hour and a half into my visit my phone rang. It was my dad. Immediately I felt panic rising, as I nearly always did. I didn't want to answer it. I felt like he knew where I was, and that I would receive hell for it, but my aunt gently put her hand on mine and nodded to the phone. I answered.

"Hey," I said shakily, trying to hide my nervousness.

"Louie," he said, as if he didn't know who he had called. That was typical of people his age.

"Yeah?"

"Those messages," he said. "I found out where they are coming from."

"Where?" I asked, but in the space it took me to say one word I felt myself leave my body. My soul floated to the ceiling, and I looked down at my terrified husk. It was all over. Everything would flood out now, nothing was safe, I was exposed, and my life was over. Good thing I had the rope ready. When I got home, I was going to use it, before the ridicule of my family and the entire society set in.

I watched myself respond to his answer. I didn't know what it was until I settled back into my body, but I saw from afar that it was not the world-ending news I was expecting.

"All of the messages come from an internet cafe downtown," he answered. "This scumbag hides his tracks well. Are you sure you have no idea who it is?"

"I'm sure," I answered, "Just some scumbag probably. Waiting for me to pay them to make it stop." Slowly I began to reinhabit my body.

"That's what I thought too," he said in reply. "I'll let you know when I find out more."

There was a strange relief that coursed through me. I truly had no idea who was behind all of those hateful messages, but finding out seemed like a death sentence. Whoever they were, they had to know I was gay. Why else would they target me? They knew I had something to lose.

My hands were shaking as I hung up the phone, and I remembered where I was. My aunt was looking at me with deep concern, and she gently set down her teacup.

"What's going on, sweetie?" she asked, and in her voice was a gentleness I hadn't heard for what seemed like eternity. Crying, I told her all about the rumors and the fake profiles and the hateful messages. She brought me in for a hug, and I sobbed into her shoulder. I hadn't experienced compassion for so long, I had forgotten what it felt like, and I bawled and heaved for breath as I expelled every bit of emotion I had. But that reprieve was short lived, because tomorrow was my first day back to school, and my routine of lonely pain started back up in force.

John picked me up every day, and almost always wanted a blowjob. When I had first met him, he was a cool, suave, outlaw figure. Now when I looked at him, I saw a walking bag of bile, stinking of rot and despair, and he sickened me.

When he pushed my head down in the car, I threw up all over him, his pants, and his leather seat. Smack. He hit me so hard the left side of my vision blurred out, and all I could see were flickering specks of light. People call it "seeing stars" but it's more like a fracturing of one's vision. Smack. He hit me again, then once more, then growled at me.

"Clean this shit up."

That became my go-to. Every time I puked on him, he hit me harder, but it was better than having his dick in my mouth. Every night I would slink back to my room, my head throbbing with pain, and I would take long looks at my balcony. My rope was still ready, stashed on the top shelf in my closet.

One day it was pouring rain when John picked me up. I could tell he was in a bad mood. There was a darkness—more than usual—hanging over his brow, and his face was hooked into a hawkish frown.

"Hey," I mumbled, flopping into the passenger's seat. He didn't say anything at first, and the sound of the rain filled the silence as the weather intensified.

"I'm pissed off," he said eventually, pulling away from the university's steps. I thought he might say more, but instead he just clenched his jaw. I was terrified, and I shrunk as far as I could into the corner of the seat.

He drove for a little bit, winding down into a residential area not too far from the university, and finally pulled up alongside a tall condo building under construction. There was nobody around, and the rain had reached its peak, pelting down in torrents. The sound of the huge drops slapping the slick black roof was nearly deafening.

"A blowjob would really make me feel better," he said finally. "But I don't want to deal with your bullshit."

I didn't reply. I thought he was finally going to kill me, and there was a small part of me that was ready for it. About fucking time. I was done.

"Get out of the car," he said.

"The rain—" I answered feebly, not understanding.

"Get the fuck out," he snapped, reaching over me to open the door. It swung open and the curtain of rain shouted louder, screaming at me to stay in the car, but before I knew it he had kicked me from my seat and I landed cheek down in a streaming puddle, the rain striking so hard it looked like a boiling pot of water.

I pushed myself up, looking back as the passenger door slammed shut behind me. John rolled the window down a bit and looked at me with those cold, vampire eyes.

"Start walking," he said.

"What?" I asked, blinking, and trying to rub the rain out of my eyes.

"Start walking," he repeated, and he began to roll the car forward. "If you walk far enough, you can get back in."

I struggled to put together what was happening until the car was a good four yards ahead of me, then I hurried to catch up. My feet slushed through the wide puddles of the dirt, and the rain poured over my eyebrows and down my face. I trudged after him, never quite catching up before he kept rolling forward.

He led me out of the residential area and down the street, the storm worsening and the thunder roaring as my hot tears met the cold rain on my chin. He led me around like that for nearly two miles before finally letting me in, a towel already draped over the seat. He drove me home in silence, and just as he was about to let me out at the gate he turned and said, "That made me feel better."

When I got to my room, I stripped off my wet clothes, letting them fall on the bathroom floor. I was freezing, and felt a cough welling up in my chest. I went to my closet and reached for my homemade rope, threading one end around my bed's leg and fixing the other around my neck.

I dragged my feet toward the balcony, the rain still pelting outside, and was about to slide open the glass when my laptop signaled a new Facebook message. I knew it was probably bullshit, but curiosity dragged me over to my desk, the sheets still tied around my throat.

It was Adam, and I smiled.

Hey how's it going over there?

What's your email? I shot back, and as I waited for his reply, I created a new email address, one John could never know about. When he messaged me back, I copied his email into the address bar, and told him everything that had happened that day, but I left out the fact I had a noose hanging loosely around my collarbones.

Then I paused, looking down at my laptop. John was going to look through it eventually, he always did. In a panicked rush I signed out of the account and deleted my browser history. I had to play this smart.

I took the sheets off my neck and threw on some sweatpants, ruffling my hair with a towel so it looked like I had just taken a shower. I crept downstairs to my dad's office and found nobody around. My brother's car out front told me he was home, but he was probably gaming on his computer with those big headphones on.

I logged back into my new email account on my dad's desktop, and emailed Adam a few more times. I found myself smiling each time a notification popped up with a new email from him. There was nothing joyful about the correspondence. I was recounting habitual rape and emotional abuse, but he was listening, and that in itself made me feel better than I had in more months than I could count.

Adam's last email that night read, *Start saving for a plane ticket. You have to get out of there.*

I was sick as hell for the next two weeks, coughing and dragging my heels everywhere I went, but I kept talking to Adam on a daily basis. I only logged in from my dad's computer, and always deleted the pages from the history.

I started taking cash out of my dad's wallet when he left it sitting on the kitchen counter or on his desk in his office. Only a little bit at a time, so as to not arouse suspicion, but within a few weeks I had about six hundred dollars squirreled away in my closet, sitting in a neat pile next to my homemade noose. That little shelf was my way out, one way or another. Somehow, the thought comforted me.

My mom had left me a good chunk of money, but it was all wrapped up in a trust that I couldn't access until I was thirty. I didn't completely believe I could escape. John was more than just my tormenter, he was a phantom, a supernatural being that I could neither outsmart, nor escape from. He was everything to me, in the worst way imaginable. Still, I stole and saved the cash because Adam had told me to. I didn't want to disappoint him.

The rumors and messages were constant, and it almost seemed like they were escalating. They would flood in when I was sitting with school friends, and they would all look at me in shock, but see that I wasn't the one sending them. Robert started spreading the rumor that I was paying someone to send them when I was with friends so I could look innocent. I tried to tell him how ridiculous that sounded, but he didn't hear a word I said, he had made his mind up.

On the second anniversary of my mom's death I went to visit her in the cemetery. Part of me expected her to have been moved again, but as soon as I entered the space, I could make out her memorial on top of the hill.

As I approached, I saw spray paint scrawled on the base. Frowning, I got a little closer. When I read it, I was more confused than angry. It didn't make any sense to me—yet. It was just a few words, slanting up diagonally from the lower left corner. In large, blotchy, red letters, it read: *LOUIE IS GAY.*

Chapter Seventeen

THE CEMETERY WAS STARK and quiet while I stared with a dumb face and a slack jaw at the paint scrawled across the side of the gravestone. The paint shone in the light, and when I leaned in, I saw that it was still wet, dripping down from the bottoms of the letters. As I moved closer, I caught the smell of a cigarette, and I saw a few tendrils of smoke snaking up from the grass.

I wouldn't have paid it any more mind if it hadn't been a Parliament. I recognized that strange hollow end of the filter from all the stubs sticking out of John's ashtray. Confused, I made a ruffled face and twisted the cigarette cherry into the dirt, and while I had my head down, I heard a rapid rustling of leaves, combined with a hurried grunt.

There was a man by the fence, struggling to haul himself over the four-foot-tall, vine-entangled chain link. He had some kind of dark hoodie on, and his backpack rang out with the jingle of paint cans as he tried to get his left leg over the top.

"Hey!" I called, taking a step forward. "Hey!"

He kept fumbling, getting his torso over the top, shooting a quick hooded glance my way before turning back.

"Hey! Stop!" I yelled, stepping faster now, almost marching. "Stop!"

He gave another grunt and flopped over the other side of the fence. I broke into a run, crossing the last hundred yards to the barrier while he stood up on the other side, and opened the door to a hulking white SUV that was sitting there waiting for him.

He threw the backpack in the passenger's seat, jingling all the way, and hurried around to the driver's side just as I reached the fence.

"Fucking stop!" I screamed, planting my hands on the top of the fence just in time to see him peeling out and speeding away.

It was as nondescript as a car could be in the capital—a clean, white SUV with tinted windows. There were probably one of those for every five people in the city. Hell, even my shithead cousin had one parked in our compound. The only distinguishing mark I could make out was a small circular sticker on the back windshield.

I watched the car speed down the little road along the side of the cemetery before it disappeared with a screeching left turn and was gone. As I stepped back from the fence, I realized I was sweating and panting, my heart was racing. I was seething, feeling anger now in place of intrigue.

Defeated, I trudged back up the hill to my mom's grave. Standing there, looking at the graffiti, I replayed the car driving away over and over. Why didn't I move faster? I could have caught that fucker. Who the hell would do this? I stuffed my hands in my pockets to stop them shaking as I took deep breaths, reading the line again and again. *LOUIE IS GAY.*

I stood there for a long time, kicking the cigarette butt around with my shoes. My left hand wrapped around my Xanax supply inside of my pocket, my thumb hovering on the lid's release tab.

The sound of a car broke through the stillness of the cemetery, and I looked up to see my aunt's car coming down the loop. My thumb came off the lid. Suddenly I was in a panic. I had to do something. I couldn't let her read that. I frantically started scrubbing at the paint with my hands. Most of it had dried by then, but the bottoms of a few letters came up in a big smear, obscuring most of the lettering as the stone scraped my palms.

"Go away!" I grunted at the words, scrubbing at it with my fingernails.

"Louie?" My aunt was walking up to the grave now. She had a huge bundle of flowers and a confused look on her face. "What are you doing honey?"

"I—" I tried to answer but couldn't, and I fell back onto the grass, nodding to the paint-smeared mess on the gravestone. "I was trying to clean it."

My hands were shaking again, and I looked down at them to see my fingertips were cut open and bloody.

"Oh, honey," she said in her controlled, calm tone, "What happened?" she asked as she set down the flowers and crouched beside me.

"There was a guy, a guy with spray paint," I mumbled, still looking at my hands. "I was trying to clean it."

"We're gonna get this sorted, don't you worry," she said softly, placing a hand on my back. "It's all right."

"Okay," I whispered back.

She got her phone out and made a call. A little while later one of the caretakers showed up with a bucket and a sponge and scrubbed away the paint. I sat there until it was clean, holding my hands in my armpits to hide all the smeared blood and paint on my fingers. Then I went home, took some Xanax, and fell asleep before dinner.

When I woke up, I had a pleasant surprise waiting for me. A text from John read, *Going out of town for the week. Behave yourself.*

A week to myself! That was worth a quick smile. Then I felt the pain in my fingers and looked at the damage I had done the day before. The smile turned into the frown as I washed them and wrapped my fingertips with band aids.

For that week without John I felt almost whole. He still lingered over me in everything I did, but being able to talk to Adam whenever I wanted and drive my own car was like an elixir for my soul. I told him all about my mom's grave, and he said:

Damn, man, I'm so sorry. That's awful.

It's okay. I replied. *It's cleaned up now.*

But you saw the guy who did it?

Just for a second. He jumped over the fence.

Why would they do that?

I don't know, I don't really care. I'm just happy to have all week to myself.

You know, now would be a perfect time to get away. He's gone all week?

Yeah.

You need to just go to the airport and come over here. Now's your chance.

I don't have enough cash saved, I replied, and I frowned a little bit. I probably did have enough cash tucked away up by my noose for a one way across the Atlantic, but something in me wasn't ready to run. The idea of running away was a grand one, an exciting one, but it was also daunting. I hated my family, I hated John, and I hated the Kingdom. What was stopping me? Running away was the only thing that really made sense.

Yet, just as it was my salvation, it was also a cliff. If I jumped off into the unknown, I could never get back here. Everything I knew would be gone, and I would be truly on my own, and while that was the whole point, it was also what was stopping me.

How much longer do you need?

I don't know.

You have to be careful. If he finds out you're going to leave he's going to snap.

Yeah.

Pretend to submit, make him think he won to get his guard down. Then you can get away when he's not expecting it.

You think he'll believe me?

It's all he wants right? He'll believe you.

I decided to give Adam's idea a try. It made sense, and it wasn't far from the truth. I was already a husk of a human, subject to John's sadistic will. If I leaned into it, I might escape a few beatings and keep a low profile until I was ready to run. If I ever did.

The first night that John was back in town he picked me up and took me straight to his dad's office building. It was clear what he wanted. I could practically hear him salivating in the elevator. I heard him click the lock on the office door behind us, and before I could turn around, he had his hands on the back of my neck, pushing me toward the flat of the desk.

"All right, hold on, it's fine, just don't hit me," I said, squirming under his grip. He stopped in his tracks, his hands still tight on my neck and my head.

"What?" he sounded confused.

"Why are you doing this?" I asked, looking forward at the big office windows and the city beyond. "You can do whatever you want, just don't hit me."

"Don't you get it?" he growled. "I own you. If I can't have you, nobody can."

"I—" my voice cracked as I tried to get the sentence out. "I'm not going to leave you."

He was silent for a minute. I had thrown him off. Adam was right.

"Then you have to earn my trust," he finally answered. "Take off your pants."

"All right, it's fine," I said back, dropping my jeans. "It's fine," I repeated as he pressed my face against the cold top of the desk and fumbled with his belt. After he was done, he went over to the mini bar, took a shot of something, and gave a little woot while I slowly pulled my pants back up.

"Let me see your texts," he ordered, holding out his hand.

"Sure," I whispered, zipping up my jeans. I handed over my cell phone and he scrolled through the messages. There wasn't much for him to look at, just a few random texts from my dad, brother, and a few people from school. I only talked to Adam through my new email account, and only from my dad's computer. When he was satisfied, he tossed the phone back to me and said, "Good. Now let's go. I want to meet Omar for a drink."

He locked the office, and I followed him out of the main door. Then weeks went by, and before I knew it, Christmas was in full swing.

My dad and my uncle went all out that year. They hired some decorating company to turn our compound into a winter wonderland, minus the snow of course. The guys setting it up took all day, stringing line after line of lights along our gutters and the top of our wall. They wound lines of lights down the bars on our gate, striped like a candy cane. There were huge inflatable snowmen around the edge of the pool, model reindeer on our roof, and half of a Santa Claus sticking out of one of the chimneys. All along the base of the wall there was a procession of little elves, carrying all sorts of classic toys. It made me want to puke when John dropped me off that night, all lit up and garish.

Christmas meant something when my mom and I decorated the tree together. We had fun and laughed about the ornaments she had from two decades ago. Christmas was alive when my mom woke us up at 7:00 a.m. on Christmas Day and we rushed down to the tree and opened our presents. Christmas came to life when she baked cookies and showed me where to leave them with that glass of milk for Santa. After her suicide, Christmas died.

We had a small gathering with everyone in the compound for Christmas Eve. I was fidgeting the whole time, wanting to explode every time a new Christmas song came on the stereo. It was undoubtedly worse than last Christmas. We were all gathered in the grand living room, clustered around the extravagant tree, pretending to be some sort of typical family. Cigarette smoke floated up toward the star on the treetop and ice gently clinked against the sides of glasses.

My two youngest cousins were giggling about something on their phones, probably one of those dumb chain texts that they found so amusing. My brother was snacking at the kitchen bar, popping stuffed olives into his mouth every few minutes. My dad, uncle, their sister, and my uncle's wife were in their half circle of chairs, smoking and chatting away. I sat silently, shifting uncomfortably in my seat.

Eventually I got fed up and started up the stairs. When I was about halfway up my oldest cousin, Nathan walked through the room, looking up from his phone as he went. As he glanced around I caught his eye. There was something cold and strange in his gaze, and I felt unsettled by his energy. After half a second, he broke eye contact and continued through the living room.

I hurried up the stairs, feeling my heart racing from that icy stare. I needed air, so I stepped onto the second story balcony that looked out over our courtyard. The whole place dazzled with light from the overabundant decorations, and I winced. It was almost brighter in the courtyard than it was indoors.

I heard the front door shut below me, and I looked down to see my older cousin step out onto the front patio. He lit a cigarette and leaned against a post almost directly beneath me, smoking silently for a few seconds then pulling his phone back out of his pocket. Whatever he was waiting for had arrived, because after glancing at his phone he tossed his mostly intact cigarette and walked briskly to the gate. A car pulled up out front. It was black, and its headlights were bright LEDs, but that's all I could make out from where I stood. Something about it made me shiver again as I watched my cousin go through the gate, get in the car, and disappear. After that I went back inside and lay around my room until everyone left.

Christmas was relatively quiet, but not New Years. My dad threw a massive party for the whole family, distant relatives and random friends included. I felt claustrophobic in that huge house and went up to my room several times to get a moment of peace, but even there I felt trapped. Eventually I had to step outside, so I slipped out the back and started slowly walking the perimeter.

The noise was inescapable, but I stuck to the shadow of the compound's wall, where there were no people. I was going to soak up as much of that brief reprieve as I could. Not that they wanted me in there anyway. Everyone had heard at least a few of the absurd rumors floating around on Facebook, everyone knew that I had been in the hospital for a drug overdose, and everyone knew that I had wrecked my mom's car. They looked at me with somber disdain, as if secretly they felt pity but enjoyed shaming me more than anything else.

There was a mass of cars squeezed into our courtyard, and others parked down the road outside of our gate, which sat open, its candy cane lights welcoming people in. My dad had opened up one of his garage doors and set up a few plastic tables for all the chauffeurs. I could see them all sitting around, laughing, smoking, playing cards, and I couldn't help but wonder how much better their lives were than mine, or those of my whole family for that matter. They looked genuinely happy, and I envied them bitterly, fairly certain happiness was a feeling I would never have again.

I kept walking around the property, killing time away from the crowd until John inevitably picked me up. I wanted to talk to Adam, but there were too many people everywhere for me to use my dad's office. I could tell he was frustrated and worried that I hadn't come to the States yet, but we still exchanged messages almost every day. For some reason he hadn't given up on me. I would have, a long time ago.

I leaned up against my cousin's white Escalade. He usually parked in the garage, but it looked like he had gotten home a little late and found a row of cars in his way. If I hadn't been so high, I might have scraped some of the paint with my jacket's zipper, just because he was a little fucker, and though I smiled at the thought of it, the actual deed required far more energy than I possessed.

John texted me. *On my way, be outside.*

Frowning, I tried to pull myself off the side of my cousin's car. I was higher than I thought I was, and I sort of rolled around from the side to the rear of the car, giggling to myself a little as I sat down on the rear bumper.

"All right," I mumbled. "Stand up." Pushing with my legs, I slid my back up the rear windshield, reaching out with my arms on either side to steady myself. I felt balanced after a few moments and took a breath as I pushed forward until I was standing.

But as I came away from the car, my left jacket sleeve stuck to something, and I heard that soft but distinguishable sound of something separating from a sticky substance. Puzzled, I ran my hand down my sleeve until I felt the small patch of gooey residue just past my elbow, and with a frown I turned to look at the car.

There was a small circle of dirt and dust stuck to the window, clinging to that sticky substance left behind when you tear off a sticker.

A sticker. My brain tried to put everything neatly into place, but I was high as a kite, and I was overwhelmed by what I was seeing. I thought of the car speeding away from the cemetery, the little sticker on the window, the sticker that wasn't on my cousin's car anymore.

There was a flash of movement in the corner of my eye, and I looked up at my uncle's villa just in time to see a shape disappearing from one of the second story windows. A cold dread dripped down my spine. What did this mean? Before I could make sense of it, John's car revved up to the gate, and he gave his horn a quick honk. I had to go.

When I told Adam about the sticker he was really concerned.

God damn it, Louie, you have to get out of there! He wrote.

But what does it mean? I don't get it! It's driving me crazy!

I don't know, but it's not good. Have you saved enough yet?

Maybe, I don't know. What would I do in Texas? I still have school. The longer I waited to run away, the more absurd the idea seemed. There had to be a way to fix things, to get John out of my life. I couldn't just leave my whole world behind, but I also couldn't tell Adam that, because I didn't want to let him down.

You would be safe here, he wrote back. I didn't reply, I didn't know what to say. After a few minutes, he sent another message, reading, *You could go to school here too.*

How? I asked. I hadn't thought about that before.

Transfer here, get a loan for tuition.

I don't know how to do any of that.

I do. I can help.

Okay.

Adam did everything. He told me what to send him, and what to get from my school. He filed all the admissions paperwork from his address in Texas so nothing would come to my house. It was too late for me to enroll in the spring term, so he signed me up for the fall semester. I still didn't know if I was going to go, but I got accepted.

The Facebook rumors and fake profile attacks spiked as February started, sending me down another Xanax spiral. For a few days I just stayed in my room until John came to get me, even missing some classes. I probably lost five pounds from not eating. A fake profile in my name and a few other fake ones bombarded my friend's walls with shouts about prostitution, sex trafficking, and heroine.

It got so bad that one of my friends' moms called the police. I was a few days out of my drug binge, and I had just showered and stepped outside for a few minutes when I saw the cop car pulling up to our gate. I saw the cop leaning out of his window, talking into the speaker, but the gate stayed closed. I winced as I heard my uncle's door open.

"What the fuck is wrong with you?" my uncle bellowed, marching across the courtyard in his bathrobe, his big hairy belly sticking out the middle. "You know why he is here? Huh?" he yelled, pointing to the police car that was pulling into the courtyard. "They are here for you!" Then he stomped over to the gate and let loose a string of curses at the cop, ordering him to leave. "You do not have permission to be here! This is a private road!" I heard him yelling.

Eventually the police car pulled a lazy U-turn and slunk away down the street, and my uncle turned back at me, his face bright red and cheeks puffed out from all his shouting.

"Is it your ambition to destroy our reputation? Is it?" he screamed. "You do nothing but shame us! You and your bitch mother!"

"Shut the fuck up!" I screamed back at him, stomping my foot. "Don't you ever mention her again you fucking pig! Fucking monster! You're a piece of shit! You talk about our family? You have a pedophile living in your house!"

"My family is a role model!" he shouted back, the veins in his forehead protruding like angry worms trying to reach the surface of his skin. "You are trash! Worthless!"

"Shut the fuck up!" I echoed again. I wanted to shout out everything I knew about Nathan. How he touched me when I was most vulnerable. How he tried to rape me when I was only six years old. I wanted to tell everyone in the Kingdom about the monster living only a few steps from where I lived.

In all our shouting we had failed to notice the gate swinging open, and both of us were oblivious to my dad getting out of his car until we heard him cry out.

"Enough!" and his command fell over the courtyard like a blanket, startling us both. Poor Ron, our chauffeur, stood by the driver's door with a blank look of shock. "Louie, go inside! Now!" my dad snapped.

"Fuck this family!" I yelled over my shoulder, slamming the front door as loud as I could behind me.

I was crying as I ran up the stairs, and in my haste, I tripped on the top step, smacking my knee against the marble floor. Still crying I limped into my room and opened my laptop on my bed. I knew I shouldn't log into my other email from my own computer, but I was so distraught I didn't care. I just wanted to talk to Adam, and I felt a pang of excitement when I saw that I had a message from him waiting for me. It read simply: *Louie, I think I have feelings for you.*

I was still crying when I read it, but I found myself smiling.

Chapter Eighteen

IRST, EXCITEMENT BOUNCED AROUND my chest cavity, like a pinball machine it just kept going, mixing in dashes of hope and sprinkles of romance. I read the line again, letting that pinball tear its course through layers of emotions, but soon it began to twist. Guilt and shame roared up, swallowing the good, and cast me into a nervous quagmire. My fingers were shaking as I typed out my reply.

I think I have feelings for you too, I wrote, *but this isn't a good idea. I'm a fucking mess, everywhere I go, shitty things happen. I don't want to get you involved with all of this. John is dangerous.* I sent the email and let out a few nervous sighs, tapping on the edge of the laptop's keyboard. I waited for about ten minutes, slowly assuring myself that Adam had finally bowed out, and that I would be left to languish in the Kingdom. It was probably for the best. I would have fucked everything up anyway. Running away? Who did I think I was? That shit didn't actually work in real life, no way. Then the blip of a new email shook me back into the present.

You got me involved when you told me what was happening to you, he wrote, *Things are bad over there, but once you get out here everything will be different. There, you're surrounded by evil people, here it would just be me. I know what I'm getting myself into. You need to get out of there as soon as you can.*

I smiled again reading his message. That excitement and hope returned, swirling up all sorts of random images of adventure and my flight from the Kingdom. This was real, this was going to happen. I was going to make it.

I know, I'm trying. But my dad has my passport and green card in his safe, and I don't know the combination.

Shit! Can your brother help you?

His are in there too, my dad keeps everything locked up.

I stared at my inbox for a few minutes while Adam figured out something to write back.

Finally, he sent: *Didn't John want to take you on a vacation somewhere? Like in Eastern*

Europe? Your dad won't suspect anything if you go on vacation, right?

Yeah, maybe that could work, I wrote, dreading the thought of going anywhere with John, but it did make sense.

You just have to be out here before August 10, so you have some time still.

I'll do my best, I replied.

A few weeks went by. Spring was just around the corner. Adam and I talked every day. We even figured out a few times in the week when he could call the landline at the house, and I would chat with him in the dining room about random nothings, and it always made me smile to hear the slight inflexions in his voice.

"You know," he said one day, "If you drop out before the semester is halfway over, you can get, like, a half refund."

"Wait, really?"

"Yeah, I just read that on your school's website. That would be enough for a plane ticket and some startup money."

"How much is tuition over there?" I asked, drumming my fingers against the dining table, scanning the courtyard through the large windows to make sure nobody would walk in while I was on the phone.

"A lot," Adam laughed back at me. "What do you think of that idea?"

"I could probably get it in cash, right?" I said.

"I am not quite sure. I don't know how schools over there go about that."

"That's a good idea," I agreed. "I'm failing all of them anyways."

In the middle of March, there was another flurry of Facebook activity. It didn't really hurt anymore, I had grown pretty numb to the online harassment, but it was still shitty when Robert called, screaming and cursing at me.

"What the fuck, Louie?" he bellowed over the phone. "What the fuck is this shit?"

I didn't even know what he was talking about until I flipped open my laptop. An anonymous profile with my name had posted a picture of my mom's grave with the LOUIE IS GAY graffiti and me standing next to it, captioned: *Robert helped me discover who I am. I am so lucky to have him as my boyfriend.*

"This is totally fucked up!" Robert screamed. "You can go and self-destruct all you fucking want, but leave me out of it!"

"Robert, you know this isn't me, right?" I protested. "This is the same shit that's been happening for a year now."

"Oh bullshit, Louie!" Robert snapped. "You're sick in the head, you know that? Even your mom fucking hated you, that's why she killed herself. You're a disgrace. Stop trying to ruin everyone's lives!"

"Fuck you! You're an asshole for thinking I would do such a thing! I have known you for almost eighteen fucking years!" I fired back. I didn't usually have the energy to argue, but he had gotten me all fired up. "You're a piece of shit, Robert, you can't even see what's going on around you. At least Adam loves me, and he's gonna—"

Fuck. I hung up the phone. I shouldn't have said that. I knew that Robert talked to John sometimes, and I had just put my whole escape in jeopardy. I felt like an idiot, so I took a some Xanax and went to sleep at one in the afternoon.

A few days later I was out with John. We walked back to his car from the cafe, and the second I shut my door John looked at me and asked, "So do you keep your passport on you?"

My heart may as well have just stopped. I was so terrified. I could only think that my slip of the tongue had undone everything, and that John was going to brutalize me in retaliation.

"No, my dad keeps it in the safe," I answered, trying to keep my playing nice voice on an even keel.

"Do you think you could get it for a trip?" John asked musingly.

"A trip?" I asked, my heart beating with increasing speed. This was it. It was all over.

"Let's go to Bulgaria," John said unexpectedly. It was a mixture of relief and dread. My communication with Adam hadn't been revealed, but John wanted to go to Bulgaria. What the fuck was in Bulgaria? "Ask your dad for your passport, we'll get tourist visas. Doesn't that sound exciting?"

"Yeah," I said, trying to steady myself. "It does." Exciting wasn't the way I saw it. Exciting to John was horrifying to me.

A couple of days later it was March 21. I remember that day specifically because of two things. It had been two years since I met John, and it was my second Mother's Day without my mom. I felt like the most miserable person on the planet. I wanted to go visit her grave, but I was petrified by the thought of encountering more graffiti. Instead I walked into her huge closet, still with all her clothes hanging like some fucked up snapshot in time, and I sat there and cried, dragging some of the plastic sleeves off her clothes so I could smell her, crying out for her, pleading for help.

The phone was ringing somewhere. "Sir Louie?" one of the housekeepers was calling out. The phone was for me. Fuck. I dragged myself off the floor of the closet and down the hall to the top of the stairs. "Sir Louie? Phone call for you," she said from the bottom of the steps, holding up the receiver like it was the Olympic torch.

"Thanks," I said, taking the phone and slipping out the back door. "Hello?"

"Hey, it's me," Adam said, and I immediately felt a shred of relief.

"Hey."

"I just thought today would be really hard on you, thought I'd call," he said. We chatted for ten minutes or so until I saw my dad's car pull up out front.

"Hey I gotta go," I said.

"All right, think of me today if things get tough."

"I will, love you," I said, and hung up the phone. The second I hit the button I felt my face flush. Had I really said that? I love you? Fucking idiot. I knew we had feelings for each other, but that was a step too far. He hadn't said it, I had just hung up. I was such an idiot.

I got a text from John: *Take yourself to school today, I'm busy. I'll see you tonight—be ready to earn my trust.*

I frowned. What did that even mean? Earn his trust? It's what I had been trying to do by playing nice, and I had no idea what he meant. Whatever it was, it couldn't be good, and I shivered.

I went to school, but I didn't go to class. Instead I went up to the admissions office and asked for a cash refund. The woman behind the desk glanced over my student profile on the computer, clicking a few things, and I saw her eyes go a little wide when she scrolled over what was probably my academic record. She didn't say anything else as she counted out my cash on the counter.

I couldn't believe how much money it was. She just kept stacking bills, counting them off. I lost track after she hit two thousand. Finally, I scooped up the money and walked out the door, feeling like I had won the lottery. Who knew school was so expensive? I had the money to move, now all I needed was my passport and green card.

I drove home and was surprised to see my dad's car still parked in the courtyard. He usually only stopped home for a few minutes at a time. I walked in, and he looked up over his newspaper, his brow furrowing.

"Didn't you just leave for school?" he asked.

"My first two classes are canceled today," I answered. At least I had gotten good at lying.

"Mm," he mumbled, glancing back down to the paper.

"You know," I said tentatively, tiptoeing my way into the subject. "Some of my friends from school were talking about going to Varna, Bulgaria this summer, for a vacation. I was wondering—"

I didn't even finish before he was out of his seat. He marched straight past me to his office and returned in a few moments with my passport. I was about to ask for my green card too, but I peeked inside the first page and saw it sitting there like a present under the Christmas tree.

"Thanks," I managed to mumble.

"It's good, you should take more trips," he said back. "See the world, enjoy yourself. You said Varna? You know your uncle has a house there. Here, I have a key," he went into a kitchen drawer and rummaged for a minute before he brought up a small keychain with a little info tag. "The address is there, have fun for once!" he clapped me on the back, smiled a little bit, and went back to his newspaper.

The day that had started so awfully was becoming one of the most hopeful days I had had in years. I had cash—a real pile of it—and I had my passport with my green card. My escape was a go.

Then the night came, and John picked me up. I was playing nice as much as I could, and I leaned over and gave him a kiss on the cheek after I swung my door shut. I could see it threw him for a loop. He sort of recoiled and frowned.

"What the hell was that for?" he snapped, looking at me blankly.

"I feel safe with you," I lied. "It's been two years, I feel like you protect me." He looked me up and down, confused, then smirked.

"We'll see how you feel after tonight."

"I trust you," I lied again. "I'm not worried." I was terrified.

"Well, all right," he grunted, shifting gears and pulling away from the front gate.

We pulled up to his dad's office building. I knew what was going to happen, at least I thought I did. We were silent in the elevator and up to the office door. As he clicked the key into the lock, I saw a shadow move behind the glass.

"Wait," I whispered. "There's somebody there, a janitor or someone."

"Shut up," he growled, dragging me by the arm. The shadow was gone when the door opened, and John dragged me inside. He tossed me up against the desk and I looked around frantically. I could have sworn there was someone else in the room, but I couldn't see anyone. "Put this on."

John handed me a thick blindfold, and I felt my panic rising. Just play it cool, I told myself over and over. Play it cool, and soon I'll be free. After the blindfold was in place I felt John moving my arms behind my back, then tying my hands together, then taking down my pants, then nothing. Fear overwhelmed me as I lay with my stomach against the desk in the dark, naked, and vulnerable.

Then all I could smell was this distinct cologne. It was strong and unique—it wasn't John's. Then it clicked as I felt a man behind me, forcing his way in. There had been another man in the room. This wasn't John. He was smaller and rougher, more hateful, and the smell of his heavy cologne was suffocating as I took ragged breaths, gasping for air until John's dick blasted through my lips, and then I was just trying not to vomit. I knew what would happen if I threw up. They shared me for an hour or so, though I have no idea how long it really was. It was the most violating and violent thing I had ever been forced to experience.

When the blindfold came off the other man was gone. I never even saw him. My body felt broken as I tried to get my clothes back on, each little movement hurting. I felt vulnerable. My mind was racing with thoughts, and I felt violated more than ever. My body was just a toy for John and that strange man. I felt like an object.

Neither of us said a word as we rode the elevator back down and started driving to my house. My thoughts were running wild. I wanted to grab the steering wheel and crash the car and kill us both. I wanted to scream and hit John as hard I could. I wanted this nightmare to end. I wanted my mom to tell me that everything was going to be all right. When we were almost there, John broke the silence.

"Good boy," he said, his hawkish eyes staring out over the steering wheel, the night lights dancing over his face in haunting patterns.

"I told you, you can trust me," I replied, trying not to throw up all over the seat, trying not to burst out in tears.

"Did you get your passport?"

"Yeah."

"You got it with you?"

"Yeah," I answered before thinking about it. Then I immediately despaired as I realized what I had done.

"Good, give it here," he said, holding out his hand without looking at me. I slowly pulled it out and passed it to him, feeling like a piece of me was dying as I relinquished my freedom. It vanished as quickly as it had appeared. When we got to the front gate, I smiled weakly.

"Have a good night," I whispered, gave him a quick kiss on the cheek again, and tried not to limp through the courtyard. I got up to my room, curled up in the shower, and cried. I fucking hated crying. It had been the most brutal violation yet, and all I wanted to do was grab the noose from my closet and toss myself over the balcony.

I felt like there was nothing else I could do. My life had been deeded to John and there was no escape. One stupid move, and I could end up either homeless or dead. Taking my own life felt very comforting. I felt like a plane running on reserve fuel while crossing the Atlantic. A skilled pilot would know how to land it gently on the water, but I was not one. I had two options: keep flying until I saw an island with a runway or say my peace and surrender to reality. But something was stopping me. An invisible force that kept injecting me with endurance and persistence. An invisible force that supplied my plane with fuel.

After dragging myself out of the bathroom, I grabbed for my laptop loosely, my fingers were weak. I wanted to say goodbye to Adam. It didn't matter if I was using my laptop anymore. No need to delete my history. It was all over. I flipped open the computer, and the first thing I saw was an email from him, reading simply, *PS I love you too!*

There was a flickering of hope in my world of darkness and agonies, in my decrepit dungeon of despair, and maybe that was enough to hold onto. Enough reason not to die right then. I curled into a ball on top of my blankets, and fell into a feverish, thrashing dream.

Easter was almost here. Our whole family, and I mean everyone, did a huge Palm Sunday brunch, taking up an entire convention room at one of the downtown hotels. There were second cousins, uncles once and twice removed, and whoever they brought along with them. Everyone was in designer suits and custom dresses, Italian shoes, and overpriced ties. All of the staff were invited too, from the whole compound, and their families. There must have been at least thirty tables set up in the room with elegant white tablecloths and expensive floral centerpieces.

I was mostly numb the whole time, experiencing all the surrounding conversation as a background buzz, sipping on ice water, and waiting for the Xanax to kick in. My phone lit up with a text, and I frowned as I read it.

In Bulgaria, I want you to wear diapers. What the fuck? I didn't understand. Another text. *And a pacifier.*

Okay no problem, I replied, shivering. I looked up and saw my cousin Nathan smirking at me from across the table. What was up with him? We hadn't spoken or interacted with one another since he touched me in my room at the funeral. I looked away, shrugging it off, and shut down for the rest of the day.

My birthday was the month after. It had been the worst day of last year, and there was no reason to think this year would be any different. I had a bunch of texts from friends, from my aunt and grandma who apparently called me before their flight to Beirut for the summer, and of course, from John telling me to go find the gift he left for me under the tree. Of course. I didn't want them, but I had to find them before anyone else did.

I threw on a shirt and some shorts and hurried down the stairs. I was almost out the door when I saw through the front window that my dad's car was gone, and I redirected to his office to see if Adam had emailed me. I was halfway down the hallway when I heard the maids frantically whispering to each other from the kitchen.

Poking my head around the corner I saw a pair of them clustered in front of the pantry, and they jumped when I stepped into the room. They looked flustered and embarrassed, as if I had caught them in the middle of something. Frowning, I glanced around the room and immediately saw a deflated red balloon. It stood out on the black counter like a flare in the night.

I marched out of the kitchen, my face reddening. My dad was throwing me a big classic birthday party. That was the last thing I wanted. Some gaggle of half-drunk chain smokers clapping me on the back. Was he trying to be caring? Fatherly? It was a little late for all that.

There were no new emails. I wanted to stand there and refresh the page for ten minutes, but I dragged myself away to grab John's secret present. There was a box under the tree, and I carried it up to my room under my shirt. In the box were diapers and a card, reading, *for Bulgaria, take yourself to school today.*

I was freaked out by the whole diaper thing, I didn't know what it really meant, but going on this trip was the only way to get my passport back, so I would have to endure it. Not wanting to leave the box laying around my room, I brought it out in my backpack and stashed it in my trunk. I had to pretend to go to school.

John had been dropping me off and I had mostly been walking around campus and sitting in the library on one of the computers until he came and picked me up in the afternoon. That day I had my own car, and it felt good to drive the long way with my windows open. I walked around campus a little bit and got some coffee, playing the role of student in case anyone was looking. I was watching people walk by from the cafe when I remembered the party. What if my dad had invited some people from school? They would know I had stopped attending classes. I began panicking, and hiked toward the engineering department at a bold pace.

Halfway there I stopped, realizing that none of my "school friends" had ever been to my house. I had never told anyone their names. They weren't even my friends, just people I talked to on campus and occasionally hung out with at bars or malls.

I was relieved and deflated by the realization, so I turned around and began dragging my heels toward the car, unsure what to do with myself. I got a text as I flopped down into the driver's seat, and was surprised to see it was from Joseph, that got a little smile out of me.

Hey Birthday Boy! You got time today for your favorite person? Dinner maybe?

Dinner sounds great!

5:30?

Sure, see you then, I sent. It was weird he wanted to have dinner so early. In the Kingdom you didn't eat until later, but it really didn't matter. I was excited to see Joseph, and I got out of my car and paced around campus for the rest of the "school day" in anticipation.

I was ready by 5:15, and he picked me up a few minutes early. He was all smiles and cheer, and it felt good to be around such positive energy. We drove to this Italian restaurant down the street from the American Embassy, got a nice little table and chatted for a bit, swapping family small talk before we got into the Facebook rumors.

"You know I got some of those," he said, doing a little flourish with his fork. "Some nasty shit."

"You know it's not me though, right? Because I—"

"Of course, buddy," he said, setting down his silverware. "Don't even fret it."

"You know Robert just thinks I'm fucking nuts," I griped. "He's telling everyone that it's me, and I'm just a psycho."

"I know, dude, let's just leave it lay," he said. "We both know the truth, that's gotta be enough."

"You're right," I said, shrugging. I hadn't eaten anything, I was still holding a shiny silver fork, and I realized I was gripping it so tightly my knuckles were white. Setting it down, I asked, "Is that why you've been distant lately though? The rumors? All the shit online?"

"Um," Joseph said, awkwardly shifting in his seat. He took a drink of his beer and said, "I don't want to hurt your feelings, Louie, you know, I guess I just felt like, well, like you only ever hit me up when you were in trouble, which is like, good you know, better than being in trouble, but well, you know."

"I'm sorry," I said, blushing and looking down. It was horribly embarrassing, but it was true. "I'm sorry Joseph, I didn't mean to be like that. You're right. I was just going through so much shit, you know, I—"

"Hey, it's all good," he said, giving his wrist a little flick. "I get it."

"I guess I just felt like I couldn't trust anybody except for you," I confessed.

"And you can trust me," he reassured me. "How are you doing now? Is everything all right?"

"Yeah," I lied. "Everything is cool now. I'm going to Bulgaria with John next month."

"Wow, back with John?" he said, raising his eyebrows. I shrugged and tried changing the subject. "This food is really good," I said.

"Yeah," he agreed, breathing slowly through his nose, "it is."

I ate a little bit of food, pushing it around to make it look like I ate more than I had. I didn't want to be rude, but I was rarely hungry those days. Joseph paid the tab and we walked outside, and I distinctly remember the American flag flying from the embassy.

It was backlit by a setting sun and bristled in the wind with a stiff elegance. It was my future, my escape, my new life, and in that moment, it was captivating.

"You coming?" Joseph called out from his car.

"Yeah," I said, shaking myself back to the present. "Let's go."

When we got within a few blocks of our compound I started seeing the parked cars, all up and down the street. I had a creeping dread as I counted them, imaging how many people were going to be crammed into my living room.

"Goddamn it," I whispered.

"What?" Joseph asked.

"All these cars," I said, "They're here for my party."

"Wait, you know about the party?" Joseph spat out.

"You were in on it too?!" I balked.

"Guilty," Joseph said, shaking his head. "I fucked that up. Your brother called me, but I still wanted to reconnect with you, you know? It was good."

"Stop the car!" I shouted, and he slammed on the brakes, lurching to a halt with a screech.

"What?" he barked, surprise all over his face as he looked around. "Was there something in the road?"

"No," I said softly. I couldn't keep it in anymore. I had said it myself, Joseph was the only person I could trust. "Listen, I have to tell you some stuff."

"Like what?" he asked.

"I'm only with John because he's blackmailing me," I said, and it all started tumbling out. "He's got a sex video of us, and he's gonna send it to my dad if I leave him. He rapes me, like, every day, beats the shit out of me, shares me with I don't even know who—"

"What the fuck!" Joseph shouted, reeling from the information. "Wait, what?"

"I didn't want to get you involved, you know? But listen, I have a plan, I'm running away to America—"

"Louie! Slow the fuck down! This is not okay! We—"

"Stop," I said briskly. "I don't want to cry right now. I fucking hate crying. Let's just drive to the house and pretend this fucking party plan worked."

We drove lazily toward the tall black compound gates, I could tell Joseph was freaking out because he had his hands squarely planted on the wheel, his knuckles white, and he couldn't say anything. We passed even more cars, and the compound came into view around the bend in the road.

"When we get in there, just act normal," I said, not fully aware of how ridiculous that sounded. I had been trapped in the cycle of abuse for so long, I was able to carry it in a way that Joseph couldn't figure out. In his mind he was reeling. "Joseph!" I hissed.

"What?" he asked, sounding surprised.

"Did you hear me?"

"What?"

"Just act normal," I said again, shaking my head as he parked by the front gate.

The courtyard was deserted and dark. I knew they were going to jump out when we walked in the door, and I gritted my teeth in anticipation. Joseph was straggling behind, pale with shock. He couldn't make sense of anything, and I guess I couldn't blame him. It was a lot to take in.

"Joseph!" I hissed. "Snap out of it, nobody got killed. It's my birthday. We have to act cool." He looked at me for a second with a blank face and then said, "How?"

"You just do," I shot back. "After a while, you get used to it." I turned to the door, straightened my collar, and walked into the "SURPRISE!" as lights went on and at least a hundred faces lit up.

"Fuck," I whispered as I faked a big smile. You can do this, I thought to myself.

I had to hug everybody, and it became a tedious process as I waded into the house toward the kitchen. I saw my dad clap Joseph on the back, chuckling about his plan working like a charm. My dad was all smiles, and Joseph looked like he was trying his best to match him. There were so many people, many of them that I hadn't seen for years, and for a few moments I was actually caught up in the whirlwind of it all, and even found myself smiling. I saw one of the maids from that morning and she gave me a wink, and that made me chuckle.

I was finally twenty-one. In all my misery I had forgotten what a milestone that was, and I realized it made sense for my dad to do something so extravagant. At least he was trying. It still wasn't going to stop me from running away. I didn't fit in. I didn't belong. My life had been hijacked and I was lost.

I had a sort of fun time for about an hour—I was able to have some drinks and a few fun conversations without thinking about John or my trauma for the first time in a long while. Then it all came crumbling down like the loose sandcastle it was at the first collision with a wave. That wave was my cousin Nathan. He had been strange to me lately, more than normal, and he made his way over to me just before we did the gifts.

"Twenty-one!" he cheered. "Well done," and he leaned in for a hug. "You're not the family baby anymore."

As he spoke into my ear I got two full nostrils of his cologne. It was that same haunting, dominating smell from the night with the blindfold, and I felt my stomach wretch as I quickly recoiled. He could see how thrown off I was, and he smirked as he stepped away from the hug, but I couldn't let him get away with it that easily.

"Family baby? Do you want me to wear diapers?" I shot back, feeling emboldened by the crowd and by the afternoon with Joseph and my impending escape. In a weird way, it felt like a victory.

He gave me a sour look while two people next to us laughed and began to slink away. "No, no, Louie, he said you're not the baby anymore!" one of them babbled drunkenly. I flashed them a smile and a chuckle and walked away.

I was still shaking from the encounter, but I was determined not to let it show. I wanted to scream and kick and punch and let the whole world know about the sick, twisted piece of shit in front of me. But it wasn't time for that, it wasn't the place. I had a plan, and outside of that, everything could wait. Of course, it was fucking Nathan. How else would John have targeted me in the first place? Where did it all come from? I always knew Nathan was a monster, but this was a whole different level of fucked. My mom was right, I would understand when I was older.

We gathered around the living room while gifts got handed over. I hate the gift portion of a party, it is always weird and dull and difficult to endure, especially in the moment. Everyone clapped when I opened the gifts, one at a time. I had a pile of gift cards, new shirts, and cologne. Every other gift was a repeat of one of those, and still everyone kept clapping. It was horrible. At least I could sell the gift cards for some extra escape cash.

I thought we had finally finished, and I was relieved the party would be over soon, but someone said, "Wait, there's one more on the table here."

"Oh, who's it from?" someone else said.

"No card," the first answered, handing it up the line. It was as if the gifts were more important to the audience than to me.

"Very exciting," a third person said, and the small square box wrapped in silvery grey paper was dropped in my lap.

I took up the corners and ripped away the paper. It was a box like you would get a bracelet in or something like that, and I was confused. Probably just another gift card. Then I lifted the lid and froze.

It was a fucking pacifier, sitting on top of neatly folded tissue paper.

"A pacifier!" Someone laughed.

"I suppose he is still the youngest," another chimed in, and the whole room laughed it off as a clever joke. I gave a little smile, as if I were in on it, but other than that I couldn't move. My eyes rolled across the room, scanning for Nathan, wanting to catch his reaction, but I couldn't find him.

He was gone. I stared down at the pacifier. John's gift had come in two parts.

Bulgaria. It was my only chance of escape, but it could just as well be my final doom.

Chapter Nineteen

THE WEEK FOLLOWING THE party was bleak and bland. Adam emailed me the day after and apologized for missing my birthday. *It's all good*, I told him, *don't worry about it.*

I saw Robert on campus yesterday, Adam wrote. *He was all pissed off.*

Yeah, he gets like that these days, I replied with a frown. *I can't really talk to him anymore.*

I was at one of the bars on campus, and he just came up all angry, yelling about you. He blames you for all that shit online. He was asking about us, you know, asking if you were really coming to the States.

What did you say?

I didn't really say anything, I just sort of left.

He's just trying to get you riled up, I wrote, *you just have to ignore him.*

Yeah, I am.

John picked me up the following evening to go on a drive. I tried to ignore the Robert stuff. I knew that bridge had been burnt for a long time, but it still nagged at me. He had gone from my best friend to whatever he was now. An enemy? No, it wasn't that extreme, but he certainly wasn't my friend, and it hurt.

"Did you hear anything I just said?" John barked, snapping his fingers in front of my face.

"What? Sorry, no, I—"

"Just shut up," he sighed, slumping further into the driver's seat, waiting for the light to change.

"Sorry," I mumbled again, waiting for the inevitable slap. Instead, he changed the subject.

"How was that birthday party? It was a surprise right?" he asked, seemingly out of the blue. "Did anything interesting happen?"

"How did you know I had a party?" I asked, trying to work it out in my head.

"Hard to hide all those cars out front," he answered. "I saw them when I drove past."

"Oh," I said softly, thinking of Nathan's cologne, and a shiver ran down my spine.

"Anything fun happen? Anything interesting?" John probed again. He wasn't going to let it go.

"No," I said, "It was just a party."

"Huh," John grunted, shifting out of neutral and continuing through the intersection.

We drove in silence for a while, winding up the hills back into my neighborhood as the last traces of the sun faded from the horizon. When we pulled up to my gate, he stopped the car, turned to me and said, "Just make sure you bring that pacifier to Bulgaria."

"I will," I whispered back, feeling those nerves rising for the millionth time.

"Good," he said with an abrupt nod. "All right, I'll see you tomorrow," and he switched the child locks off, letting me out of the car.

The last three weeks of school went by as I prepared for my journey. John still dropped me off and picked me up, so I spent a lot of time bumming around campus, dodging people I knew. I didn't want to talk to them, to explain anything, even if the explanations were a lie. It was too much effort. Mostly I sat in the library, hoping for an email from Adam while I browsed the website for the University of Texas. It was the only thing that mattered anymore. My way out.

The last day of school came and went. I had about a million missed calls from people I knew on campus, but that was fine, I would be gone soon enough. It was liberating, not to have to go to campus every day, pretending to be enrolled. It had gotten pretty old by then.

I spent the last week before Bulgaria lounging by the pool. I felt like I had been ready for months. Part of me wanted to talk to people, say goodbye to my brother at least, but I knew I had to act like everything was normal. It wasn't hard—I had gotten damn good at acting over the past two years.

Two days before I was supposed to leave, I saw Nathan's car parked in the center of the courtyard with the hatch open. One of the housekeepers was carrying a few small bags from my uncle's door to the car. Curious, I walked over to one of the nearby gardeners.

"Where's he going now?" I asked casually, trying not to sound suspicious.

"I heard them say something about Europe, sir, an expedition."

"An expedition, huh? In Europe?" I asked in a high pitch, raising my eyebrows. Nathan walked out the front door and headed for his car. He had a small but bulky bag slung around his shoulder, lined with little zipper pockets and a shiny stripe of protective aluminum, looking like a wedding photographer.

"I remember now, sir," the gardener said, scratching at his chin. "A camera expedition in Eastern Europe."

"Well let's hope he doesn't get eaten by wild animals," I joked softly, feeling a creeping fear. He wasn't the only one going to Eastern Europe. That night I emailed Adam, worried about the trip.

I think Nathan's going to be there, I wrote. *I saw him loading up his car this morning.*

Are you sure?

I don't know anymore, just a hunch I guess. Eastern Europe? Coincidence?

I know it's scary, he wrote back, *but you're so close. Do you have your ticket yet?*

I'm going to buy it the minute I get back. If I get Ron to pick me up from the airport, and tell John my dad sent him, he'll leave me alone. Then I can go back inside and buy my ticket and leave.

Got it all figured out huh?

I sure hope so.

Hope was the best I could do. I wasn't sure of anything—if I could make it through Bulgaria, or if I would have the courage to walk back into the airport and leave the Kingdom behind. It had all seemed so distant, so abstract, but now that the trip was here I was terrified. I couldn't escape the dread of failure, of which I was so accustomed. If I failed with this, I would be doomed. I probably wasn't going to live long enough to get a second chance.

We left for Bulgaria on June 15. I had a small backpack with my laptop and a suitcase of clothes. They sat in a neat pile by the door, and I listened to the ticking of the clock while I waited for John.

"Hey! You're taking off, huh?" my brother said, bouncing into the room with half of a sandwich in one hand.

"Yeah," I replied, my voice soft and pensive, "Just waiting for my ride."

"Have fun, man," he said, taking a bite of the sandwich and talking through a mouthful of food. "I'll see you later," and he started trotting up the stairs.

"Yeah," I echoed, "I'll see you later." Then he was gone from view, and my heart sank. I couldn't even give him a real goodbye.

"You have everything you need?" my dad asked, poking his head in from the kitchen. "You need any money?"

I almost said no, but I caught myself. More money couldn't hurt when I landed in Texas.

"Sure," I answered. "If you want."

"Of course," he said, and walked briskly to his office. He came back with what must have been close to a thousand dollars, folded into a little bundle. "Here, I want you to have fun."

"Thanks, Dad," I said, taking the money gingerly. I picked up my backpack and opened it. There was a little zipper pocket tucked up under the main compartment, and I slid the money in there next to my other wad of cash from the college, plus what I had saved and my green card. Glancing down at my stash, I was confident I had enough to get away and start anew.

"It's not a problem," he said, flashing me a smile. "Go on, have fun! Enjoy yourself. You have the key to your uncle's house?"

"Yeah, I got it," I said, hoisting my backpack over my shoulder. "I'll see you later."

"Goodbye, son," he said, holding the door open for me.

"Bye, Dad."

The door shut behind me. That was it. I was gone. I took a huge breath, trying to steady myself as I walked around to the trunk of my car. I shivered as I slid the diapers into my suitcase, glancing around to make sure nobody saw. What the fuck were they for? It was all sick. I wanted to throw up right there in the courtyard, but I was so close. I could make it through a weekend, even if it was a hellish one.

John picked me up outside the gate. I remember the heat from his tailpipe on my leg as I loaded my suitcase into his trunk and the smell of the fumes.

"You excited?" he asked, a devilish grin on his crooked face. "This is gonna be fun as hell."

"I'm excited," I lied, shutting the door as I settled into my seat. "It's gonna be great." It was going to be hell.

When we got to the airport John parked in one of the garages and handed me my passport. "No funny business," he said, coldly handing it over. "I get that back after we go through security."

"What about customs and immigration in Varna?" I asked.

"I'll give it back to you for that," he snapped. "Now let's go."

My panic spiked as the airplane lifted off. I was committed now. There was no getting out of this. Even if I didn't run, I was going to Bulgaria.

We got through customs pretty quickly. Whenever I traveled, unless it was to the US, the casualness of security always surprised me. The Kingdom had that shit locked down. They took everything seriously. The Varna airport, on the other hand, waved us right through.

We got into a rental car, and John demanded my passport. He threw it into his bag, zipped the compartment shut, and clicked one of those little luggage locks over the zipper. There was no getting it back, not until we landed in the Kingdom.

I checked my phone as we pulled out of the airport. No roaming. Of course. Leave it to backwater Eastern Europe to be out of my coverage area. This was going to be a long week.

We didn't say much as we drove. I leaned my head against the window and watched the rolling landscape wash by. There were goats everywhere. Where the hell were we?

"What hotel are we staying at?" I asked, looking at the world outside of the car.

"No hotel," John answered.

"What?"

"Look there," he said, pointing with one finger from the top of the steering wheel. "That's where we're staying."

It was a big house, modern with white walls and chrome accents, and sat on a hill overlooking Varna. It wasn't completely in the middle of nowhere, there were street signs and houses scattered around, but it was definitely a rich, secluded suburb.

"Whose house is this?" I asked, looking it up and down as he pulled to the side garage.

"I rented it from a vacation agency," he answered, bringing the car to a stop. "Got it for the week."

"Oh, cool," I said, my voice hollow. It was a big house, and the closest neighbor wasn't that close. I dreaded what would go on in there.

We brought our bags inside and settled in. The rooms were big, but I could tell the house was old, likely remodeled recently. I stepped onto the terrace to get a breath of air. It was a beautiful view as the sun set over the city and the Black Sea, and for half of a second I forgot my problems.

"You're my baby," John's voice came from over my shoulder, disgusting me, and his arms wrapped up around my torso.

"I am," I said back, clutching my vomit in my chest.

"That's right," he whispered into my ear. Then he withdrew suddenly and pulled the car keys out of his pocket. "There's food in the fridge if you're hungry. I'm going out."

"What?" I asked, blinking, but before I could get another word in, or an answer, he walked back into the house, scooped up his backpack with my passport in it, and walked out the front door. "Wait!" I called after him, running to the door, but as soon as I touched the handle I found it locked. "John!" I called again from the front window, but it was also late. I watched the rental car pull out of the garage and disappear down the block. "What the fuck," I whined.

I looked around the house from where I stood. The doors were locked. If I really wanted to get out I could jump off the terrace, but it was at least a fifteen-foot drop—not my best option. I started poking around, exploring the space, but I didn't find much of anything.

There were no pictures on the wall, but I saw little nails sticking out and little holes where others had been removed. Where were the pictures? Someone had taken them all down, but John and I had just gotten there. On the mantle over the fireplace I found marks in the dust from where pictures might have sat, but there wasn't a picture frame in sight. My phone was still without service.

"What the fuck," I muttered, cracking my fingers one at a time as that nervousness came back around. What kind of prison was this? Even thousands of miles away from the Kingdom, I was a captive. As long as I was with John, I would never be free.

Eventually I flopped onto the couch, frustrated and bored. I had no idea when John was coming back, or where he was. I just wanted to talk to Adam, to be in the States and away from all of this, but I wasn't there yet.

I tried to turn on the TV and frowned when it didn't work. Opening the cabinet underneath I noticed the TV's cord didn't go anywhere, and I was about to start fumbling to find an outlet when I spied the internet router.

I got excited. The internet was within my reach. Maybe I could talk to Adam, even figure out where I was. I plugged the router into the closest outlet and hurried to my laptop, powered it up, and tried to get on the network.

Password required. "Fuck," I spat, staring blankly at the screen. What was I supposed to do now? My eyes trailed from the computer to a box of cables and cords that stuck out of the cabinet I opened earlier, and I remembered my brother.

"No password with this shit," he had said, clicking the ethernet cable into the back of his machine. "It's a closed loop. Cable is the word."

I jumped up and tore through the box until I found a pale-blue ethernet cable. Within seconds I was online, and I felt good about figuring out a solution. It wasn't often I could give myself a win, no matter how small.

Adam had emailed me asking about the flight and if everything went off all right. I told him it was all fine, but that John still had my passport, and I was stuck in this empty, creepy house. We started chatting a bit back and forth, and my mood started improving quickly. Even if I was alone and locked in this weird house, I could talk to Adam and surf the web. That was plenty to pass the time.

I poked around the kitchen after I had started feeling better, and in between emails with Adam, I poured myself a few drinks. There may not have been any decorations, but the house was chock-full of liquor, and I got drunk pretty quickly.

Hours passed. Another drink. Another email. Another smile. This was the happiest I could get. John wasn't back, and it was getting late. I was starting to think I had the night all to myself. That was worth another smile, then another drink, and then another. I tried to make some food at one point, but I just ended up eating slices of cheese out of the fridge, curled up all drunk on the kitchen floor. I laughed at myself. I was the king of the world. More drinks. More Adam. More smiles.

I started getting drowsy, feeling my eyelids flutter as I poured another. Just one more drink, then I would go to bed. Ping, another email, another smile. I could stay up a while longer, but damn I was getting tired. The keyboard went click, the ice in my glass went clink, and a few minutes later I was fast asleep.

I woke up to the sound of a door slamming somewhere upstairs. I had fallen asleep on the couch, and sweet fuck I was hungover. The morning light came in the big windows and struck me in the face, warming my cheeks and battering my eyelids.

"Shit," I mumbled, sitting up. John's keys were on the counter, his shoes were at the door. I heard the shower turn on. "Ughh," I groaned, rubbing my temples. My computer was on the coffee table in front of me. I tried to wake it up, but the battery was dead.

Dragging myself upstairs I sorted through my suitcase, looking for my computer charger. As I looked, I realized my stuff was all out of place, like it had been sorted through. Fearing John had searched my backpack, I quickly reached into the pocket to make sure he hadn't found my green card and stash of escape money. It was still there, and I breathed a shaky sigh as I zipped the pocket shut. Fuck, I was hungover.

The shower turned off, and John stepped out of the bathroom in a towel. "Hey," I said weakly, squinting his way. "How was your night?"

"Take a fucking shower," he said coldly. "You reek of booze."

"All right," I mumbled, grabbing my towel out of my suitcase. "Sorry."

I stepped into the bathroom and fumbled with the doorknob for a few moments until I realized it didn't have a lock on the handle, just an old school keyhole, and I didn't have the key. Frowning, I took my clothes off and turned on the water. The shower sat next to a big window that had a view of the Black Sea, facing away from the city. It was beautiful, but I was too hungover to appreciate anything.

I was in the shower for a few minutes when the door opened. I jumped in surprise as John walked in, completely naked, and flung open the shower curtain.

"Didn't you just take a shower?" I asked, cocking my head.

Slap! Harder than usual. My face stung and I nearly slipped, but then his hands were around my neck, pressing me against the side of the shower window, squeezing like hell. It hurt. I could barely breathe. "Did you fucking forget?" he screamed into my face. "Huh!" I tried to answer but I couldn't speak through his iron grip. "Remember that I fucking own you!" His teeth were in my face, his spit splashing onto my nose as his grip got tighter and tighter. Did he see the emails? When did my computer die? When did he get back to the house? I was such an idiot. A drunken idiot. He was going to kill me. "You got that?" he hissed, slackening his grip so I could speak, and I choked for air.

"I know," I wheezed. "I'm yours."

"Damn right," he growled. Then he lunged at my neck, biting and kissing me before he forced me down to the bottom of the shower and had his way, my face splashing in the small puddle of water that formed around the drain so that I had to hold my breath for a few moments at a time. When he was done he stepped out and grabbed my towel, wrapping it around himself. "Now clean yourself up," he said.

Later that day we went to the beach. It was nice out as we sat in the sand watching the vacation scenes unfold around us. There was a group of kids making sandcastles, maybe fifty feet down the shore from us, and I kept seeing John's eyes wander their way.

"Do you like kids?" I asked out of the blue.

"What the fuck does that mean?" John asked, whirling around on me. "You—"

"I mean," I stuttered, trying to cool him off, "Would you ever want kids, like, you know, in the future."

He turned his gaze back to the sea slowly, readjusting his persona, and said, "Maybe one day, but you know that's impossible, at least in the Kingdom."

"Yeah," I said, "I guess you're right."

"Come on let's get cleaned up," he said, standing abruptly. "We got reservations."

"Reservations?"

"Dinner, idiot," he shot back, scooping up his beach towel. "Let's go."

He drove us to a huge fancy hotel on the water, backlit by Varna's scattered skyline, and the hostess brought us out to a nice table on the veranda with a view of the sea. As we walked through the hotel lobby I saw John glance at a guy sitting by the elevators. I couldn't make him out really. He was wearing sunglasses and reading a newspaper, but his bright blue baseball cap stood out. I felt like I had seen it before, but I couldn't place it for the life of me. Whoever he was, he had John's attention.

We were drinking beers and snacking on appetizers for a little while. John was talking about something, and I pretended to listen. I was damn good at pretending.

"And then I—" John interrupted himself as his phone lit up next to his silverware. "Hold on a second. I'll be right back." He scooped up the phone and stood up from the table, walking into the hotel.

I leaned over the table to watch him walk toward the lobby. I guess I just couldn't help myself, maybe fueled by the confidence of my impending escape, but either way I got up from the table and followed him.

Poking my head around the corner of the lobby I saw him walking out the front door and down the steps. I hurried to keep up and hid behind one of the pillars that supported the roof of the valet area. I could hear his voice, he was arguing with someone, but I couldn't make out the words. I peeked over a big shrub in a fancy ceramic pot and saw him. He was talking to the man in the blue baseball cap. Who the hell was that? His back was to me, so I had less of a view than when I had seen him in the lobby. Whoever he was, he had John upset about something.

John tossed his cigarette with an annoyed flick and brushed past the guy in the hat. I was so fascinated by their conversation that it took me a few moments to realize he was headed my way. I ducked behind the shrub as he scurried up the steps back to the hotel lobby. Shit! I wasn't at the table.

I power walked to the bathroom as soon as he was out of sight, breathing heavily with nerves. I still didn't understand what was happening here, but I couldn't risk screwing anything up. I stood in the bathroom for a few seconds, then washed my hands, and headed back to the table.

John was standing next to the table, tapping his lighter anxiously against his palm. When he saw me come around the corner he clenched his jaw, then said, "Where the hell were you?"

"I just went to the bathroom," I said, trying to move around him to get back to my seat, but he grabbed my arm and held me fast.

"You couldn't wait five fucking minutes?" he said through gritted teeth.

"I had to go, I mean, John—"

"That's it!" he snapped. "We're out of here, get your shit, let's go!"

"I—" I tried to protest but when he became angry I became an item, just a possession he controlled.

"Now!" he screamed, grabbing my coat off the back of my chair and shoving it into my arms. The whole veranda had gone quiet. Everyone was looking at us like that scene in *Scarface*, and I was the drugged-out wife getting dragged along, but in my world I didn't have her courage. I couldn't walk out of there without him. Instead he dragged me by the elbow to the car, tossed me in, and drove me back to the house so he could beat the shit out of me.

He threw me up against the front door so hard I thought I might break the windows at the top, and pressed my neck against it with his elbow while he unlocked the door.

"You think you're fucking slick? You piece of shit," he spat into my ear.

"John, I—"

"Shut the fuck up!"

He opened the house door and forced me through, pushing me to the floor in the foyer. I felt my elbow smack on the hard tile and pain shot up my bicep. Slamming the door shut behind us he grabbed me by the hair on the back of my head and started dragging me toward the kitchen, my stomach squeaking against the tile as I cried out in pain.

"You and Adam!" he bellowed down at me. "You thought I wouldn't find out?"

"It's a rumor, a fucking rumor Robert started—" I tried to protest but he cut me off with a hard kick to my ribs.

"I read the emails, you dumb bitch!" he screamed, kicking me again, and again.

"Please," I wheezed, clutching at my ribs, "I—"

"Shut!" Kick.

"The Fuck!" Kick.

"Up!" Kick, kick, kick. Crack went one of my ribs.

"Stop," I cried, clutching my stomach as I curled into a ball on the kitchen floor.

"You don't get to fucking talk," John seethed down at me. "Get the fuck up," and he grabbed the back of my hair again, hauling me up the stairs. Each limp of a step hurt both my hair and my ribs, and I leaked tears as he dragged me over the top step.

"John, wait, please," I begged. Smack. I saw stars.

"I told you to shut the fuck up. You gonna stop doing what you're told right now? You want to do that?" he hissed into my ear. All I could do was cry. Smack. Things were fuzzy, it hurt like hell to take a real breath. I heard clicking, felt the bathroom tile beneath me as my arm was lifted up. There was a ratcheting sound, and pressure on my wrist, then click!

John stepped back. I tried to wipe my tears away so I could see. "Look at me!" he raged. "Look!" and I tilted my head up like a man getting a glimpse of his executioner. Smack! My head lashed back from the blow and cracked against the metal radiator I had been handcuffed to.

"Wait," I mumbled, disoriented, dizzy, and hurting. I could make out his feet shuffling from the room, and hear him tearing through luggage. Then he reappeared and threw the diapers and pacifier down on the bathroom floor beside me.

"You're going to need those later, baby," he said coldly. "Now shut the fuck up," and he slammed the door. I heard the click of the key in the lock, then his footsteps disappearing down the stairs, and finally the faint sound of the front door slamming behind him.

Chapter Twenty

M Y RIGHT ARM WAS handcuffed to the old-style radiator against the wall, with the shower to my right and the sink to my left. A massive bruise was forming on my ribs, and it hurt to breathe. The back of my head stung, and my right ankle was swelling. I was alone, and I cried until I couldn't. Sometime after that, I fell asleep.

There was a split second when I woke up in which I thought it had all been a bad dream. Then I opened my eyes and saw the pale tile, illuminated by the large window, and felt pain all over my body, except in my right arm. It was completely numb, and there was a small line of blood dripping down from my wrist, pressed into the handcuffs.

I gave a little groaning sound as I moved into a sitting position, trying to get some blood flow to my arm. John must have been waiting for me to wake up because the door opened right then, and he walked in wearing nothing but a towel, holding a big cup of water. At the sight of it, I felt a horrid wave of dehydration slam into me, coupled with hunger, but mostly I just wanted a drink of water. I was so thirsty I could feel the air in my throat gliding over dry, caked tissue.

"Thirsty?" John asked casually. I nodded as best I could, afraid to say anything. "You can have this when I trust you again," he said, crouching down. He placed the plastic cup of water a few feet from the diapers and pacifier, well out of my reach. Then he dropped his towel, whistled while he took a shower, and left me alone in the bathroom again.

I nodded off for a moment until the pain in my ribs brought me back. I had no idea what time it was. The house was quiet. I stared at the water, taunting me from across the room, partly hiding behind the pack of diapers.

I started clawing around, seeing what I could reach. I could get to the cabinet under the sink, and the edge of the shower—that was about it. The longer I looked at the water the more I started to think I could reach it with my feet and drag it over the tile floor.

I stretched as far from the radiator as I could, feeling the handcuffs cut into my tingling wrist, and gritting my teeth as my rib cage screamed in protest. I was so close, so close! Almost there! My shoe was only an inch away. I could do it. I was going to drink that water. I had never been more excited about anything in my life. There! I had it! I hooked the edge of my shoe around the back of the plastic cup, pain screaming out of my wrist and ribs as I strained, and then—*Splash!*

There came the unmistakable sound of water spilling over tile. I twisted around to see the plastic cup rolling across the floor. I would have cried if I had tears to spend, but instead I just withdrew, leaning up against the shower, drawing myself into the tightest ball I could without squeezing my ribs.

It was as if the floor had opened up beneath me. There was nowhere left to stand, but I didn't even feel like standing anymore. I was ready to fall. I hadn't really been on my feet for two years. I had been limping along, sometimes crawling. Now there was nowhere left to crawl, nowhere left to even roll. It was easier just to fall into blackness, so I did.

I have no idea how much time passed while I sat there, void of all hope and drive. I nodded off a few times, but I don't know how long. Eventually the light began changing, and I knew sunset wasn't too far away. John would come with the darkness. I knew he would. I didn't have to wait much longer.

What was that? I could hear something, or was it someone? The fuzzy edge of a voice, floating through the room, mumbling something I couldn't make out.

"John?" I called toward the door. "John is that you?" The house was silent, but the bathroom grew louder as my auditory hallucinations spiked. "Hello!" I screamed as loud as I could. "Who's there? Fucking help! Help!" Nobody answered. "I don't want to die," I grumbled to myself, but I wasn't so sure about that. I had thought about dying for a long time. Maybe this was it, maybe this was the best way to check out. This way, I didn't have to leave a body lying around the family compound.

Who's to say I would ever be found? I was in fucking Bulgaria. But then I wouldn't have a funeral. Fuck a funeral. Who would even be there that I cared about? Just my brother really, Joseph, and the very few friends who didn't betray me would probably show. Adam wouldn't be there though, no way he would make it from Texas. He wouldn't even find out until way later probably.

Adam! Shit, I couldn't die in Bulgaria, I had to get to the States and see Adam. "Duh," I chuckled to myself, falling into the full embrace of delirium. "You gotta see Adam, you can't die." At the time, talking to myself made the most sense. "You gotta get out of here, this shit is old," I said, tugging on the radiator and feeling the sting of the handcuff on my lacerated wrist bones. "I can break this shit."

I started tugging at the hunk of metal, calmly at first, like it was a casual thing, but as I pulled and pulled I got more furious, more visceral, gritting my teeth and yelling all sorts of discombobulated shit at the inanimate object.

"Fuck you, brave little fucking toaster, fuck that, fuck you! Argh!" I yelled at the wall, pulling and kicking and screaming, but nothing came of it. A few minutes later I ran out of steam. I stopped hearing the mumbling buzz in the background, I stopped thinking entirely, and I slumped back down into the darkness with nothing but five new gashes on top of my right hand from the handcuffs.

"Shit," I mumbled, then I nodded off again.

There was no dream, no reprieve from the bleak bathroom, only flashes of darkness that consumed an unknown amount of time as I continually lost my sanity.

"Hey, that's my cat," I mumbled at one point.

"You make chandeliers?" I said at another when I flopped over onto my stomach, pressing my other cheek against the cold tile.

"Yeah, I guess I like butterscotch," I croaked through my rasping, dehydrated throat.

Then a smell grabbed me by the scruff of the neck and yanked me up like a puppy who took a piss inside. It was like a rocket, and I was a goddamn astronaut getting hit with all the Gs of takeoff, shaking my very soul to the edges of my eye sockets. It was the smell of my mother's walk-in closet, of the pillows on her bed, of her nightstand and her purse and her car before I wrecked it. It was her, in all her glory, and it was stronger than sulfur.

My eyes snapped open as I hauled in a huge breath, gasping for whatever life was left in the room. My left cheek was pressed against the tile, and I was looking at the little space between the bottom of the sink cabinet and the floor.

There was something there, sitting there in the clustered dust. A fucking bobby pin. My left hand slapped out like a frog catching a fly, and I started cramming the bobby pin into the handcuffs, furiously jabbing and grinding. I had no idea how to undo locks, but popular culture told me that this could work. Some thirty minutes later, it did.

The handcuffs clicked off and clattered to the tile. My right arm fell like a dead log against the floor, and I laughed at the change of sensation. Slam! The front door told me John was back.

"Fuck," I mumbled, trying to stand up. My whole body hurt and cramped and groaned as I steadied myself against the sink. The spilled water on the floor squelched under my shoes.

Thump thump thump thump went the stairs. He was coming.

My hands ran out around me over the surfaces, frantically searching for something I could use as a weapon. *Thump thump thump.* Toilet paper. Toothbrush. Soap. *Thump thump thump.* Toilet.

My fingers wrapped around the top of the toilet tank as his footsteps reached the bathroom door. The key slid into the lock, and I hauled the hunk of ceramic upward and spun around.

He didn't have time to get a word off, but for a split second I saw the sheer surprise on his face as he walked through the door and the slab came up to meet his jaw. It made a hollow thunk as it slammed into his face, and the recoil of the strike rippled through my elbows. I couldn't hold on, my right arm was still partially numb, and the piece shattered with a spectacular crash on the floor as John crumpled like a kite caught in the rain. Then all was still.

I stood there, blank and panting, leaning back against the sink, trying to process the blood pooling between the broken shards of ceramic and John's motionless body.

"Fuck!" I finally managed to say out loud. Then the panic flooded in, and adrenaline pushed me out of the room. "Gotta go, gotta go," I muttered to myself, tripping over my suitcase in the next room and coming down hard on my wrist. "Fucking killed him, fuck fuck fuck!" I groaned as I scratched the carpet for my backpack. "Gotta go, gotta go."

Over the next three minutes I threw all my shit into my suitcase, shaking all the while. I saw my MacBook sitting on the bed and tossed it into my pack. Passport!

"Fuck!" I said again. Where was John's bag? There it was. I clawed at the lock on the zipper like a harpy, but to no avail, and I dragged it downstairs as fast as I could and reached wildly for a kitchen knife. I hacked into the bag, tearing at the fibers, and dumped the contents onto the kitchen counter, frantically pawing at all the shit. A bottle of pills rolled past and dropped onto the floor as I grabbed my passport. Time to go.

I burst out the front door and slammed it shut behind me. I had my suitcase in one hand, my passport in the other, and my backpack slung over one shoulder. Suddenly I was struck by how still the night was. The chaos inside the house didn't exist out here. I was free. But where do I go now?

"Your uncle has a house there," my dad's voice said in my head, and immediately I unslung my pack, fishing through it for the house keys.

I held them up under the porch light and looked at the address: 962 Redlon St. I shivered as I read the numbers. I had seen them before.

"It's not possible," I breathed to myself.

I turned around slowly, feeling my heart beating out of my chest, and looked up at the numbers next to the doorframe: 962. Just as slow I swiveled my head to the street sign on the corner. Redlon. Despair taking over, I slid the key into the front door. It opened with a clean click.

"Fuck!" I shouted, kicking the doorframe. Then I heard a car, and I turned to see headlights pulling up the long driveway from the road. Grabbing my suitcase, I hurried to the hedges on the far side of the front garden as the car pulled up in front of the house and parked. I could hardly breathe. Whoever it was, they weren't going to find John the way they had expected.

The car door opened and there he was, the man in the blue baseball cap. I couldn't make out his face in the dark, but I watched him pull a bulky bag from the backseat before walking up the stairs to the front door. It had a metallic stripe around it that shone in the porch light, and I started getting a strange feeling of recognition as I watched the man.

He stopped at the door, gingerly nudging the doorknob with his hand. Shit! I hadn't shut it all the way. The man gave a long look around, standing under the porch light. As he turned his face toward the driveway I saw my cousin Nathan clear as day, wearing that camera bag over his shoulder, surveying everything with a serious look. Fucking Nathan. Then he walked inside and shut the door behind him. The second I heard the click of the door, I bolted down the block.

I must have looked insane running down that road, flailing my free arm and screaming for a taxi. After a few blocks I got to a bigger street, and found a cab in a couple of minutes.

"Накъде?" the elderly driver asked in a gruff, cigarette groomed voice.

"English?" I gasped. "You speak English?"

"No English," the driver shook his head.

"Fuck!" I yelled, and the old man's eyes widened a bit. "Ah, shit, uh, airport, you know, fucking planes, airport!" Universal language my ass.

"Airport," he said back with his heavy Bulgarian accent, squinting at me through the rearview mirror.

"Airport," I affirmed. He said something back in Bulgarian, but I couldn't understand any of it and I just waved him on, and eventually he drove after I stuffed a hundred-dollar bill into his hand. Then he got really friendly.

I watched the lights of Varna pass by as we retraced the route to the airport, but when we got there the cabbie spouted off a long rant in Bulgarian. I just wanted him to shut up, so I handed him another hundred and got out of the car. He drove off as I walked up to the door and rattled the handle. Locked.

I could see a security guard on the other side of the glass, and I waved to him. He looked up with a sour face, tapped his watch, and walked away. I looked around, and saw the hours posted on the glass beside the door. What international airport closed at 10:00 p.m.? Fucking Bulgaria.

I dragged my suitcase over to one of the parking lots and sank down onto the curb. I had nowhere else to go, I just had to wait. I sat there for a while, trying to keep an eye out for John's rental car or the car Nathan had shown up in. Neither showed, and at some point, I fell asleep with my knees tucked into my chest on the concrete.

"Трябва да се събудите, сър," a voice said, yanking me out of my slumber. Squinting through the morning sun I saw a cop standing over me, poking at my knee with the butt of an assault rifle.

"English," I squeaked, trying to sit up. My ribs still hurt like hell. The cop gave an exasperated sigh and waved over his partner.

"You cannot sleep here," the other officer said in a thick accent.

"I got here last night," I mumbled, forcing myself to stand up. "It was closed."

"You are flying?" he asked, looking me up and down. I looked like shit, there was no doubt, and I tried to keep my sleeve over all the wounds on my right hand and wrist.

"Yes, flying, to America," I grunted, picking up my suitcase.

"Airport is open now," he answered. "Go on."

"Thanks," I said. As I limped toward the doors, I heard him and his partner laughing together in Bulgarian.

"Welcome to Lufthansa, how may…" the lady said, her voice trailing off as she looked up from the ticket counter to see me standing in front of her.

"I need a ticket," I croaked. "To the States."

"Oh," she said, her face going a bit flush. "I am sorry sir, I thought I had seen a ghost!" she gave a little laugh. "Um, where in America?"

"Austin, Texas," I said, full of determination.

"Hmm," she said, scrolling through her computer. "I can get you to Frankfurt, and a connection from there to Houston, then to Austin on United. Will that work for you sir?"

"That will work fine," I said, flashing a hollow, beaten smile.

"Passport?" I slid it over to her, and she looked it over twice before she punched a few keys and then said, "And do you have a green card? I see that citizens of your country need a visa to enter the States."

"It's there," I wheezed. "Just turn the page."

"Ah, so it is," she said, holding up the little piece of plastic that dictated my future. "Two thousand, eight hundred, and thirty-five Lev," she said, punching a few final keys. Then she stopped, frowning as my plane tickets printed. "I'm sorry sir, this green card is, um, well it's expired, you see?" she was blushing in embarrassment as she gingerly pointed to the dates in the card's corner. It had been expired for two months. I felt like the world's biggest fool. My plane tickets sat on the other end of the counter, taunting me.

"No, it's not," I tried to plead with her. "It's American, so the dates are backward," I gestured to the month and the day printed on the card.

"Sir, I have to void the ticket," she said, her face still red. Panicking, I did the only thing I thought might work.

"Please, I need to leave today! How much do you want?" I asked feebly, sliding my stack of escape cash to her over the counter. She went a bit redder and quickly counted through the money, setting aside about two thousand dollars. She slid another couple of hundred dollars into her pocket and handed me back the rest with my tickets. I had never bribed anyone in my life before.

"Security is that way," she said, nodding around the corner, then added with a slight smile, "Good luck."

I got some more ghostly looks as I passed through security. The Kingdom would have never allowed someone so disheveled through, but I was in Bulgaria, and nobody seemed to give a fuck about anything.

I had two hours until my flight. After I was through security I looked for Wi-Fi and found a little breakfast cafe in my terminal where I ordered some juice and breakfast. I poked at the breakfast sandwich without any interest as I waited for the laptop to charge and pictured John lying still on the bloody floor. I had killed him. I was sure of it. Part of me felt sick, and part of me joy.

The loudspeaker chimed. Shoes squeaked on the floors. Somewhere a baby cried. My computer chimed as it finally turned on. Instinctively I typed in my password, but it was no good. Feeling strange, I tried it again, but still nothing. Frowning, I looked at the screen—it wasn't my computer. The username stood out bold and imposing, screaming at me from the dead: John. Incorrect Password.

"Damnit," I muttered, shutting the computer, and sliding it back into my pack. My phone still didn't have any roaming signal. I would have to wait until I got to Germany to contact Adam, and I hated that. All I wanted to do was hear his voice.

"Lufthansa flight 806 to Frankfurt, this is your primary boarding call, anyone who needs additional..." the loudspeaker droned on. That was me. I threw out my uneaten sandwich and my untouched juice and walked toward the gate like I was walking the green mile.

Everything inside me was collapsing. Each step I took chunked away another piece of my soul. I kept thinking about my brother and even my dad. He wouldn't understand, there was no way he ever could. I felt bad for him. He was as oblivious as John's dad must be, I thought, and as I thought on that, I nearly turned around.

I thought of the country house, sitting around the table with my dad and brother eating steaks. It wasn't so bad. Then I heard the thud of John hitting the floor, and saw his blood flowing around the hunks of broken ceramic, and I took another step.

"Lufthansa flight 806 to Frankfurt, this is a secondary boarding call, now boarding groups one and two at gate…"

I stood at the gate, watching group after group board before me. I couldn't do this. I had to go home. I was free of John, he was gone, I could go home now. Everything was fine. I couldn't run away! How crazy was I?

"Now boarding group four," I heard. I looked down at my ticket. This was me. I couldn't do it. Shit! I was going to cry in the middle of the airport.

"Are you in line?" A man with a thick Danish accent asked from behind me, lugging his bulging backpack behind him.

"I…I'm not sure," I laughed out nervously, fighting against tears.

"Yeah, that's you, you're in the right place," he said, peering over my shoulder to glance at the ticket I held in my shaking palm. "After you."

"No, go ahead," I said, giving a little gesture toward the Jetway.

"As you like," he said, and shouldered ahead. As he walked past, I caught the smell once more, as if it were trailing off of his shoulder, tugging me to follow. Suddenly I could see my mother, waiting for me at the airport in the Kingdom, welcoming me home from the States three years ago with a huge hug while my father stood there, stalwart as he ever.

"It's not true," I had cried into her shoulder. "It's not fair."

"I know sweetie," she whispered back. "Everything is going to be all right. You'll go back, I promise."

"Last call for Lufthansa flight 806 to Frankfurt…" the loudspeaker broke through, and I saw my mom cheering for me as I walked to the gate with a confidence I had never had before, brandishing my boarding pass like it was the winning ticket at the races.

"Welcome aboard," the woman said with a smile, handing my ticket back.

"Thanks."

I walked down the Jetway as a million thoughts raced through my mind. I stored my backpack in the overhead bin and sat by the window. As the plane took off, and Varna became smaller and smaller beneath us, I took gasping breaths, just trying to settle down. I thought I would feel excited, or even happy, but instead I was racked with fear, doubt, and gut-wrenching anxiety. Even now that there was no going back, I was unsure of my course.

I shut my eyes while the plane climbed higher, trying to hold myself together. Damn it if I was going to cry. I couldn't believe I actually left everything I knew behind. Well, not everything. At least Adam was waiting for me, but was that enough? It had to be.

Escape was the only way I would survive, the only way to find peace. For so long I had clung to my crumbling sandcastle as John's evil waves ate piece after piece away from the foundation, but now I understood that my castle was lost. There was always a new beach, somewhere far away from John and the Kingdom's oppression, and I was off to find it.

Or so I thought…

To be continued...

Acknowledgments

To MY BELOVED HUSBAND, Misha, words cannot express my love and gratitude. You have stood by me through the deepest lows and the tallest heights and held my hand as I struggled with depression and PTSD. I would not be here today without your love and support; thank you for being such a piece of my life. I love you always.

To Alan Janbay, you believed in me, you saved me. Some thirteen years ago I was defeated, exhausted, and hopeless. I had lost the will to survive until you lifted me up and showed me the way. Thank you for saving me, and for being the person you are.

To Debbie Nau Redmond, thank you for your energized support and guidance on this journey. You have taught me so much, and I treasure our friendship.

And to everyone who helped this book materialize, thank you from the bottom of my heart. This is a dream come true.